If I Could Give You A Day

Dave Richards

If I Could Give You A Day
By Dave Richards

www.daverichardsbooks.com

Copyright © 2017, Dave Richards

Second Edition, published 2017

Cover: ShutterStock image license 24588826
Author photo by Joel Sackett

ISBN-13: 978-1-942661-53-5

Published by Kitsap Publishing
P.O. Box 572
Poulsbo, WA 98370
www.KitsapPublishing.com

Printed in the United States of America

TD 20170405

50-10 9 8 7 6 5 4 3 2 1

For Marigene, with all my love.

Acknowledgments

*Many thanks to Jennifer Hager, Victoria Skurnick,
Alice Acheson, Steve Grabowsky, Alan Corner,
Ralph Cheadle, and my late great friend,
the amazing and magical Bob McAllister.*

*Plus an extra special, super-sized helping of
appreciation to my wife Marigene, without whose
unwavering support this novel wouldn't exist.*

"The two most important days in your life are the day when you were born and the day when you find out why."

— Mark Twain

"Self-sacrifice is the real miracle out of which all the reported miracles grow."

— Ralph Waldo Emerson

Chapter 1

SCOTT

It was raining the morning Scott Northwood pulled his silver Range Rover into the gravel lot of Danny's Tavern. Although September was one of the drier months in western Washington, it was a soggy fact of life here that it could rain any time of year.

Scott switched off the engine and glanced at his watch. Eleven o'clock. Opening time. He smiled at the thought of the good ale coming his way, even if it was still morning. Danny was forever mixing and matching new ingredients and experimenting with different brewing techniques. On the first Monday of each month, he would make the virgin pour from his latest "brew-storming session," as he liked to put it. Only Scott was invited to these initial tastings. It was a ritual he'd been enjoying for a couple of years now. Since Scott had moved west, Danny had become his closest friend.

A few years back, Danny and some of his pals had renovated what had originally been a rickety old house into a small but comfortable pub. To enter it was like stepping into a welcoming cave of blonde wood. The ales he conjured up here were always quite good, and, every now and then, truly wonderful, like last year's award-winning pale ale. It had placed Danny's Tavern firmly on the map of up-and-coming craft breweries. The number of local bars and restaurants with Danny's Pale Ale on tap had grown to more than forty. Even some high-end Seattle restaurants were selling it.

Danny, used to brewing in small batches, had recently begun looking for larger digs so he could expand his operation and keep up with demand.

As Scott climbed out of the car and headed toward the tavern, he had no way of knowing that, on this rainy Monday morning, his life was about to change. As time went by, he would occasionally think back to this moment and know it as the dividing line between the person he had been and who he was destined to become.

Scott pushed open the door and walked across gently complaining floorboards, past the two pool tables, past chairs and tables made from maplewood the color of honey, to the polished mahogany bar. What he saw there surprised him. Instead of Danny, Barbara—the tavern's head barmaid—sat on a stool staring without expression into the antique mirror over the bar. In front of her was a half-finished schooner of ale. There was no sign of Danny.

Danny had always been there to welcome him with a gravelly shout and a wave, his faux surly biker exterior transformed by a luminous smile creasing his scruffy goatee. And Barbara should have been bustling about, getting the place ready for customers. Besides, Scott thought, Danny didn't like his employees drinking on the job.

Scott sat on the stool next to her. "Hey, Barbara."

She didn't look at him, but watched his reflection in the mirror.

"Hi, Scott," she said, her voice flat. She was a thickset woman in her forties, with dull blonde hair and a wide pale face framed by black horn-rimmed glasses. Danny would joke that he hired barmaids on the basis of how many pints of ale they could carry on a tray. If it ever became an Olympic event, he would say, Barbara would be a serious contender for the gold.

"Where's Danny?"

She turned to look at Scott, allowing him to see that behind the thick lenses, her eyes were moist and red. "Pam called me last night from the hospital. I'm afraid I have bad news."

"Did something happen to Danny?"

Barbara's words were halting. "He had an accident. Yesterday. At home."

Scott felt a knot of concern forming in his stomach. "What happened?"

"He was changing a light bulb at his house. He fell off the ladder and hit his head."

"Is he all right?"

"No, he's not. They airlifted him to Harborview Medical Center in Seattle."

"Danny's in the *hospital*?"

She nodded and took a deep swallow of ale. "He hasn't woken up. They've got him on life support."

Scott expelled a lungful of air that he hadn't realized he was holding in. "...Jesus."

"Pam and the girls are there with him."

Danny and his wife had two daughters. Amber was a freshman at the University of Washington. Crystal still attended North Kitsap High School.

"They spent the night at the hospital. They're going to run more tests today."

"Why in the world was he using a ladder to change a light bulb?"

"They've got recessed lighting. You need a ladder to reach the sockets."

"I still don't see how—"

"One of his shoes was untied." A tear was spilling down her cheek. "They think he tripped on the way down. He fell and hit his head on the coffee table. Pam heard him fall. She found him on the floor."

"Oh, man..." breathed Scott. "Poor Danny."

A sad chuckle escaped Barbara's lips. "Can you believe that guy?"

"What do you mean?"

"Danny worked twenty years as a roofer before opening this tavern. Never got more 'n a scratch."

Scott found he couldn't say anything. The idea of his friend—robust, irreverent, only forty-five years old and so full of life—lying in a coma in a hospital room on the other side of Puget Sound, seemed improbable. Monumentally absurd. As if the universe were pulling some twisted, cosmic prank.

Scott shook his head as if to clear it. "This is crazy," he said.

"You got that right," Barbara answered. She downed the rest of the ale and wiped her mouth with the back of her hand. "I'm going to have another." She got up and went behind the bar, wobbling a little as she did so. "Let me pour you one. I don't think Danny would mind, considering."

She set a drink down in front of him and refilled her own glass.

Scott stared into in the mirror. He saw a fifty-two-year-old man with thick copper hair going now to silver looking back at him. You look more like forty, someone had said to him recently. Taking in his own boyish, unlined face, he realized it might be true. But inside, his shock and horror was making him feel like a bitter old man. He had kept himself trim and fit, working out and taking a long walk every day, but the horrifying news about Danny made him wonder why he even bothered. The possibility of another loss penetrated the depths of Scott's psyche, something he rarely allowed. But he couldn't stop himself; he felt a depth of sadness that was as painful as it was familiar.

He stood up, his ale untouched. "Thanks, Barbara. I'm going to head out."

She nodded.

He placed a hand on her shoulder. "Are you going to stay here?"

"Sure. I guess. I mean, I don't know what else to do... Where else to go..."

"Can I call you for updates on Danny?"

"Of course," she said.

He headed for the door.

Danny could die, Scott thought as he drove home. He wondered what possible lesson was supposed to be learned by someone exiting this world in such a pointless way. Here was a man in his prime, a good person for whom things had been going so well. In a careless moment, all of that could be gone.

And if Danny died, he thought with a slight shudder, what, exactly, had the man's life meant?

And what about his own life? If he got run over by a bus tomorrow, what—if anything—would his life have meant?

Scott had spent the last five years living just outside Poulsbo, a town of 8,000 located at the head of a sheltered bay on the western edge of Puget Sound. He had no plan in mind when he'd arrived. At the age of forty-seven, he'd sold his Silicon Valley technology company to a Seattle-based global software corporation for 30 million dollars. Although such a sum was pocket change to the giant conglomerate, to Scott it was a fortune. He'd worked hard all his life building up his business, and he'd assumed that would be the case for many years to come. He was happily mistaken.

As the deal moved closer to being final, the realization sank in: he would soon be able to live anywhere and do anything he wanted. When he flew to Seattle to sign the papers that would complete the transaction, he'd decided to stay on an extra day and explore the area. He had never been to the Pacific Northwest and was stunned by its natural beauty.

That afternoon, he drove onto the Bainbridge Island ferry in his rented car. After making his way around the island, he rode across the tiny Agate Pass Bridge, which connected Bainbridge to the Kitsap County mainland. And then he stumbled across Poulsbo. He was enchanted by the quiet town. At a particularly verdant turn in the road, he pulled over to the side and got out of the car. Looking around, he was surrounded by views of water, forest, and snow-capped mountains. There and then he decided that this was where he wanted to live.

Within the year, he'd bought ten acres of land in the hills outside of town and built a house. To get to the property, there was a drive to the end of a steep and winding country road called Ridgetop Lane. From there, it turned into a narrow gravel driveway bristling with signs that read "Private Property," "No Trespassing," and "Keep Out," and continued through a forest of Douglas firs so tall and thick it was like driving through a tunnel.

After a couple of hundred yards, past the trees, was a wide bluff that dropped sharply away to a broad, tree-covered valley. The valley was bordered at its far edge by a ribbon of water known as Hood Canal. Thrusting abruptly up from the other side of the canal was the Olympic Mountain Range. The view from this bluff was jaw-dropping. Some days, the mountains seemed so close that he felt as if he could reach out and run his fingers along their jagged, snowy peaks.

Perched near the edge of this bluff was his house. Constructed of wood, glass, and rock, the simple one-story structure was laid out in a clean, rustic, open style of architecture, loosely defined as "Northwest."

One of the first things he had done after moving in was head to the local animal shelter. When he was a boy, his family had adopted Sam, a smart and gentle Labrador retriever. Scott and his sister Shelly had fallen in love with the dog. In fact, just about everything was perfect at that time—Scott had a happy family, a sister he got along with, and now Sam, the *piece de resistance.*

But life was not about to stay perfect. It was years later that Scott heard the saying "Bad things come in threes" for the first time. He'd never been the superstitious type. He believed that coincidences could and did occur. But in retrospect, he had to admit that the expression was eerily prescient.

At age fourteen, Scott was about to experience bad thing number one.

He was taking Sam on his morning walk when two dogs came running toward them. They belonged to the couple in the yellow house across the street, and these pit bulls were the bane of the neighborhood, barking furiously whenever anyone passed their house. Scott would heave a sigh of relief everyday as he'd pass the locked gate to their yard. But, he realized much too late, today the owner had left the latch open.

He stood frozen in horror as the animals charged full-speed around the corner of the house and fell on Sam in a frenzy of gnashing teeth. Scott's desperate attempts to kick them away only resulted in several deep puncture wounds to his own calf. He could do nothing more than writhe, helpless, on the ground, clutching his leg and screaming for help, while Sam died a violent and bloody death a few feet away. Just as the pit bulls were turning their attention to Scott, a man ran out of a nearby garage with a baseball bat and beat them off.

He'd always wanted another dog, but for years had been way too busy to care for one. But that was then—now he had all the time in the world.

At the Kitsap County Animal Control Services, he viewed row after row of cages, overwhelmed by the number of dogs who needed a home. Each of them seemed special in its own way, and he felt an emotional pull toward just about every one of them. It was so hard to focus on only one dog. Scott was prone to overthinking things from time to time... and this was one of those times. Unable to make a decision, he ended up going home alone that day. He had every intention of returning to the shelter, but before he had a chance to do it, the decision was made for him.

It happened a couple of days later as he was heading home. Darkness had fallen and there was a driving rain. He had a takeout pizza in the back seat, and he was starved. Out of nowhere, he glimpsed a pair of eyes shining from the side of the road. The steamy aroma of pepperoni filling the car was making his stomach growl, but something in those eyes made him turn the car around.

With the flashlight he kept in the glove box, he located a

scruffy brown mutt who was lying in a puddle of mud. Blood flowed from a gaping wound in his side where a car had hit him. The dog was sopping wet and shaking uncontrollably, but he stared into Scott's eyes with unblinking calmness.

All thoughts of eating pizza evaporated.

Scott draped his coat over him, lifted him up as gently as he could, and carried him to the car. He made a beeline for the twenty-four-hour emergency veterinary clinic he'd driven by a number of times. The vets cleaned and stitched the dog's wound and kept him overnight.

When Scott went back to check on him the next morning, the dog looked at him with that same oddly serene gaze and began to wag his tail. The vet filled him in on the dog's overall condition as best he could. He appeared to be a terrier mix, maybe five years old, give or take a year or two. He hadn't been wearing a collar or a name tag, nor was there an identifying microchip implanted in him. From his emaciated condition and deeply matted fur, the vet guessed he was a stray who must have been scavenging to survive for some time. He weighed twenty-five pounds, but when he regained his health, he would weigh a good ten pounds more.

"Other than that," smiled the vet, "everything else about him is pretty jake."

Scott had found his dog. He took him home and nursed him back to health. And he named him Jake.

Later that month, Scott added a "Beware of Dog" sign to the collection at the beginning of his driveway. He also had to buy earplugs; he learned the hard way that Jake snored.

It wasn't until after he stopped working that Scott realized how burnt-out he was. As CEO of a software company that was forever having to reinvent itself just to stay competitive, each day had been more demanding than the last. His life had felt out of control and it seemed he never had time for anything but work.

When he sold his business, everything changed overnight.

The hectic schedule disappeared. Now he had all the time in the world. Even better, he had the power to regulate the ebb and flow of the daily events of his life. He found this deeply comforting. He'd always heard the phrase peace of mind, but he'd never had any idea what it meant. Now he had an abundance of it, and he loved it.

His most surprising discovery was that he enjoyed the pleasures of solitude. Finding out he could immerse himself in isolation whenever and for however long he wanted was a revelation. If he wanted to, he could choose to do nothing but sit and stare at a wall all day long, and knowing this left him giddy. He found himself looking forward to being left the hell alone—for a while, anyway.

He had begun his new life, one that would be lived on his terms. Work had required him to be hyper-connected at all times to the Internet, to employees, to competitors, and to vendors, so now he decided to do the opposite; one of the first things he did after moving into his new house was bury his cell phone and laptop in the back of a closet.

Instead, he got a landline with an unlisted number, mainly so he could stay in touch with his sister Shelly, who lived in Atlanta. He had always been a news junkie, but hadn't had time to do more than glance at the headlines. These days, he would linger over *The Seattle Times* with a cup of coffee—something he hadn't done in decades. He had always liked movies, but could rarely fit one into his schedule. Now, he decided to get DVDs from the local video store. No streaming from the Internet for him. These decisions made him smile. If his former employees could see him now, they would say he'd become a Luddite.

For the first twelve months, he would do absolutely nothing. That was his most radical decision. He figured he'd earned it. By the time a year of complete idleness went by, he assumed he would become so bored that he'd be eager to rejoin the world of human commerce, and do something stimulating and useful with his time. He might even want to start another company.

Except it didn't turn out that way. The stress-free existence he had designed for himself proved too seductive, too deliciously comfortable. His planned year of doing just about nothing stretched to two years. Then three years. Then four.

It was now coming up on the end of his fifth year.

Scott's daily routine was little more than variations on a theme. For the most part, his activities consisted of: working out in his home gym; returning and/or picking up DVDs at the video store, where he might spend a few minutes discussing movies with Jeff, the owner; returning and/or picking up books at the library; dropping off and/or picking up laundry at the dry cleaners; buying groceries at Central Market, where he and Mike the produce guy would trade friendly insults.

On a sunny day he often went mountain biking on one of the local trails, or hiked in the Olympic Mountains. If it was raining, he might drive out into the country with Jake or kick back in his massive leather armchair with a book and a glass of wine. For better or worse, Scott was more in control of his life than he'd ever been. He relished the sensation.

One of his routines had only recently come to an end, reluctantly so, on his part. From the first week of his new life, he had enjoyed treating himself to a martini and steak dinner once a week at the Viking Broiler, Poulsbo's finest dining establishment. Over several months, he had gotten to know Betty, the pretty, recently divorced cocktail waitress. What had started as mere flirtation had progressed to casual sleepovers.

Betty was fun and sexy, even a little goofy, which Scott found endearing. She was also honest. From the very start, she'd told him in no uncertain terms that she didn't want to be in a serious relationship, that theirs would remain casual and non-exclusive. And this was fine with him. He had no desire to form a deep romantic attachment to anyone at this point in his life.

For a few years, it had been a mutually pleasurable and

convenient arrangement. Only once did they even touch on the subject of their emotions. It had shocked Scott at the time and he hadn't dwelled on it since, but it was there, in the recesses of his mind.

He and Betty had been sitting outside, drinking an Oregon pinot noir and enjoying the warmish night. She had given him an odd smile. "Scott, have you ever been in love?" He hadn't quite known how to answer. They had always been honest with each other, and there was no reason to begin lying now. "Maybe," he'd replied. "Maybe not. I guess I'm a loner at heart."

She turned to him. "Yes," she'd said. "Perhaps that explains it."

"Explains what?" he'd asked.

"Well," she'd answered, taking her time to form her response. "Explain why it is you always seem to be looking through a window, even when you're sitting right next to me."

The discussion had ended there, but her perception haunted him. Yes, that was a perfect description of how he'd always felt – like a man looking through glass, rather than really being with any other person in the room. The image of himself as a little boy came into his mind – playing with his sister, laughing with his parents. Okay, he acknowledged, perhaps he hadn't always felt that way, but he wasn't about to dwell on how Scott the happy boy turned into Scott the solitary man. He was doing fine, he told himself, living the life he'd chosen.

One night a few months after that conversation, Betty nonchalantly mentioned that she'd met a man at the Viking who owned a high-end steakhouse in Scottsdale, Arizona. He had offered her a job, one that would pay substantially more than she was making now. Plus, she would be done with Washington weather. She had said yes and would be moving to Arizona in a couple of weeks.

Scott's reaction surprised him. An unexpected sadness settled into his bones at the thought of her moving away. It was only with great effort that he had been able to keep his feelings to himself. On the day she left, he said goodbye and sincerely wished her well. Then he stood in the road outside her apartment and watched her drive away.

He vowed to never go back to the Viking Broiler.

Returning home from Danny's Tavern, Scott pulled up to the house and parked in front of the garage. He could see Jake lying down in the narrow window adjacent to the front door, watching the Range Rover with quiet expectation. Because the dog stood a compact 18 inches high from toenails to the tip of his pointed brown ears, it was good that the window extended all the way to the floor so that he could see out.

Scott stepped out of the car and called to him. "Ready for a walk?"

Jake stood up, his tail wagging steadily from side to side. The dog's disposition had remained as calm and serious as ever. He never got overexcited about anything. Didn't chase sticks or balls. Didn't splash through mud puddles. Rarely played with toys. Scott had to admit that he liked those qualities in his four-legged companion.

Jake was affectionate in his own way. He would move to whatever room Scott happened to be in and present his head for scratching. He would turn it this way and that, staring with a serious expression into Scott's eyes, his tail going back and forth.

When Scott opened the front door, Jake headed straight for the Range Rover. Scott lifted him onto the passenger seat and got back behind the wheel.

In the five years he'd lived in Poulsbo, the one thing that never varied was the walk he and Jake took every afternoon down the same network of paths. Every day, rain or shine, they made their way to an obscure, rarely used county park called Autumn Lake, located deep in the woods.

Because Kitsap County was surrounded on three sides by

the tributaries of Puget Sound, it had no shortage of parks. Most of them had stunning water and mountain views and came equipped with amenities like boat launches, fire pits, picnic tables, bathrooms, campsites, and park rangers.

Autumn Lake was different. Though technically a park, the 500-acre preserve had zero facilities, not even a garbage can. It had been donated to the county by an elderly and eccentric heiress with the caveat that the land remain in a wild state with no improvements.

The woman's motive for this unusual requirement had long been a subject of local conjecture, but the reason was simple. She was descended from a timber baron who had mowed down many of the state's old-growth forests. In her twilight years, this left her wracked by a late-blooming yet profound guilt. Her gift was an effort to attain some kind of karmic redemption for her ancestor's clear-cutting ways.

Whether the creation of the park helped assuage her conscience or not, the lack of amenities did ensure that Autumn Lake was one of the least visited parks in the state.

This suited Scott just fine.

The heiress had made one concession to the county. She allowed a network of trails to be built so that visitors would have decent access to the forest. Once a year, a county work crew would go through the park removing downed trees and limbs from the trails. Other than that, Autumn Lake remained in its natural and increasingly shaggy state.

The woman died shortly after the county took over the land. Then, as time went by, something odd and a little spooky happened; people started claiming that they had seen her ghost wandering among the trees, as if she were haunting the forest she had ensured would be forever protected. Scott didn't believe in ghosts, but, if the ghost story helped keep visitors out, so much the better.

He pulled into the small dirt parking lot at the end of the gravel road and looked up, as he did every day, at the sign nailed to a tree:

Autumn Lake County Park
Boating, Fishing, Swimming Prohibited

He went around to the passenger side, let Jake out, and the two headed for the unmarked trailhead at the edge of the lot.

The chilly drizzle of the morning hadn't subsided. Scott buttoned his faded green field coat to the neck and shoved his hands deep into its pockets. Made of water-repellent canvas and lined with soft brown flannel, the coat was roomy, dry, and warm. It was the first item of clothing he had bought after moving here. It was the most practical outerwear for the cool, watery clime of the Northwest.

The lake—if it could even be called that—was located a quarter-mile down the main path. In reality, it was little more than a shallow, ten-acre pond, much of it overgrown with reeds and water lilies. The warnings on the sign at the entrance to the park were unnecessary. Although the water was pleasant to look at, it was about the last place anyone would want to boat, fish, or swim.

One of the best things about the park was its near-total absence of visitors. This meant Scott could let Jake roam free without fear of running into officious citizens carping about his dog being off-leash. On the rare occasion they came across another person, it was almost always another off-leash dog walker.

Even though the park was the high point of his day, Jake maintained his usual low-key style. He didn't chase squirrels up trees or go bounding after deer. He was content to stay by Scott's side, stopping now and then to sniff something along the trail.

The walks were often the apex of Scott's day as well. They never failed to make him feel at peace with himself and the world. But today, something was very different. He couldn't stop thinking about Danny. One minute the man was doing chores around the house, living his life, maybe thinking about the pasta and salad Pam was going to make for din-

ner. The next minute he was in a coma fighting for his life.
All from changing a light bulb! Scott shook his head at the
mind-boggling pointlessness of it.

He thought back to the first time he had walked into Danny's Tavern three years before. Despite its rainy reputation,
in the summer western Washington experienced its share of
hot, humid days, when the air would be so thick and still, it
felt like you were being held under warm water. It had been
just such a day when Scott was driving back from a walk
with Jake and saw the new neon OPEN sign. Without much
thought, he pulled into the lot and went in.

The tavern had been open for only a couple of days. Word
hadn't gotten out yet, so there was a mere handful of customers in the place. Barbara and another younger barmaid
were tending to them, so Scott took a seat across the bar
from a grumpy-looking guy reading a newspaper, dressed
in a too-tight black Harley-Davidson T-shirt that covered
a slight paunch. He looked to be in his early forties, with
squinty eyes and a salt-and-pepper goatee. His thinning
hair was cut short and spiky. Scott assumed—correctly, it
turned out—that this was Danny.

The man glared up from his paper and growled at Scott in
a voice heavy with exaggerated sarcasm and malevolence.
"Can I help you?"

Scott figured he'd wandered into the wrong place. He
started to climb back off the stool. "Well, actually, no. I
think I've changed my—"

"Danny." It was the younger barmaid.

Danny and Scott both glanced in her direction. Using her
index finger, she made the 'cut' gesture across her throat.

"Not him?" said Danny. She shook her head no.

What happened next could not have surprised Scott more;
one of the biggest, sweetest smiles he had ever seen lit up
the man's face.

"Hey, man, sorry 'bout that," said Danny. "Didn't mean
ta freak you out. Grace is havin' serious problems with her
ex-boyfriend. In case he showed up here, I was gonna try

and discourage him from bothering her. Guess you're not him. Which I shoulda been able to figure out on my own, 'cause you're an old dude, like me." He extended a hand across the bar. "I'm Danny."

Scott, feeling relieved, smiled at the good-natured insult and shook hands. "My name's Scott."

"Well, then, Scott. What'll ya have?"

Beneath Danny's gruff façade was one of the nicest people Scott had ever known. He began stopping by the tavern on a regular basis where, over schooners of ale, the two men engaged in blunt, freewheeling conversations. But as time went by, that became harder and harder to do; Danny's Tavern had become such a popular place, it was nearly impossible to catch him alone. This was one of the reasons Scott had come to relish the first Monday of each month; that was the time he'd be sure to have Danny to himself, at least for a little while.

Scott continued wandering down the trail deep in thought as Jake followed a few paces behind. Walking into the tavern earlier that morning and hearing what had happened to his friend felt like being struck by a bolt of lightning. It brought home the reality that—except for Danny—he had no friends. In fact, it had been many years since there had been anyone he considered a friend.

An image of Harry Higgins came into his mind, and Scott smiled. He hadn't thought about his childhood pal in a long time. The two boys had looked nothing alike—Harry was skinny, terrifyingly nearsighted, and wore braces on his teeth. But, like Scott, Harry was terrifically bright. They sat next to each other in just about every class, and both were especially good at math and science. The two had become inseparable.

At this point in his musing, Scott stopped smiling; if only that wonderful friendship had been allowed to continue.

After Sam's death, Scott had been devastated, and both his parents and Harry's parents were worried about him. So, a few days after it happened, Marge and Phil Higgins had asked Scott's parents if he could come with them to their vacation rental on Lake Sonoma for the weekend. He had accompanied the Higgins family several times in the past and always had a great time. They thought it might help take his mind off Sam. Scott's parents readily agreed.

Harry had been the one to instigate the kayak race. The frantic windmill oar strokes of his friend's scrawny arms made Scott think of a giant spastic grasshopper. He started laughing so hard that he wasn't able to keep up, which allowed Harry to pull a couple dozen feet ahead. Because he'd taken off his coke-bottle glasses so they wouldn't get wet, Harry never saw the powerboat filled with partying water skiers rocketing toward him from the side.

The fluke death had been the second terrible thing to happen in less than a week, and in those few days, Scott began to change. He had been an optimistic, outgoing boy; now he was learning to face his sadness by keeping everything inside. His mother noticed this immediately, and his father had come to agree with her. They were smart, loving parents, and they talked about ways to help their son. But they also figured that in time, things would get better.

As it turned out, fate was just getting warmed up.

Scott walked faster in an effort to force these memories out of his head. Right now, he couldn't bring himself to think about what happened next.

Instead, as he covered the trails of Autumn Lake, he came to a startling conclusion. Five years of a structured routine had lulled him into believing he could actually control what happened to himself and to those around him. The cold reality was Scott had very little power over anything. At this realization, it suddenly felt as if the earth were shifting under his feet.

Danny never in a million years deserved to have something like this happen to him. But it was such a stark reminder of how stupidly arbitrary, how shatteringly unfair, fate could be. And that there wasn't a damned thing Scott could do about it.

It infuriated him. He wasn't a religious man. He didn't believe in a Supreme Being. He didn't think there was a heaven or a hell. He'd never belonged to an organized religion, finding them either rigid or silly. Sometimes both.

But neither was he an atheist. For him, to even consider the possibility that all of life was an accident of chemistry and physics was nothing short of terrifying. He couldn't think of a bleaker viewpoint of existence. He had concluded long ago that he was somewhere in between.

Like everyone else, at some point in life, he pondered the Big Questions: Where did they come from? Where did they go when they died? What was the meaning of life?

Scott had come to believe that it didn't matter if a person were the most extreme religious fanatic, the most diehard atheist, or the most ardent agnostic; he still had to come up with answers he could live with. Everyone needed to believe in something to get them through the day. Everyone needed a philosophical framework of some kind to guide them while they were on this earth, if only for the sake of maintaining a baseline of ethics and morals, of being civil, of not murdering fellow human beings in the street for their wallets.

His own framework was straightforward. He possessed an active and searching mind that favored logic and reason, was partial to cause and effect, and was steeped in the notion that every action had an equal and opposite reaction. It was important to his psychological well-being that everything in the cosmos ultimately had to make sense.

He believed in an inherent and fundamental *balance* to the universe, that a karmic equilibrium was always working in the background. He had faith that if something happened that didn't make a lick of sense, it would throw the balance out of whack. But it would be only a temporary glitch, one that would, at some point in eternity, be corrected, and the celestial balance restored.

But he had never been able to understand or accept why such blatant and obvious cosmic mistakes happened in the first place.

After the events of his fourteenth year, Scott had spent his entire working career in the realm of science, math, and computers. Although the hours could be—and often were—long and exhausting, it was an environment in which the stability of numbers reigned, where things always made sense. As CEO of his own software company, he had striven to create order from chaos. He loved it when a sustained and logical effort resulted in the predicted outcome.

He knew that the world of human beings wasn't like that, but still, that didn't stop him from wishing there existed a means to alter the absurd and tragic equations that determined the randomness of life and death. He longed for a way to game the system in favor of those who were guilty of nothing more than being in the wrong place at the wrong time.

But how in the world do you keep a person from slipping off a ladder and hitting his head?

For that, he had no answer.

Scott had been so consumed with these thoughts that he lost track of time. He looked up in surprise to find that he and Jake were approaching the parking lot.

When he got home, a little before five o'clock, he picked up the phone and dialed. Barbara answered, "Danny's Tavern."

"Barbara, it's Scott. I thought I'd call to see if you'd heard anything more."

He heard a deep sigh before she responded.

Oh no, he thought.

"They ran a bunch of tests this morning, and Danny didn't have any brainwave activity at all."

Scott closed his eyes. He could feel it coming...

"Pam had them turn off the life support machines at three this afternoon." Barbara's voice cracked. "He's gone, Scott."

He couldn't speak. Could only stand there with his eyes closed. Finally he said, "I'm sorry, Barbara."

"Me, too."

Hanging up, he walked over to the big picture window. In the distance, the clouds had lifted to reveal the darkly forested lower skirts of the Olympic Mountains. He stood before the window a long time, staring out.

His body began to tremble; Danny's death triggered memories of the third unthinkable tragedy. Now there was no escaping the memory.

After Harry's death, Scott was in an emotional tailspin. His parents tried everything to cheer him up, but nothing seemed to work. He began suffering from acute anxiety and depression, and lost all interest in school. His parents agreed to let him to stay home until Harry's funeral, which took place on a Sunday. By the time Scott got home from the service, he was worse than ever. He shut himself up in his bedroom and refused to come out, not even for dinner.

The next morning, his parents both stayed home from work. They sat down with Scott and told him he needed help, that he should see a psychologist. Scott didn't like the idea at all. He told them they would have to drag him kicking and screaming. His parents had known that his reaction might be something like this. They had one last idea about how to make him feel better, at least for a day. Not only had his mom and dad taken the day off, but they had kept Shelly home as well. All of them would play hooky this one day, would do something fun as a family. This was so out of character for his hard-working parents that, for the first time, Scott was able to see through his own pain to how upset his parents were, how desperate they were to help him.

The Northwoods spent the day pretending to be tourists in San Francisco. They visited Fisherman's Wharf and Chinatown, toured Alcatraz, rode the cable cars, walked across the Golden Gate Bridge. His mother suggested a late lunch at Scott's favorite place, a high-end restaurant in a section of the city known as Japantown. It had become a popular area and construction was booming. The eatery was a place they set aside for special occasions such as birthdays and anniversaries.

Lunch service was open until three. They arrived at 2:30, famished from the busy day. There were few customers, so they sat exactly where they wanted, in an area enclosed by glass, extending partway over the sidewalk. They chose a corner table.

They ordered a meal with copious amounts of sushi, miso soup, chicken yakitori and salmon teriyaki, finishing it off with green tea and fortune cookies. One of the features of the restaurant was the large, well-stocked koi pond located near the front desk. During their visits over the years, Scott and Shelly would always check out the koi fish as their parents settled up with the waiter. They would then come join them at the pond.

As Scott pushed back from the table, he gave his parents the first smile they had seen since before Sam died. He thanked them for the fun day and the super meal, and told them he would go back to school the next day. Then he went to join Shelly who was already at the pond.

While watching the colorful fish scurry about in the water, Scott happened to glance at the glass atrium where his parents were waiting for the waiter to bring back the credit card. They were both watching him, pleased smiles on their faces. Then something strange happened.

A giant shadow passed over the restaurant, accompanied by a loud screech of metal-on-metal. The grating sound suddenly turned into a deafening roar. Scott watched his mother and father look up in uncomprehending fear just as the counterweight of a construction crane crashed through the atrium, landing directly on top of them.

Chapter 2

DANNY

Danny's memorial service was scheduled for one o'clock the following Sunday. Because he hadn't belonged to a church, it would take place in a barn on a bluff overlooking Puget Sound. A native of Kitsap County, he had plenty of family in the area, and an uncle had offered his property for the occasion.

Sunday morning dawned warm and clear. Late summer days in the Northwest could be magical, and today was one of them. Because Scott didn't know when he would get back from the service, he took Jake for an extra-long walk that morning. He knew the dog would snooze through the afternoon.

Arriving at the service early, he found only a couple of cars parked in the lot. He left the Range Rover and headed toward the barn, feeling a little odd in his suit and tie. The last time he'd dressed so formally had been the day he'd stopped working. He did so today out of respect for Danny, though he was pretty sure the man wouldn't have cared if he'd shown up in flip-flops, a snorkeling mask, and a pink thong. In fact, he might have preferred it.

Inside the barn, there were a couple dozen rows of baled hay in place of chairs. A small knot of what Scott assumed were family members stood just inside the doorway, talking. He exchanged nods with them and took a seat in one of the middle rows.

A trickle of people soon began filing into the cavernous

space. The trickle became a stream, and then a river as folks from all walks of life poured in. Young and old, wealthy and poor, blacks, Hispanics, Asians, Native Americans, they were dressed in everything from expensive suits and dresses to scruffy jeans and frayed T-shirts.

Scott caught Barbara's eye as she walked through the doorway. Divorced for a number of years, she had come alone. He motioned for her to join him, and she headed his way.

"I'm glad you came," she said.

"I sure miss that guy."

"We all do. Terribly. It's been really hard at the tavern."

Scott watched in growing amazement as people continued to fill the barn. Among them was Mike from Central Market. Scott waved him over.

He took a seat on Scott's other side, throwing out one of his usual barbs. "What are you doing here? Take a wrong turn-off looking for the Casino?"

Scott found the silly banter to be a welcome relief from the pain he was feeling, and he responded in kind. "So this is how you get Sunday brunch? Go to funerals where you can scarf free food?"

"Beats sitting at home in my underwear watching cartoons over a bowl of soggy corn flakes."

Scott smiled. "I suppose."

The two were quiet a moment. Then Scott said, "I take it you knew Danny."

"Went to high school with him."

"No kidding. What was he like then?"

"Seriously?"

"Seriously."

Mike thought for a moment. "Danny was a hell-raiser with a heart, if that makes sense."

Scott nodded. "I can see him being like that as a teenager."

"Danny went through a lot in life. But we always stayed in touch. He patched my sorry-ass roof more times than I can count. For free. I was glad, though, when he opened the pub. He was getting too old to go up on a ladder every day. Then again, after what happened, I think Danny would appreciate the irony."

Barbara, who had been listening to their conversation, broke in. "Speaking of ironic," she said, "did you hear the one about the recovering alcoholic who went on to open an award-winning micro-brewery?"

Scott was surprised to hear this. "Danny was an alcoholic?"

"Big time," interjected Mike.

"I don't get it. He and I had drinks together. Many times. He always seemed fine."

A reflective smile crossed Barbara's face. "Danny once told me it took him thirty years to learn how to drink."

Scott was beginning to think that maybe he hadn't known Danny as well as he'd thought. Barbara saw the look on his face. "He never said anything to you about that."

"No. He didn't."

"As open and friendly as Danny could be, he was actually a pretty private person. But I'll tell you one thing, Scott."

"What?"

"He genuinely liked you. He would talk about you sometimes. He was flattered that someone like you would take the time to come to the tavern and hang out with him."

On hearing these words, a wistful smile appeared on Scott's face.

People continued to arrive until every row in the barn was packed. Even the standing room along the walls and behind the bales was filled up.

Scott was amazed. "Look at all these people."

"Danny knew a lot of folks."

"I guess."

Danny's younger brother, Casey, stepped up on a make-shift platform at the front and leaned into the microphone. Clean-shaven with close-cropped hair and dressed in a three-piece suit, he looked like a Wall Street version of Danny.

"Thanks for coming, everyone. I thought I would start

Danny's memorial service by drawing your attention to the fact that it's taking place inside a barn, and not a church. In case you hadn't noticed."

Polite laughter rippled through the crowd.

"You're probably wondering why. Well, there's a reason. I'll tell you what it is in a minute. But first, a little background information about my brother."

The crowded room became quiet as Casey began his eulogy. "As many of you probably know, Danny went through a lot of phases in his life. Some good. Some not so good. There was the drinking phase. The drug phase. The muscle-car phase. The biker phase. The hippie phase. And then there was his religious phase, which I think was the one that had the most impact on him. In that time, Danny explored just about every religion there was. Christianity. Islam. Judaism. Buddhism. Hinduism. Shinto. He even dabbled in some of the more exotic belief systems, like Druidism and Paganism. He tried religions on the way some people try on shoes."

Knowing smiles appeared on some of the faces in the crowd.

"Then, one day, just like that, Danny's religious phase was over. I asked him what he had learned. He told me he'd learned three things, all of them pretty basic. He said we should all strive to be kind to others, because each of us, in our own way, carries a heavy burden. He also told me that it's important to do the best we can with what we are given. And finally, he said you don't have to be inside a church to pray or worship or meditate. A house, a cave, a forest—even a barn—work just as well. That's why we're here today."

Casey let the words sink into the hushed crowd. Scott saw more smiles appear as people nodded in appreciation.

"Danny went through a lot as young man, not all of it good. But by his early twenties, he'd managed to turn his life around. He went to work as a part-time roofer and did so well at it that he eventually had his own business, which he ran successfully for many years. Then the economy tanked, the work dried up, and his business was suddenly gone. Not being one to sit around and feel sorry for himself, Danny decided to go back to his first love—beer."

There were chuckles from the crowd.

"When he was in high school, he started brewing beer in our garage. He made it so strong, it was actually more like ale. I remember some interesting after-school get-togethers... Anyway, that went on for about a year, until the day Dad came home early from work. When he opened the garage door, there was Danny sampling his latest batch. Needless to say, my brother's little operation came to a screeching halt.

"But just as every cloud has its silver lining, the recession that cost Danny his roofing business also led him to return to his first passion, the result of which is a little establishment called Danny's Tavern. For all the time I knew him—which, by the way, is my whole life—I can honestly say that I never saw him happier than during these past three years when he was at the tavern, busily crafting and serving his ales.

"Danny was a good person. He was a good husband. A good father. A good brother." Casey's voice began to quaver. "He touched a lot of lives in the short time he was here... and he's going to be deeply and profoundly missed..." Casey had to stop a moment to compose himself before continuing.

"What our family would like to do now is present a slide show of moments from his life."

The lights went down. A series of still photos was projected onto the sheet-covered wall behind the podium, accompanied by a sound track the same vintage as the photos.

There were pictures of Danny's early hard-partying years; of him in a tie-dyed shirt and a flower in his shoulder-length hair; posing with tricked-out cars and Harley-Davidson choppers; as a Hare Krishna, with shaved head and orange robes; of his wedding to Pam; of their camping in the rain; of the births of his daughters Amber and Crystal; more shots of them celebrating birthdays and Christmas; photos of

Danny repairing or replacing roofs; of him and Pam, building houses for Habitat for Humanity; shots of him clowning around in the tavern; a recent photo of him in the lotus position meditating over a cask of ale.

As Scott watched the slideshow, it dawned on him that there was a side to Danny he knew nothing about. Over many years, Danny had put in countless hours helping other people, all on his own time. Scott felt a deepened sense of loss at the fact that he had missed this whole extraordinary part of his friend.

After the slideshow, Casey invited anyone who wanted to come to the podium and share his or her memories of Danny. Dozens of people did, including Mike and Barbara. The stories were poignant, hilarious, and irreverent, eliciting by turns tears and laughter.

As Scott listened to the stories, he found himself thinking about the circumstances of Danny's death.

Falling off a ladder while changing a light bulb.

A wave of outrage swept through him at the incredible unjustness of it. But then a wrestling match broke out in his mind: What, exactly, was so unjust about it? *It was an accident.* Like it or not, they happened every day.

But for a person like Danny to die so pointlessly, so *stupidly*—it just wasn't right!

Who was to say what was right and what wasn't? Certainly not Scott.

It didn't make any sense.

Not everything had to make sense.

Why not?

Was he saying bad things shouldn't happen to good people, and good things shouldn't happen to bad people?

Inside his head, Scott was shouting: *That's exactly what I'm saying!*

He was so immersed in his inner dialogue that the words came out in a fierce whisper. Both Barbara and Mike turned to look at him. He forced himself to calm down, though his hands were trembling.

The last person spoke. The service was winding down. Casey got up to say a few final words about how much Danny was going to be missed.

While Casey spoke, Scott got a strange feeling that someone was staring at him. He tried to ignore it, but the sensation grew stronger until it became an itch that had to be scratched.

His eyes did a quick sweep of all the people filling the barn, then fell upon a man standing with the crowd in the back. He was staring at Scott.

The sunlight streaming in the open doorway behind made it hard for him to see the man's face. The only thing he could clearly take in was the dark gray overcoat the man wore. Odd for such a warm day, he thought.

He returned his attention to the podium. When he looked back a few moments later, the man was gone.

That night, Scott sprawled in his big leather chair, working on his second bottle of wine, half-watching a rerun of *The Wonder Years* with the sound turned off. He decided to call his sister.

He didn't see Shelly nearly as much as he would have liked. She was his only remaining family. Long ago Scott had told her that she had a standing invitation to visit him and bring her family, that he'd be happy to pay their expenses. But she and her husband Ben both had hectic schedules. Together they owned a small restaurant and were raising two teenage boys. Besides, they lived all the way across the country, and a trip to the Northwest seemed like a big deal. So, once a year, Scott would fly down to see them. But again, because of their packed schedule, even then he saw very little of her. In the meantime, they spoke on the phone every month or so.

He picked up the phone and dialed.

In Atlanta, the phone rang four times before an answering machine clicked on. Shelly's voice had a mild southern accent.

"You've reached the Crenshaw residence. Sorry we can't get to the phone right now, but if you'll leave your name and number and the time you called, we'll get back to you as soon as we can."

"Hey, sis, it's me," said Scott. "I was really kind of hoping you'd be there. I went to a memorial service for a friend today. Yeah. Imagine that. Your brother actually has a friend. ...Or *had* a friend, I should say. His name was Danny. He was only forty-five."

The wine was making him ramble, but he didn't care.

"You should've seen all the people there, Shelly. I mean, there were hundreds and hundreds! It got me thinking. When I die, I seriously can't think of anyone who will come to my funeral... Not one person... Except you, of course. At least, I hope you'll come. I'd be really mad if you didn't."

He reconsidered his last statement. "Well, I'd be dead. I don't know if you can be dead and still be mad, but you know what I mean. I've had some wine—I hope I'm making sense. Anyway, I guess what I'm saying is, if I'm living the kind of life where no one's going to bother to show up for my funeral, what kind of life is that, anyway?"

He didn't say anything else for a long moment. Suddenly he began shouting into the phone. "The way Danny died was so goddamned ridiculous, Shelly! You know?! Sound familiar?! It makes me crazy! It makes me want to—to—I don't know, do something! Anything! So that—so that—"

Scott noticed Jake looking up at him in alarm. He dropped his voice to a drunken whisper. The words came out passionate and intense. "Wouldn't it be great if there was some way, some magical process, where I could give up a piece of my life—say a month, or even a year—to Danny, so that he could have lived a little bit longer? If I could give him a day even, one measly day... I mean, that would still be something, right? Anyway, I would have done it. I swear I would have done it. It would've been my gift to him."

He sighed. "I know, life isn't fair. But, dammit, that still doesn't make it right—what happened to him. Does it? I mean, don't you think life should be more fair? At least for people like Danny? I think absolutely it should."

Suddenly drained, he gave an embarrassed laugh.

"Sorry. Didn't mean to go off on a rant like that. Anyway. On that cheerful note, I bid you good night. Call me when you can. I love you. Bye."

He took Jake outside one last time. As he stood swaying in the backyard, waiting for the dog to do his business, he looked up at the sky. The night was perfectly clear. The stars formed diamond swirls and clusters against the black velvet of space.

Scott lurched back into the house and turned off all the lights. He managed to strip down to his T-shirt and boxer shorts before collapsing into bed, where he fell into a deep sleep.

Chapter 3

PATRICK

Next morning dawned cool and gray. Scott woke up and looked out the window with bleary eyes to see a steady drizzle sifting down from leaden skies. Visibility was less than a hundred feet, in marked contrast to the burning blue skies of the day before.

It was Monday, exactly one week since he had first heard the news about Danny.

After a shower, breakfast, and a couple of Advil for his hangover, he and Jake headed for Autumn Lake where the misty drizzle was even thicker. The forest was eerily still, as if encased in gray crystal. The only sound was that of fat drops falling from the trees.

He felt depressed this morning and couldn't think very clearly. The chill damp air felt good against his face. As he and Jake padded quietly along the trail, he was content to let his mind wander.

Suddenly the dog jerked to a halt, standing perfectly still, peering down the mist-shrouded trail.

"What is it, boy?"

A long, low growl sounded from Jake's throat. Scott looked down the path.

Someone was coming toward them.

Probably another dog walker. As scarce as they were when it was warm and sunny, they were practically nonexistent on damp, cold days like this. He wondered who else was crazy enough to be out here in such dismal surroundings.

As the person emerged from the gloom, Scott could see

a man walking by himself, moving at a steady, unhurried pace. His hands were buried deep in the pockets of a charcoal Burberry overcoat. Beneath the coat he wore a black turtleneck, and, instead of boots or outdoor shoes, he was wearing Brionis—not the best choice for a muddy trail.

The man had a lean, six-foot frame and stared at the ground as he walked. His black hair was combed straight back from a receding hairline. He looked around forty, give or take.

Now that Jake saw the man clearly, he stopped growling, sat on his haunches, and watched with curiosity.

The man drew closer. Knowing that some people were frightened of dogs, Scott chose to put the man at ease.

"Don't worry. My dog's friendly," he called out.

Just a few feet away, the man looked up at Scott with eyes of startling depth and intensity.

"You could still do it, ya know." The man spoke in a gruff East Coast accent.

Confused, Scott said, "Excuse me?"

The stranger didn't break stride as he shouldered past. "What're you, deaf or somethin', Northwood? I said, *you could still do it.*"

"Now just hold on a minute," Scott said, unsettled. "Do what? And how do you know my name?"

Still moving, the man turned his head back toward Scott. "Danny's gone," he said. "It's too late for him. But you can still give a portion of your life to somebody else. And never the hell mind how I know your name."

Scott was too stunned to speak. The man continued down the path, disappearing back into the gloomy mist of the forest.

"Hey," Scott said, breaking into a run after him. "Hey!"

But the man was nowhere to be seen.

Scott halted and stared down the empty path, the beating of his heart mingling with the sound of raindrops dripping from the trees.

By the time he and Jake made it back to the parking lot,

his mind was racing. There could be only one explanation.

He made the call as soon as he got home. He wasn't so much angry as annoyed. Once again the answering machine came on. Once again he left a message after the beep.

"Okay, Shelly, what's up with the prank? Why in the world would you do something like that? Did you have that guy follow me just to creep me out? I mean, I know Halloween's coming up, but really. I've never known you to pull a stunt like this, and frankly, I'm disappointed. I didn't find it funny at all. If anything, it was just plain weird."

He hung up the phone, feeling better for having vented.

Needing to run some errands, he grabbed his coat, gave Jake a rough pat on the head, and headed out the door. He spent the next hour going by the library and buying groceries at Central Market.

It was getting dark by the time he got home. Jake sat framed in the window, watching for him. It was his dinnertime, a sacred period of the day.

As Scott unlocked the door, the phone rang. He managed to get to it before the answering machine picked up.

"Hello?"

"What on earth are you talking about?" It was Shelly. She didn't sound happy.

"So you got my message."

"Yes, I got your message. We were out of town for the weekend. Just got back a few minutes ago."

It took Scott a moment to put it together.

"A few minutes ago? But that means—"

"It means I only just now listened to both your messages. And I don't know anything about any prank."

It felt as if an ice cube were sliding down the length of his back.

"Scott, you know what I think?"

"What?" He was only half-listening. If it hadn't been Shelly who put that guy up to it, how in the world did...

"I think you've been living out there in the rain too long. It's starting to leak into your skull!"

"Look. Shelly. I'm sorry. It's just that something very strange happened today and—"

"And how dare you to think I would even think about doing whatever it is you think I did!"

She hung up. Scott stared at the phone in his hand. He placed it into its cradle and looked down at Jake.

"What the hell's going on?"

After feeding Jake, Scott put on his pajamas and robe and went outside. He stood in the backyard. The thick cloud cover had vanished. It was a moonless night. The air had been washed clean and the stars burned with unusual clarity. Though the Olympic Mountains were hidden, they still made their presence known as a deep, black silhouette in the distance.

He pulled his robe tightly around him and folded his arms to ward off the chill. For a long time he remained that way, staring out at the night.

Disturbed by his encounter with the man on the trail, he spent a restless night. Still, he was up early the next morning, determined to try to find him and get some answers. After a shower and a quick breakfast, he and Jake headed for Autumn Lake much earlier than usual.

The day was clear and cool in marked contrast to the moisture-saturated gloom of the previous day. Bright autumn sunlight filtered down through the trees, illuminating the ferns that sprouted like green fountains from the damp forest floor.

Scott walked every trail in the park without any sign of the man in the dark coat. After several hours, he began to wonder if he'd imagined the whole thing, though the notion that he had been hallucinating was hardly a desirable alternative.

He looked down at Jake. Much as the dog loved his outings, he, too, was dragging.

"I don't know who that guy was," he said to the animal, "but tramping around out here all day isn't getting us anywhere. Let's call it a day."

They turned in the direction of the parking lot. "I hope Shelly isn't too mad at me," he said, continuing to address Jake. "I'll call her when we get back to the house and try to patch things up."

They were almost to the car when the man in the dark coat appeared. He was walking right toward them, wearing the same clothes as yesterday, and moving in the same unhurried gait. He looked at Scott with those dark, unnerving eyes.

About ten feet away he stopped and stood gazing at Scott as if sizing him up. The man seemed in no hurry to speak, so Scott broke the silence.

"Okay. I'll go first. You obviously know my name, but I haven't had the pleasure. Who are you?"

The man replied in a clipped East Coast accent. "You can call me Patrick."

"All right, Patrick. What's going on?"

He grinned a moment, though Scott thought it looked more like a sneer. "I think what you really meant to ask was, 'What the *hell* is going on?' Am I right?"

"Won't argue with that."

Patrick spoke clearly and distinctly, as if talking to a child. "What's going on is exactly what I told you was going on. You wish there were some way you could have taken time from your own life and given it to Danny."

Scott struggled to remain calm. "How could you possibly know that?"

"Let's just say it's one of my special talents. The point is, you weren't making idle conversation with your sister. You were dead serious."

"Yeah, I was serious. What else do you know about me?"

"Lots of things."

"Like what?"

"Like when you were twelve, you and Mark Harrington used his dad's twenty-two to go hunting in the fields near his house. It was your first time. You shot a rabbit, but it didn't die right away. You had to shoot it a couple more times. That night you felt so bad you cried yourself to sleep."

A chill ran through Scott's body. "I never told anyone about that."

The sneering grin again. "Like I said. One of my special talents."

"Are you a psychic or something?"

"Or something. As I said yesterday, what's going on is Danny's gone. That can't be changed. But I'm here to tell you that you can still give a piece of your life to someone *like* Danny."

Scott was dumbfounded. He finally managed to say, "You expect me to believe that?"

"I don't give a shit what you believe. The fact of the matter is, it's true."

"But how is that even possible?"

"I don't know why it works. I don't know how it works. What I *do* know is, it works."

"If what you say is true, you're asking me to do this for a complete stranger."

"So?"

Scott was incredulous. "Why should I shorten my life so somebody I've never even met can live longer?"

"I'll tell you why. There are only so many Dannys in the world. By that, I mean people who put in a lot of time and effort helping other people. Unfortunately, now and then a Danny expires before he's had a decent chance to fulfill his potential. Unless, of course, someone like you comes along who's willing to transfer a slice of time to him—or her, as the case may be."

Scott thought about that a moment before responding. "So, basically... you're saying that the Dannys of the world are more deserving to live than I am."

Patrick's mouth opened in fake awe. "I'm talkin' to a regular Einstein here!"

"But that's ridiculous! I've got just as much right to live as anyone else."

"Technically, you do. Realistically, you don't. Not if *you know* you possess the ability to extend the life of another Danny. I mean, come on, Northwood. Look at yourself. All you do is sit around on your ass." Patrick's voice brimmed with disdain. "Who do you really think is more deserving to live? Someone like Danny? Or someone like you? Take your time answering. I got all day."

Scott felt a hot surge of anger, but forced himself to remain calm. "If it's so important to you," he said, "why don't you transfer time from your own life?"

"I would if I could. But that's not where my abilities lie. What I can do, though, is help others to do exactly that. You could think of me as an *Enabler.* Do you follow me?"

"But isn't an enabler someone who—"

"Who helps an addict stay addicted? Isn't that what you were going to say? Well, crap on that noise. The word has been corrupted. Try looking it up in the dictionary. It means *one who enables or empowers others.*"

"To do what, exactly?"

"Listen carefully. I'm going to lay it all out for you just this one time. First, there's me—the Enabler. Then there's you, the Implementer. Then there's the unwitting Prospect, by which I mean a Danny who is about to kick prematurely. I am here to enable you to implement the process by which the Prospect's life can be extended. You with me so far?"

"That's the craziest thing I ever heard."

"It sounds off the grid, but, trust me, it's real."

"But how is it even possible?" And why was he even talking to this lunatic? Then again, the guy knew things about him no one else could possibly know...

"Like I told you; I don't know how or why it works, but it does. Think of me as a set of jumper cables. Danny's a dying battery. You're a fully charged one. You and me team up to jumpstart him so that the car—meaning all the stuff that he's doing—will keep running a while longer, maybe even make it to a gas station."

Scott said, "Okay, just for the sake of argument, suppose such a thing were possible, and you persuaded me to extend the life of another person. What do I get in return? Besides having my own life shortened?"

"You get the chance to put your money where your mouth is."

"Not good enough."

"Then how about this: you get the satisfaction of knowing you actually did something worthwhile with your otherwise meaningless existence."

That sneering grin again.

"But what if I've only got a couple years left to live myself?"

"You got nothin' to worry about. You're slated to live into your nineties."

Patrick said this so matter-of-factly that Scott found himself believing it for a moment. *Forty-plus more years...*

"How in the world would you know something like that?"

"Again, one of my special talents. Actuaries would kill to have it."

The cold black liquid of Patrick's eyes became still and deep as he fixed Scott with a stare so unnerving it sent a shudder through him.

"So that's what's going on. Like I said, it's too late for Danny. He's moved on. But there are other Dannys out there. It's not too late for them. In fact, I got a Prospect right now who's going to need help soon. How about it, hotshot? Want to be an Implementer?"

Not in a million years. Scott felt an overwhelming urge to get out of there. "No thanks. I've got to be going." He and Jake moved past the man and down the trail.

"Don't be a jerk-off, Northwood! For once in your life, you have the chance to do something worthwhile! I suggest you take it!"

Scott quickened his pace and called back, "Goodbye, and don't bother me again."

Patrick voiced a response. Scott couldn't be sure, but he thought it sounded like, "We'll see about that."

Scott spent the rest of the day trying to put the encounter out of his mind. But the harder he tried, the more he thought about it and the more troubled he became.

That night he called his sister once again. For once, he was thankful that her answering machine came on.

"Hi, Shelly. Look, I just wanted to say that I'm really sorry for the message I left you the other night. I accused you of something you didn't do, and I apologize. I don't know what I was thinking. Except for my hairy brown beast of a dog, you're the only family I've got. Please don't be mad. I love you."

He hung up the phone, yawned and scratched Jake's scruffy muzzle.

"It's been a long day, old bean. Time to hit the hay." He got up and they headed for the bedroom.

Chapter 4

MEGAN

Next day, Scott and Jake took their walk at the usual time. Wondering if he would run into that man again, Scott felt anxious as they set out on the trail. Sure enough, halfway through their walk, Patrick stood on the path ahead, waiting.

Scott found himself getting angry. "What part didn't you get when I told you to stop bothering me?" he called out. "Go find another park to play in where you can mess with somebody else's head."

"Do you like cheeseburgers, Northwood?" Patrick asked.

It was about the last thing in the world Scott expected him to say.

"Excuse me?"

"Everybody likes cheeseburgers. I know a place that makes the best one in the county."

"What in the world are you talking about?"

"Cedar Rock Restaurant in Seabeck. You should check it out."

Then he turned and walked away. Scott watched him disappear down the trail, more mystified than ever.

⌒⌒⌒

After this last encounter, Patrick stopped showing up at Autumn Lake, and Scott was greatly relieved. For the first few days, anyway. But after several weeks went by, he couldn't get out of his head what the man had said.

Do you like cheeseburgers, Northwood?

What the hell was that supposed to mean?

The guy was beginning to bother him more by his absence than by his presence.

Cedar Rock Restaurant in Seabeck. You should check it out.

Finally, in late October, after one particularly rainy walk, Scott gave in. He dried Jake off with the towel and loaded him into the Range Rover. "What do you say we take a little drive?" he said.

Kitsap County roads were uncrowded and inviting, which made driving a great pleasure for Scott. After Silicon Valley, it was a novelty to drive at the speed he wanted and not have another car twelve inches from his rear bumper. Plus, it was great to take long, rambling sojourns down the rural back roads. After an hour of cruising past fields and forests, half hidden in somber autumn mist, he came upon a road sign for the town of Seabeck.

"As a matter of fact, I do like cheeseburgers," said Scott as another sign materialized:

Food - Next Right

It listed the names of several places to eat. And there it was: Cedar Rock Restaurant. He took the exit.

The restaurant was set back from the road in a grove of giant cedars. The building was at least forty years old, constructed of enormous beams of wood and boulders. It looked as if a landslide had ground to a semi-symmetrical halt directly in front of the paved parking lot.

Even though it was after one on a weekday, the lot was almost full. That seemed odd for a funky restaurant this far off the beaten track.

Inside, the restaurant was a large room filled with cheap wooden tables and chairs, and the aromas of garlic, onions, and sizzling meat. The walls were late seventies faux wooden paneling. On the left was a long counter where old-timers sat on stools lingering over cups of coffee. Behind the counter, a large man with tattooed arms and a grease-streaked apron sweated as he grilled burgers over an open flame. On the right, several tired-looking booths lined the wall, all but one occupied.

The man in the apron called out, "Grab a menu and sit anywhere you like. Megan'll be right with you." He nodded at a waitress taking orders at a table across the room.

Scott slid into the vacant booth and began studying the list of foods.

"You gonna memorize that menu or what?"

He looked up into a young woman's dark brown eyes.

"Let me know if you are." She sat down across from him and tossed her order pad in the middle of the table. "Because then I could sit here and do my nails. Or I could meditate, maybe do a little downward-facing dog. Or I could have a margarita. I could tell Gus to turn on the TV so I could watch a soap. And maybe another margarita. Then I could settle in for a good long nap while you make up your mind." She closed her eyes, leaned her head back against the booth and pretended to snore.

Scott, for a moment too flummoxed to respond, stared at the waitress. She was just a girl. Her long brown hair was pulled back in a ponytail. Although her eyes were a little too big and her lips a little too thin, she possessed a quirky beauty. She looked about twenty.

Suddenly she sat upright, all business, her pen poised to stab the ordering pad. "Okay, Mister, we're both going to start to decompose here if you don't order up. What's it going to be?"

He couldn't help but smile at her. "I hear this place serves a mean cheeseburger."

She lowered her voice and spoke excitedly, as if sharing a delicious bit of gossip with her best friend. "You got that right! The ground beef Gus uses is top notch. He seasons it with fresh garlic, grilled onions, a little pepper and just the right amount of salt. Topped with a thick slice of Tillamook cheddar, it's really tasty! Trust me, you'll love it."

"Sounds good to me. Could I get a Danny's Pale Ale to wash it down?"

"You sure could."

Scott smiled. "That would be perfect."

"I don't know if we're going to keep getting it. I heard the guy who makes it died."

"So I heard."

She snapped her pad closed and stood up. "Order coming right up." She strode away, ponytail swinging from side to side.

He watched her walk away. She was tall to the point of gangly, but carried herself with a grace and efficiency of movement that was curiously sexy. She moved from table to table, dishing out an energetic onslaught of teasing abuse to all customers. Judging by people's responses, everyone loved her. Scott grinned. He had never come across anyone quite like her.

An hour later, he returned to his car, a toothpick between his teeth and a paper bag in his hand. He opened the passenger door, and Jake sat up.

"I had them make you a baby cheeseburger." He reached into the bag, pulled out the treat, and held it out. The dog quickly yet politely gobbled it down.

That night in bed, Scott lay with his hands behind his head thinking about Megan. The girl was definitely a trip. After he had gotten the hang of her insolent banter, he'd returned it in kind. It was the most fun he'd had in a long time. He wasn't physically attracted to her; that wasn't it at all. But he'd enjoyed her earthy charisma. Megan was a welcome blast of fresh air in his quiet, ordered life.

The next day he went back to the Cedar Rock for another cheeseburger, arriving just after 12:00 o'clock, the beginning of the lunch hour. The parking lot was full so he was forced to park on a side street.

Entering the restaurant, he was surprised again to see this out-of-the-way place so packed. But then he realized why that was. Yes, the food here was good, but they came because of Megan.

He spied an empty stool at the counter and slid in next to an old-timer who was deeply involved with a hamburger. There was another waitress working the room with Megan. The short, blonde, heavyset woman approached Scott, and slapped a menu and a glass of ice water in front of him. Her nametag read "Brenda."

"I don't need a menu. I'll have the cheddar cheeseburger and a Danny's Pale Ale."

"You got it."

He turned in his seat to watch Megan move from table to table, taking orders and balancing trays while cheerfully heaping verbal abuse on her customers. They were eating it up.

Even the infirm didn't escape her caustic remarks. Sitting at a booth with a group of friends was an elderly woman tethered by plastic tubing to a portable oxygen tank. As Megan set their lunch plates in front of them, she spied the tank.

"You can't fool me, sister," she said. "That's nitrous oxide. Everyone thinks you're using oxygen when I know what you're really doing is getting high on laughing gas."

"Don't tell anyone," whispered the woman with a wink.

"Only if you promise to save me a couple of hits for when I get off work. Then you and I are heading to the casino and partying till dawn." Megan smiled. "Who knows, maybe we'll even pick up a couple of cute guys and get lucky." The older woman was beaming.

As Megan passed the counter with a stack of dirty dishes, she noticed Scott. She stopped in front of him, gave him a withering look and announced, "You again. Look, mister, like I told you yesterday; the Convention for Sexual Deviants is in *Seattle*, not *Seabeck*."

This brought guffaws from everyone around him.

"And you better leave Brenda a ginormous tip," she continued, "or I'll bend you over my knee and give you a good spanking."

"Promises, promises."

As she strode away, she called back, "In your dreams, buddy. And in my nightmares!"

On Wednesday, Scott returned to the Cedar Rock for the third time in as many days. He wanted to be there when it wasn't so busy, so he didn't come until after two. The restaurant closed at 2:30.

The place was nearly empty as he slipped into a booth. Megan appeared right away. "Gus is about to close the kitchen, but if you know what you want, I can get your order in before he shuts down."

"I'll just have a Danny's."

"No lunch today?"

"I need to watch what's left of my girlish figure."

"One ale coming up." She went off to get his beverage.

By 2:25, he was the last customer in the restaurant. He sat in the booth sipping his ale while Megan cleared the last of the tables. Behind the counter, Gus wiped down the griddle.

Megan came over and slid into the booth across from him. Speaking with a directness that was both charming and disconcerting, she said, "So what is it?"

"What is what?"

"I'm going to be frank with you. You've been here three days in a row watching me and it's starting to creep me out. I hope you don't have some kind of a crush on me, because I'm not into older men and I'm sure not looking for a sugar daddy."

"It's nothing like that. It's just fun watching you work."

"So you're not stalking me?"

"Afraid not."

"Damn. I've never been stalked before. I thought you

might be the one."

"Sorry to disappoint you."

"I'll survive. You must have a lot of free time on your hands to spend your days going around watching other people work their tails off."

"I'm retired."

"You seem a little young to be retired."

"I worked in the software industry. Sold my business a few years back."

"Must be nice."

"It is, actually. What about you?"

"What about me?"

"What else do you do besides verbally harass diners?"

"I'm studying graphic design at Olympic Community College in Bremerton. Afternoon and evening classes."

"Do they have a decent program?"

"It's just okay. I'm planning on transferring to the Seattle Art Institute next year."

"I've heard it's a good school."

"It is. It's also expensive."

"Will you be able to manage it on a waitress's salary?"

"I think so. My mom is helping me out big time. She's letting me live with her rent-free. She's even offered to help pay for my tuition."

"That's nice of her."

"It is, 'cause she doesn't make a lot of money. She's a big believer in getting an education, or at least learning a good trade." She looked at him with a curious expression.

"What?" said Scott.

"I think you'd like my mom."

"If she's anything like her daughter, she'd be a handful."

"Mom's nothing like me. She's nice." Megan pushed the check for the ale across to him. "I notice you're not wearing a wedding ring. Do you have a girlfriend?"

"Not at the moment. But getting back to you. It sounds like you've got everything figured out."

"Not everything."

"Oh?"

A look of yearning crossed her face. "Ever since I was little, I've wanted to go to Europe."

Scott's eyebrows went up in surprise. "Really? Where in Europe?"

"The usual suspects. France. Italy. England."

"Why?"

Her voice suddenly colored with passion. "It always seemed so exotic and exciting to me. Don't get me wrong. I'm a red-blooded American girl through and through. But my whole life, I've had this really strong desire to go there. I want to walk down ancient cobblestoned streets. Visit medieval cathedrals. Hang out at sidewalk cafes. That's why, in addition to my savings for school, I have a secret 'E' fund set aside."

"E for Europe."

She nodded. "Mom says I need to get an education first, and then I'll have plenty of time to go to Europe."

"Smart woman, your mother."

"She's right, I know. So I need to wait until I'm through school. But then I'm definitely going."

"I'm sure you are."

"Have you ever been?"

"To Europe? Once."

"When?"

"Back when I was in college. About a hundred years ago."

"Did you go by yourself?"

"I went with a tour group of other students that was affiliated with the school."

"Where did you go?"

"The usual suspects. We wandered around London, Paris and Rome for a couple of weeks."

"Did you like it?"

"It was okay."

"Just *okay*?"

He shrugged, a little embarrassed. "I was never much for vacations. Didn't have the time."

"Now that you're retired, your whole life is a vacation."

"I hadn't thought of it that way."

"It's true, isn't it? You're still young—relatively, anyway."

"Gee, thanks."

"I mean that as a compliment. And you seem healthy. You could pretty much go anywhere and do anything you wanted. I think that's pretty cool."

"I guess."

"You 'guess'? Let me tell you something. If I had your life, I sure wouldn't be lurking around backwoods restaurants."

"Quitting time, Megan," Gus called from the kitchen.

She stood. "Sorry, but I need to throw you out now."

Scott drained the last of his ale and stood up. "Nice talking with you, Megan." He pulled out his wallet. "Allow me to make a modest donation to the 'E' fund." He pulled out a twenty and laid it on the table next to the bill. "Keep the change."

"I wasn't asking for charity." She looked offended.

"And I wasn't offering it. Consider it a ginormous tip."

She smiled and picked up the twenty. "Since you put it that way. Thank you very much, Mr.--?"

"Call me Scott. It was nice chatting with you, Megan."

"Likewise, Scott. See you tomorrow?"

"I don't think so. I'm going to stick with salads for a while. Let my cholesterol level drop back below 'stroke imminent'. So I'll be lurking a little closer to home."

"See you around."

She turned and headed toward the cash register. Scott walked out into the cool gray afternoon.

November was historically the stormiest month of the year in the Northwest. True to form, it was cool and blustery on the trail the next morning as a strong wind pushed through the forest. Trees twisted and swayed and rubbed against each other, creating an eerie racket that sounded like ancient doors creaking open and closed.

Scott smiled at his conversation with Megan. Her blend of honesty, directness, and irreverence was refreshing, especially in one so young. For all her brash exterior, the genuine warmth and kindness just below the surface was obvious.

He hadn't gotten far when he saw Patrick a few yards ahead, standing in the middle of the path with his feet planted wide and hands buried in coat pockets. The impatient look on his face made it clear that he had been waiting for a while.

Scott realized he'd barely given the man a thought the last couple days. This made him smile to himself. Indeed, it would be fine with him if he never laid eyes on Patrick again.

He halted a few feet away. "Hello, Patrick. How nice to see you again." He didn't care if the man noticed the sarcasm saturating his words.

"She's somethin', isn't she?" said Patrick.

Puzzled, Scott said, "Who are you talking about?"

"Who the hell you think I'm talkin' about?"

It could only be one person. "You mean Megan? The waitress at the Cedar Rock?"

"Like I keep tellin' ya, Northwood, you're a regular Einstein."

What Patrick was telling him suddenly came clear. "Wait a minute. Do you mean *Megan* is the Prospect you were talking about the other day? The one you said is going to need help?"

"Listen to this guy. You oughta go on *Jeopardy*. Why'd you think I told you to go there in the first place?"

"Why is she a Prospect? Is something going to happen to her?"

A gust of wind swept down the trail. Scott heard a cracking noise above and behind him. He looked up to see a large branch spear to the ground about twenty feet away. When he turned back around, Patrick was gone.

"Answer me!" Scott shouted into the air. "What's going to happen to her?!"

But there was only the sound of the wind pressing through the trees.

Scott dropped Jake off at the house, then drove to the Cedar Rock, arriving at the height of the lunch hour. Megan and Brenda were both swamped. They hurried from table to table, delivering food and taking orders.

Scott managed to catch Megan's eye as he stood near a hungry crowd, all waiting for tables. He motioned her over.

"I thought you weren't coming back for a while."

"I wasn't planning to. But something's... come up."

"Sorry, Scott," she said briskly, "but it's going to be at least a half-hour. You'll have to wait your turn like everyone else."

"I didn't come here to eat."

"Then what did you come here for?"

"To tell you something."

"Tell me what?"

He became flustered. "To just... be careful."

"Be careful? Careful about what?"

He realized that that was a real good question. "I don't know," he answered, feeling frustrated and ridiculous.

A look of mild alarm came into her eyes. "Look. Scott. I'm really busy right now. I think you're a nice man, but you're getting weird on me."

"I'm sorry. It's just that..."

"What?"

"Nothing. I better go."

"That's probably a good idea." She turned and reentered the barely-controlled chaos of the lunch rush.

His face burning, he drove home feeling like a fool. He vowed never to go back to the restaurant.

When the Cedar Rock closed at 2:30, Megan and Brenda stayed busy carrying trays of soiled dishes to the back to be rinsed and washed.

Brenda dropped off a load of plates and cups. Megan was

behind her, carrying a tray bristling with glasses.

"That's what I call a busy lunch run," Brenda said, turning to head back for another tray. "At least the tips were good."

"Yeah," said Megan, without her usual enthusiasm.

Brenda stopped and looked at her. The girl was sweaty and pale. "Megan, are you okay?"

Megan continued past her. "I'm fine. A little under the weather, but I'll live."

"Just checking." Brenda turned to go collect another tray. "Because if you want to head home early, I'd be happy to—"

There was a loud crash. Brenda whirled to see Megan lying on the floor, unconscious, surrounded by shattered glass.

"Gus!"

He charged in from the kitchen and knelt by Megan's side. "Brenda, call 9-1-1. *Now!*"

Chapter 5

LINDA

Linda Hillis was on the last hour of her shift at the Food King Market in Bremerton when, sure enough, the pain in her right knee came back. This had been happening like clockwork for almost a year now. With each passing month, the throbbing had worsened. She grimaced at the sensation. This was the last thing her otherwise perfectly healthy forty-two-year-old body needed. Funny how a skiing accident that happened half a lifetime ago could come back to haunt her now. Yeah. Real funny. Downright hilarious.

She eyed the bottle of ibuprofen that she kept handy next to the cash register. She'd take a couple as soon she finished taking care of this customer.

Pushing a strand of light brown hair out of her eyes she began ringing up the groceries of the elderly man across the counter. Trying to sound cheerful, she said, "How you doing today?"

The old man grinned at the trim, quietly attractive cashier with the pretty caramel eyes. "Just fine, young lady," he said. "Yourself?"

"Couldn't be better," she lied. She forced herself to smile through the pain.

She found herself thinking about the collision that had caused all this. It had been perfect conditions. Clear blue skies. Bright glistening slopes. The skiing trip had been her idea. It was supposed to be a celebration. She had stopped to catch her breath and was waiting for Jerry to catch up when she had been blindsided by an out-of-control snowboarder. What had begun as one of the best days of her life ended up being one of the worst.

"Linda."

The voice belonged to her boss, the owner of the market. When she glanced up to find out what he wanted, she noticed the grimness of his expression—even grimmer than usual, which was saying something. When Larry looked this way, it was certain something was wrong.

"You have a phone call," he said. "Use my office. I'll take over here." Without any further explanation, he slid behind her into the checkout stand and continued ringing up groceries.

Suddenly nervous, Linda walked to the tiny office next to the ATM machine. She closed the door behind her and picked up the phone. "This is Linda."

"It's Gus at the Cedar Rock." His voice was tight and tense. "Megan's in an ambulance on her way to Harrison Hospital."

"An *ambulance!*" A volcano of panic erupted in Linda's gut. "What happened?"

"She was working when all of a sudden she collapsed."

"What do you mean, 'collapsed'?"

"Just what I said. She was out before she hit the floor. I think you need to—hello? Linda? Are you there?"

She was already running to her car.

⁔ ⁔ ⁔

Located in Bremerton where it served the south Kitsap area, Harrison Hospital was a fully functioning medical establishment. It took Linda only a few minutes to get there. She now stood in a corner of the waiting room, terrified, watching the double doors that led into the Intensive Care Unit. She'd been there for over an hour.

A tall young doctor in a white coat pushed through the doors. His old-fashioned horn-rimmed glasses gave him an air of intelligence and authority. His eyes swept the room and locked on Linda.

"Are you Megan's mom?"

"Yes," said Linda. She was both glad and apprehensive that the doctor was finally here.

"I'm Doctor Drake. I'm in charge of the neurosurgery department."

"Neurosurgery?"

He guided her over to a couple of chairs. "We'd better sit down."

"How is she? What happened to her?"

"We've run a full series of scans on Megan. I wanted to be sure I knew what was going on with her before I spoke to you. I'm afraid it's not good. She has a large and aggressive tumor growing in her brain."

"Oh, God, no," breathed Linda, stifling a sob. "I don't understand. When she left for work this morning, she was fine."

"Megan has what's known as stage 4 glioblastoma. It's a tumor that can grow very quickly while the patient remains asymptomatic—that is, not showing any signs that she's sick. It's starting to press up against critical arteries and nerve centers. That's what caused her to lose consciousness."

"Can you operate? Remove it surgically?"

"I'm afraid the answer to that is no. The tumor's located in an area of the brain where any attempt to remove it would prove fatal."

"Oh, dear God!" *This couldn't be happening!* "What can you do?"

"We're going to try to shrink it with a combination of radiation and chemotherapy. We've already started her on an intensive regimen of both. At this point, that's the only option we have."

Linda gripped her knees with her hands. "What are the chances of it working?"

The doctor hesitated for a moment before he answered. "Not very good."

Linda's knuckles were turning white. "Tell me—*what are the chances?*"

Again the hesitation. Then, "The success rate is less than

five percent."

"Five percent…"

"Ms. Hillis, please know that we will do everything in our power to save your daughter. I'm sorry to have to bring you such painful news."

"You're sorry?" She rose to her feet. "You're a doctor, for crying out loud! Doctors aren't supposed to be sorry. You're supposed to cure!"

He stood up. "I had to be honest with you. In my experience, I've found it does no one any good if I mislead you about what's happening."

Linda took a breath, fighting to keep from breaking down. "Can I see her?"

He nodded. "Of course." He took her arm and guided her toward the swinging doors. "Megan hasn't regained consciousness since she passed out at the restaurant. Don't be alarmed if she doesn't look her best."

They entered the Intensive Care Unit. The doctor pulled aside the curtain to reveal Megan lying in a hospital bed. She looked unnaturally thin and pale. When Linda reached out and held her daughter's limp hand, the tears came in a torrent.

<p style="text-align:center">~~~</p>

Linda sat by the hospital bed for the next several hours, silently willing her daughter's body to respond to the treatment. The doctor came in to check on Megan about every thirty minutes. He told Linda that, although Megan was still in serious condition, at least her vital signs had stabilized, which meant she wasn't getting any worse. This was a good sign, however small.

It was after nine in the evening when the doctor gently but firmly insisted that Linda go home and get some sleep. He knew she lived only a couple of miles away, and assured her he would call immediately if there were any change in Megan's condition. Linda reluctantly agreed.

It was close to ten when she pulled up at the modest

Craftsman she shared with her daughter. As she unlocked the front door, she heard the phone begin to ring. Thinking it could be Drake, she hurried in to answer it.

"Hello?"

"Hello, is this Linda Hillis?" She didn't recognize the voice. It sounded like an elderly man with a soft Southern accent.

"Yes."

"Are you Megan's mother?"

"Who's calling?"

"I'm very sorry if I'm disturbing you. My name is Frank Cooper. You don't know me, but I know your daughter from the restaurant. I go there a lot and I heard what happened and I—well, I was just calling to see how she's doing."

As he talked, Linda glanced down. To her surprise she saw that there were 19 messages waiting on the answering machine.

"She's, uh, I'm afraid she's not doing very well. I wish I could say different..."

"I'm very sorry to hear that, Ma'am. I think your daughter is just the neatest gal. If there's anything I can—"

"I don't mean to be rude, Mr.—um, Cooper, but I just got home from the hospital, and I need to keep the line clear in case they call."

"Of course. I'll keep your daughter in my prayers."

"Thank you. Good-bye."

Linda hung up and pressed the Play Messages button. The first one was an early call from Gus. His normally calm voice was frantic.

"Mrs. Hillis, it's Gus. I wasn't sure if you were working today or not. I'll try calling you at the grocery store. Something's happened to Megan and, well, I'll just call you at the store."

The next call came in about a half hour later from Brenda.

"Linda, it's Brenda. I know you're probably at the hospital with Megan. I was just calling to see if you found out anything. We're all worried about her. Take care."

The next seemed to be from a very elderly woman: "Hello. I just heard what happened, and I'm calling to see how Megan is doing, God bless her. That's all. Sorry to disturb you. Good-bye."

Then there was one left in a gruff voice by what sounded like young man: "Hey, uh, hope I ain't out of line by doing this, but, uh, I was callin' to see how Megan was doing. Tell her Darryl called and that me and the lunch gang from booth four are thinkin' about her, and that if she don't come back soon, we're gonna… well, I don't know what we're gonna do, but we'll be pretty pissed and just might have to kick her ass. Get well, Megan."

Linda continued playing the messages until she had heard them all. Except for Gus and Brenda, she didn't know any of the people. She stared at the phone in wonder at all the calls from well-wishers.

The tears came again. For a brief moment, she smiled through them.

It was still dark next morning when the phone jarred Linda awake. For a moment, she didn't know where she was. She had the sensation of waking up from a bad dream. She fought to clear her head as she reached for the phone beside the bed.

"Hello?"

"Ms. Hillis, it's Doctor Drake."

Suddenly wide awake, she sat bolt upright. "Yes, Doctor."

"I'm afraid Megan's taken a turn for the worse. You need to come to the hospital."

"I'm on my way."

She had been having a nightmare, all right. Only this was one she couldn't wake up from. This one was real.

She pulled on her clothes and was out the door in under a minute.

"Ms. Hillis – Linda – remember when I told you I wouldn't mislead you?"

She nodded. They sat in the same two chairs in the waiting room, but this early in the morning it was deserted. The doctor was unshaven and haggard-looking, as if he had been up all night.

"I'm going to stay true to my word," he continued. "The tumor isn't responding to treatment. In fact, it's growing at a faster rate. This means it's pressing even harder against Megan's vital nerves and arteries. I'm sorry, Linda, but I'm afraid at this point, we're out of options."

She didn't say anything for a long moment. Finally, in a voice that was strangely calm, she said, "How long?"

"A few days. A week, at the very most."

At his words, her body was wracked by a deep and shuddering sob.

"Is there anyone you would like to call?" he asked after it passed.

She felt as if she'd just been gutted. "No," she said, her voice a whisper. "I'd just like to go sit with her."

〜〜〜

That afternoon, as a freezing early November mist enveloped the trail at Autumn Lake, Scott buttoned his coat to the neck and quickened his pace to ward off the chill. He and Jake had gone about a mile when they saw Patrick coming toward them.

In an irritated voice, Scott said, "You've got a real knack for making yourself scarce when it suits you."

"She's in trouble."

Scott felt cold electricity shoot through him. "What's wrong with her?"

"Why don't you go see for yourself."

"Where is she?"

"You're a smart guy, Northwood. You'll find her. And after you've seen her, you need to decide what—*if anything*— you're gonna do about it."

Patrick pushed past him and continued down the trail. "When you're ready to talk, you know where to find me," he called out.

All it took was a phone call to the Cedar Rock. An answering machine came on, saying that the restaurant was temporarily closed out of respect for Megan, and that if any of her friends desired, they could send flowers to room 618 at Harrison Hospital.

It was getting dark by the time Scott arrived at Harrison. He took the elevator to the sixth floor and was making his way down the wide, brightly lit hallway when he came to a nurses' station. He saw that Megan's room would be on the other side of it. He nodded politely to the young nurse behind the counter as he walked by.

"Excuse me," she called out. "Can I help you?"

Scott stopped. "I was looking for room 618," he said. "A patient named Megan? I'm afraid I don't know her last name."

"I'm sorry, but only immediate family is allowed to see her."

Not a good sign. "Why?"

The woman smiled with guarded sympathy. "Again, I'm sorry, but we're not allowed to give out information on our patients. I'm sure you understand."

Disappointed, he turned away from the counter. Walking back to the elevators, he noticed a small waiting area with a dozen chairs and some tables. An old man in khaki shirt and pants fussed over a diverse collection of vases brimming with flowers. There were at least thirty of them. The man looked familiar to Scott. He went over to him.

"Haven't I seen you at the Cedar Rock?"

The man stood up straight, regarding Scott with blue watery eyes. "Probably. I only go there about every day. Name's Greg."

"Scott." The two shook hands.

"I overheard. They won't let you back to see Megan."

"How's she doing?"

Greg gave Scott a sad tired smile. "Not well at all, I'm afraid."

"What's wrong with her? All I know is that she was in the hospital."

"Megan has a brain tumor. A big one. It's inoperable." As he said this, Greg's shoulders sagged.

Even though Scott had been expecting something like this, the reality and suddenness of it left him deeply shocked. Megan's life was about to be snuffed out for no reason at all, just as it was getting started. The unfairness of it was maddening.

"But she's so young!" said Scott.

"Too young," agreed Greg.

Scott looked around the room. "I've never seen so many flowers."

"This is just part of them. There's been so many arriving that Linda wanted the nurses to give them to other patients. I've been helping out."

"Linda?"

"Megan's mom."

"Is she here now?"

"She's been back there with Megan since early this morning. She just went down to the cafeteria to get some coffee. I offered to get it for her, but she said she wanted to move around. Poor woman. She's so traumatized." Greg turned and picked up two of the vases.

"Can I give you a hand?"

"Sure. We need to bring these over to the nurses' station. They'll take it from there."

They each carried a couple of vases to the young nurse, who set them on the floor behind the counter. Scott and Greg made several trips until finally there was just one left.

"I'll get the last one," said Greg. "Thanks for your help."

"My pleasure."

Greg turned to retrieve the last bouquet. At the same time, the nurse bent down, placing a large and particularly ornate vase on the floor. Neither of them saw Scott slip past, walking rapidly down the hall, and go into room 618.

The room was bathed in a dull greenish light. Megan was lying in the bed, unconscious, hooked up to several monitors that beeped and blinked with quiet earnestness. Scott noticed the IV drip attached to her forearm.

He leaned over the bed and looked down at her. Her eyes were closed, her cheeks sunken, her skin pallid. Her breathing was so shallow he could barely see the rise and fall of her chest.

He didn't move. Just stood there, staring at her for several minutes. Then he released a great, all-encompassing sigh and thought, Okay, Patrick. You win.

He moved closer and spoke in a whisper. "What do you say, Megan? Are you ready for this? Because I am. I didn't think I would be, but I am."

Though he was the one saying these words, Scott felt startled as he heard them. Had he only imagined his conversations with Patrick? He couldn't possibly believe that he had the power to keep death at bay. His whole life had been based on logic and reason.

He felt like rushing out of the room, but something stopped him, and he knew what that something was—he did believe it. Perhaps he had gone insane, but he felt in his bones that it was all true, that he could make it happen.

An intensity crept into his voice. "If I truly can shave some time, say, a few months, or even a year, from my own existence in this world and give them to you, I'll do it. I don't know you very well, but you deserve this. I don't even know if it'll work. But what the hell, it's worth a shot, right?"

"You're not supposed to be in here," came a voice behind him.

He turned to see a trim, nice-looking woman with the prettiest eyes he had ever seen standing in the doorway, holding a cup of coffee.

"You, ah, you must be Linda," he stammered. "My name is Scott Northwood. I know your daughter from the—"

"The restaurant." Linda entered the room and stood before him. Her gaze was clear and direct. Bold, even. Yet he saw a curious vulnerability to her fawn-colored eyes, a wounded defiance. They made him think of an old English proverb that he had heard or read a number of times in his life: "The eyes are the windows to the soul." He'd never paid it any heed, but at that moment, he became a believer.

"Look, I know you mean well," she continued. "And I do appreciate it. But if they let everyone in here from the Cedar Rock who wanted to see my daughter, this room—this *floor*—would be jammed with people."

She smiled gamely. Scott could see that she was trying hard to maintain her composure, to be strong for her daughter. He also noticed that when she smiled, one corner of her mouth went up a little higher than the other.

"I understand. I'm sorry if I intruded on your privacy."

She expelled a deep, tired sigh, and took a seat on the chair beside the bed.

"That's all right. Megan would be tickled pink to know that so many people cared about her." They both were quiet a moment, watching Megan. Then, her eyes never leaving her daughter's face, Linda asked, "What were you saying to her just now?"

"Excuse me?"

"Before I came in. You were talking to her."

"I don't know... Just telling her to be strong, that she's going to be fine. Things like that."

". . . No, it sounded like you were telling her that you..." She looked up at him with those amazing eyes, and shook her head. "Never mind. I must be hearing things. I think I read someplace that stress can cause the mind to play tricks on itself." Again, that lopsided smile. To see her strength being tortured like this was heartrending.

"I'd better go."

She nodded and resumed staring into her daughter's face.

When Scott pulled up at Autumn Lake the next day, he was surprised to see another car in the small dirt lot. Aside from Patrick, it had been months since he'd run into anyone out here. Assuming it was probably another dog walker, he didn't give it much thought.

As he and Jake got on the trail, Scott figured he wouldn't have long to wait. He was right. Patrick appeared within the first hundred yards, his characteristic brusqueness alive and well.

"You decide what you're gonna do?"

"Enough small talk, Patrick. Just come out and say what's on your mind."

"Very funny. So what's it gonna be?"

"I've decided to help Megan."

Patrick's black eyebrows shot up in genuine surprise. "No shit, Northwood. I didn't think you had it in you."

"So what happens now? Do I tap my heels together three times? Do you wave a magic wand over my head? Do I need a permit from the city of Poulsbo?"

"You're a real card. It's simpler than you think. But first I need to know how much time you're gonna give her."

"One year."

"Gee, *a whole year.*" Patrick's voice was harsh with disapproval. "Your generosity is overwhelming. Come on, Northwood. You can do better than that. This is a twenty-year-old girl we're talkin' about."

This was hardly the reaction Scott had expected, and it made him angry. "If everything you've been telling me is true, this is also the premature shortening of my life we're talking about."

"Oh, right. Let's not forget that this is all about your life. Your smug, precious, crappy little life."

Scott shook his head in exasperation. "I don't believe this." He stepped close to Patrick so that they were almost nose-to-nose, "You know something? I'm getting pretty damned sick of your attitude. The least you could do is show a little appreciation for what I—"

"Are you okay, buddy?"

Scott whirled to see a man in his thirties, guiding a golden retriever on a leash. He had a bearded, friendly face, and was looking at Scott with concern.

"I'm fine," he said, embarrassed. "We're just having a little disagreement."

The man gave him a strange look. "Disagreement with who? Your dog?"

"No. With Patrick. This guy right beside me."

The man gave a nervous chuckle. "There's nobody there, man," he said.

"What do you mean, there's nobody—" He froze in mid-sentence. He turned and stared at Patrick, who was looking back at him with wary eyes.

"If I could just squeeze on by, I'll be on my way," said the man uncomfortably, as he eased past Scott and Jake. He hurried down the trail with his dog.

Scott was looking straight at Patrick. "Oh, no," he said. He closed his eyes and covered his face with his hands. "Oh, no," he said again. He stood like that without speaking for several moments, Jake watching his every move.

"Look, Northwood, it's not what you think."

Scott removed his hands from his face and opened his eyes. He was trying not to panic. "It's not what I think? That's where you're wrong. Because that's exactly what it is—*'what I think'*. That's *all* it is. I get it now."

"I know this may seem a little strange at the moment, but—"

"I've been having conversations for days with someone who doesn't exist! And it's *a little strange?* Actually, when I think about it, it explains a lot. No. It explains everything. How you know things about me no one else does. Why you're always in the same clothes. Why you only appear out here, where nobody else ever comes. That is, until today. It all makes sense. You exist only in my head."

"No. It's not like that," said Patrick.

Scott gave a disparaging laugh. "My sister was right. The rain is leaking into my skull. I've been losing my mind the last couple months and didn't even know it."

"Listen to me, Northwood," said Patrick, his voice for once without an undercurrent of disdain. "You're not crazy. You have to believe that."

"You're not real!" Scott started to laugh. "This is great. Just great! I'm standing here, arguing with a figment of my imagination. I need help. I need to see a shrink or something. Come on, Jake. Let's get out of here."

He turned and marched back toward the parking lot, Jake trotting to keep up. Patrick's voice called out after him. "What about Megan?"

But Scott kept moving down the path.

As soon as he got home, Scott grabbed the phone book and looked up "Mental Health Services" in the yellow pages. There were numerous listings, from counselors and psychological centers to toll-free hotlines for emergency services. He picked up the phone and started to dial, but then stopped.

"I'm not crazy, Jake." He looked down at the animal. "I'm sure I'm not. At least, I think I'm sure..." He let the phone book drop to the floor. "There's a logical explanation for all this. There's got to be. First things first. I need to calm down. Get a grip. Right?"

Just talking to the dog made him feel better.

"I'm going to take this a step at a time. Today's Saturday. First thing Monday morning, I'll go see my regular doctor and tell him what's going on. He'll probably run some tests. It could be something as simple as a vitamin deficiency, or an electrolyte imbalance. But if it's not, and if he thinks it really is a mental issue, he can refer me to—"

There was a knock at the door.

He flinched at the sound. He couldn't remember the last time someone had been at his door. He got up and padded into the foyer, walking to one of the two narrow, floor-to-ceiling windows bracketing the front door. He looked out one window while Jake did the same on the other side.

Patrick was at the door.

"Oh, man." Scott ran a hand through his hair, unsure what to do. "I guess it's not like he doesn't know where I live, huh, Jake?"

The dog's tail was wagging back and forth.

"What are you so excited about? There's nothing out there." Jake ignored him and continued to stare out the window.

In a burst of anger and fear, Scott yanked the door open. "Get the hell out of here!" he shouted. "Leave me alone!"

"What would it take?" asked Patrick, his voice forceful and direct. The strangeness of the question caught Scott off guard.

"What?"

Patrick annunciated each word with exaggerated clarity. "What. Would. It. Take."

"What would *what* take?"

"What would it take for you to believe that I'm real?"

"We just went through that! You were invisible to that guy. You don't exist! You never did! And the fact that I'm even standing here arguing with you only confirms that I—"

"I'll make a deal with you. If I can't convince you I'm real, I promise I'll get out of your life. Forever. So I'm asking you again, what would it take to convince you *beyond any doubt* that I exist?"

It was annoyingly obvious to Scott that Patrick wasn't going away unless he played along.

"Okay, fine. I'll tell you what it would take. A *miracle*. That's what."

Patrick seemed unfazed. "What kind of miracle?"

His calmness only made Scott angrier. "Let's make it a good one, shall we? A real humdinger." He snapped his fingers. "I know! How about this: I want you to light up the sky. Can you do that, Patrick? I want you to turn night into day for, say, five minutes. And I want you to do it *tonight*, okay? That's the miracle I want. What do you say? Can you do that?"

"What time tonight?"

Scott couldn't believe the gall of the mental delusion standing before him. "You mean I get a choice?" he said. "Great! Let's make it two a.m. Sharp."

"Two a.m., it is."

"No, wait," added Scott, wanting to stretch the absurdity of their agreement to the limit. "Make it two oh three and twenty-seven seconds a.m."

"Okay."

"And not here at the house," Scott added. "I'm going to need witnesses. Lots of them. Because if nobody else sees this so-called miracle but me, it won't do a thing to prove that you're real."

"You're saying you wanna be someplace where there're lots of people at two in the morning."

"You got that right."

"What about the casino?"

Scott thought about it. "Yeah, the casino. It's Saturday night. They'll have a good crowd."

"Anything else?"

"Let's see. You're going to turn night into day at precisely two minutes and twenty seven seconds after two a.m. in front of dozens of witnesses. No, I think that should do it, Patrick."

"It's a deal."

Chapter 6

AT THE CASINO

Scott hadn't awakened to the buzz of an alarm clock since he'd stopped working. He looked at the time—one in the morning. He flipped on the light, sat up, and rubbed his eyes. Jake gave him the dirtiest of looks.

"Sorry to interrupt your beauty sleep, but I have an appointment to go see if I'm crazy or not. Not to mention make a total fool of myself." With an exaggerated huff, Jake dropped his head back down onto the bed. Scott went into the bathroom and splashed cold water on his face. He dressed, jumped in the Range Rover, and headed for the Eagle Bay Casino, arriving at 1:30.

He had never been to the local casino, so he lingered inside the doorway to get his bearings. The main gambling floor was directly in front of him. It was a wide, brightly lit space, filled with green-felted blackjack and craps tables, bordered by rows of slot machines. The bells, sirens, and shrieking music of the slots filled the vast room with a maniacal cacophony. Even at this hour, the crowd was loud and animated.

He made his way to the far corner of the room where a small bar provided an oasis of relative quiet. As he approached, he checked out the three people sitting at the bar.

On the left, a neatly dressed couple in their forties nursed cocktails. The man was slim and clean-shaven; the woman short and a little on the plump side. There was an easygoing manner about them.

Several stools to the right sat a very drunk blonde in her

thirties, dressed in skin-tight jeans and a low-cut black blouse. A butterfly tattoo peeked from the valley of her cleavage. Deeply involved with the video blackjack machine embedded in the countertop in front of her, when she won a couple of dollars, she cried out, "Yeah!"

No, thought Scott. He chose a seat one down from the couple and draped his coat across the back of the stool. A pony-tailed bartender appeared.

"What'll ya have?"

"Danny's Pale Ale."

"Coming up."

"Shit!" yelled the blonde, losing this time.

Scott turned to the couple and spoke in a casual, friendly manner, "You folks having any luck tonight?"

They each gave him a subtle visual appraisal before replying. This was, after all, a casino in the wee hours of the morning. One had to be wary of strangers striking up conversations. They saw that Scott was sober and wearing nice clothes, so he passed initial muster.

The woman smiled. "I'm up about a hundred dollars."

"And I'm down about a hundred," said the man. "So I guess you could say it's a wash."

There was an ear-pleasing twang to their voices that Scott couldn't place. Tennessee, or Kentucky maybe.

"How about yourself?" the man asked.

"Actually, I just got here."

"Looks like you got some catching up to do."

"I should probably cut to the chase and hand my wallet over to the pit boss now. Save myself the aggravation."

"I know the feeling," smiled the man. "My name's Bill. This is my wife Marilyn."

"I'm Scott. Pleased to meet you."

"Same here."

"Yeah!" yelled the blonde as she scored a win. She downed a shot of tequila and belched.

Scott's drink arrived, and he took a deep swallow. The cold, slightly bitter drink felt good going down his throat.

"You folks from out of town?"

"How could you tell?" said Marilyn, exaggerating her accent.

"Wild guess."

"We're from Paducah, Kentucky. Bill and I were both born and raised there."

"Here on vacation?"

"At this time of year?" said Bill. "Not hardly."

"We're visiting our son," said Marilyn. "He lives here in Poulsbo."

"Is he having any luck tonight?"

"You could say that," said Bill with a grin.

"Bill," said Marilyn in admonishment.

"Well, it's true. He and his girlfriend both work long hours. This is the only night they have off together, so we thought we'd give them some privacy, if you know what I mean."

"What nice parents you are," said Scott.

"I think so," Bill agreed.

Scott checked his watch. It was getting close to two. He took another swallow, then turned to the couple, saying, "Look, I don't mean to impose, but I wonder if I could ask you folks a favor."

The two exchanged guarded looks. "What kind of favor?" asked Bill.

"This is going to sound strange, but please hear me out. First, you need to know that I'm not drunk. I'm not on drugs. I'm not dangerous. I'm not a weirdo. I'm a pretty regular person."

"What kind of favor?" repeated Bill.

"I was wondering if you two would accompany me outside to the parking lot. Just for a few minutes."

Bill's eyes narrowed in suspicion. "The parking lot. Why?"

"Here's the strange part. Something is supposed to happen tonight. In the sky. In a few minutes. I need other people to be there to witness it."

"Why?" said Bill.

"It's... complicated. You could say it's to settle a wager of sorts."

"What's supposed to happen?" said Marilyn.

"I was told that the skies are going to light up."

"You mean like a fireworks display?"

"Something like that. Assuming it even happens."

"You don't sound a hundred percent sure it will."

"Well, I have my doubts. But I've got a lot riding on it." *Like my sanity.*

The couple studied him with wary eyes.

"You don't even need to go out to the parking lot," said Scott. "You can stay by the front doors of the casino, where the security guards are. I just need you to have a view of the sky."

"What do you think, Bill?"

"Shit!" yelled the drunken blonde.

Bill glanced down the bar at her and said, "Why not." He downed the rest of his drink. "Beats the heck out of sitting here waiting for Mark to call."

The three pulled on their coats and headed across the gambling floor. Bill and Marilyn followed Scott past the uniformed security guards and into the parking lot to a landscaped median. They all climbed onto a grass-covered mound and looked up at the sky.

Eagle Bay Casino was located on a reservation about eight miles outside of Poulsbo. Its distance from city lights ensured that the nights there were dark.

The night was cold and clear, the stars glittering an icy blue. Looking west, Scott could make out the deep black outline of the Olympic Mountains looming up from the horizon.

"What time's this light show supposed to take place?" Bill asked.

Scott checked his watch. It was exactly two o'clock.

"In a little over two minutes."

"Okay."

Scott was searching the sky. Bill and Marilyn, feeling a little silly, peered at each other, then back at Scott.

"So," said Bill. "Nice weather we're having."

"Yeah," said Scott, continuing to scan the sky. Bill and Marilyn's eyes followed his gaze up to the heavens.

Scott checked his watch one more time. He witnessed the second hand sweeping past 2:02. As it neared the 27-second mark, he said, "It's supposed to happen right... about... *now.*"

Darkness. Silence. Just the cold, star-filled sky.

"Come on," he whispered, his voice intense. "Don't do this to me."

The others heard him, and Scott saw Bill look at his wife, nod his head in Scott's direction and raise his eyebrows as if to say, This guy might be crazy.

It was exactly what Scott was thinking.

"This is not good," he said. "Not good at all."

Bill took Marilyn's hand and the two began backing away in the direction of the casino. "It's been interesting meeting you, Scott," he said. "But it's kind of cold out here, so... I think we'll head back inside."

"This is what I get..." said Scott, now oblivious to their presence. His fury built until he shook his fist at the sky and shouted, "for listening to a figment of my imagination!"

The couple hurried into the casino. The security guards heard Scott shouting, and now they kept a wary eye on him as well.

So, he had truly lost touch with reality. It terrified him. It felt as if the earth had shifted under his feet and he could no longer keep his balance. He would definitely call his doctor first thing Monday morning. He knew he should get in the car right now and head straight home, but he was suddenly afraid to be alone.

He stared up at the sky for a long time before walking off the mound and heading toward the casino. His mouth was dry and his hands were trembling. He could use a drink.

"Are you all right, sir?" a security guard asked.

"I'm fine," lied Scott. "Just fine."

The guard gave him a wary look. "If you say so. Just keep

it cool."

When Scott walked back into the casino, Bill and Marilyn were sitting side-by-side playing slots. They watched him head to the bar. He didn't see them.

"Poor man," said Marilyn. "I feel kind of bad for him."

"Takes all kinds," Bill said, feeding another quarter into the machine.

Scott took a seat one stool down from the drunken blonde. She was still playing the video black jack machine.

"Shit!" she said, as she lost another hand.

The bartender appeared.

"Another Danny's?"

"Give me a shot of Stoli instead. Make it a double. And run me a tab."

The doctor eased the door open to room 618 and stepped inside. Linda was asleep in a chair next to Megan's hospital bed.

He studied the screens of the machines hooked to Megan. He grimaced at what he saw and shifted his attention to Megan herself. Her eyes were closed, her face shiny with sweat, her breathing raspy and erratic.

He frowned at the tragic waste of it; there was little doubt that she would not make it past the next twent- four hours.

Bill stifled a yawn and checked his watch. He and Marilyn were still playing the slots. "I wonder why Mark hasn't called."

His wife muffled a yawn of her own. "What do you want to bet they fell asleep."

The blonde at the bar hit a blackjack. "Yeah!"

"All right!" yelled Scott. He sat next to her, watching her play. "This calls for another round! Bartender!"

The bartender appeared and gave Scott an appraising look. "It might be time to call it quits, sir."

"Don't worry, this is my last round."

"Are you going to be okay to drive?"

"Absolutely not. That's why I'm cabbing it home."

"Hey! I'll drive you home!" said the blonde. They gazed in mutual drunkenness at each other and then broke into raucous laughter, knowing that neither of them was capable of driving anyone anywhere.

As the taxi pulled out of the parking lot, the cab driver peered at Scott in the rearview mirror. "Tough night at the casino?"

"You could say that."

"I was in there last week. Dropped two hundred bucks in half an hour."

"That sucks."

"How much did you lose?"

Scott looked out the window at the night pressing in. "You don't even want to know."

A sudden brightness lit up the sky, blinding the cab driver. *"Jeezus!"* he cried and pulled to the side of the road. He and Scott climbed out of the car, squinting up at the light washing through the sky. Scott shook his head violently, trying to force the haze of vodka from his mind. *Was this really happening?*

Hundreds of what looked like giant flares flashed across the sky in every direction. Everything as far as the eye could see was bathed in flickering, silver light. Even the distant snow-covered peaks of the Olympics glowed in the surreal illumination.

"What the hell is going on?" The driver's voice was tinged with fear.

Suddenly feeling sober, Scott asked, "You can see this?"

The man gave him an incredulous look. "Are you crazy? Of course I can see it!"

It occurred to Scott that he just might not be crazy. "What time is it?"

"Huh?"

"I said, what time is it?"

"What's that got to do with anything?" Annoyed, the driver checked his watch anyway. "It's a little after two in the morning."

Scott looked at his own watch. "But my watch says it's just after three."

"Your watch is wrong. You're forgetting Daylight Savings Time. It ended an hour ago.

Scott closed his eyes, shook his head, and chuckled. Of course. Spring forward. Fall back. Real cute, Patrick.

He and the cabbie stood in quiet amazement, as light rippled through the sky.

It lasted a little over five minutes.

∿∿∿

When Scott awoke next morning, the first thing he did was call a taxi to take him back to the casino to retrieve his car. After driving home, he made some coffee, brought a cup into the living room and turned on the TV for local news. An astrophysicist from the University of Washington was giving a live interview:

"...the most intense meteor storm in centuries. I can't begin to tell you how rare an event like this is. People in the Puget Sound region should feel incredibly lucky for being in the right place at the right time."

"Why could it be seen in Puget Sound, but not in other areas of Washington?" the reporter asked.

"A dense but narrow band of meteors was pointed like a fire hose at one particular area. In fact, I only recently received cellphone footage taken at that location. This is what it looked like to be directly under the meteor storm last night."

The astrophysicist turned on a nearby monitor and a dazzling display of light filled the screen. All the reporters in the room gasped.

When one of them managed to find his tongue, he said,

"And where is that, exactly?"

"Poulsbo, Washington."

Scott stared at the television, the coffee cooling in his hand.

Her eyes red from worry and exhaustion, Linda sat in a chair next to Megan's hospital bed, watching the television mounted on the wall. It was a small but welcome distraction. The local news was on with the sound just high enough to hear. A breathless young reporter was broadcasting live from downtown Poulsbo. He wore a coat, gloves, and scarf against the chill of the morning.

". . . here live in Poulsbo where the meteor storm is the talk of the town. We were contacted earlier this morning by a couple visiting from Paducah, Kentucky. Bill and Marilyn Curtis happened to be at Eagle Bay Casino last night where they had a front row seat to the celestial fireworks. They have an interesting story to tell about what happened." The broadcast shifted to footage taken earlier that morning of a couple in their bathrobes standing in the doorway of a modest house.

"I'm telling you," said Bill to the reporter, "this guy knew exactly when this meteor shower was going to hit. I mean down to the minute. Down to the second!"

"That's pretty amazing," said the reporter with exaggerated seriousness.

"Well, actually, he was off by an hour," said Marilyn. "You know. Because of the Daylight Savings Time change."

"That's true," said Bill. "He hadn't set his watch."

"Can you describe him for us?"

"Well, he was a nice-looking man," said Marilyn. "Maybe in his late forties. He had a nice head of hair that was just starting to go gray. He wore one of those outdoorsy coats, like you see in an L.L. Bean catalogue? It was a faded green color."

"He said his name was Scott," said Bill.

"That's right. Scott."

At the sound of the name, Linda found herself paying closer attention to the broadcast.

"Did he do any gambling in the casino?"

"We saw him playing video blackjack, didn't we, Bill?"

"Yes. With that blonde gal at the bar."

"Did he win?" said the reporter.

"I can't say that he did," said Bill.

"Can't say that he did?" said the reporter, his seriousness turning into 'gotcha' silliness. "Don't you think a man who can predict a meteor storm down to the second would clean house at a casino? I mean, what's up with that?"

Bill realized that he and Marilyn were being made fun of. "Look, mister, we're just tellin' you what we saw. We couldn't believe it ourselves."

The TV reverted back to a live shot of the reporter smirking into the camera. "For the record," he said, "I talked to several people who were at the casino last night. No one knew anything about a man who predicted the meteor storm. In all fairness, those folks may have been enjoying their Saturday night just a little too much. And there's certainly no harm in that. Reporting live from Poulsbo, I'm Glen Hardesty for KONO news."

The camera cut to a pretty news anchor with perfect hair. With a smile and a wink, she said, "We'll be right back." As the station cut to a commercial, Linda muted the sound and stared out the window.

She had no idea how long she'd been sitting like that when Megan's breathing became very loud and labored. One of the monitors began to beep loudly.

"Nurse," said Linda, rising from her chair. *"Nurse!"*

It was late morning by the time Scott and Jake entered the trail at Autumn Lake. Patrick walked toward them.

"Well?" he said. "Are you convinced?"

"I want to know what the hell is going on," Scott growled.

"What's your problem?"

"What's my *problem?* A meteor storm!?"

"What about it?"

"How did it happen?"

His questions seemed to irritate Patrick. "Meteors are basically dirt floating through space, okay? It's just physics. No big deal."

"'No big deal' he says. I'm going to ask you again: How did it happen? Because this is all starting to—"

"Wait!" barked Patrick. "We can talk about all that later. She's out of time, Northwood. Do you understand English? Megan's dying as we speak. If you're going to help her, you need to do it now."

All that could be seen of Nurse Parker behind the surgical mask were her large expressive eyes as she monitored Megan's vital signs. Doctor Drake stood over Megan as three technicians hovered close by. Suddenly, all the machines were beeping at once. "Blood pressure dropping rapidly," the nurse said in a crisp, urgent voice. "Respiration minimal. Pulse weak and erratic." She looked at the doctor. "She's going into cardiac arrest."

"Shit," the doctor said under his breath. Then to the assembled medical team, "Get the paddles ready, people. I want a full charge." The eerie whine of a heart defibrillator charging up filled the room.

Keeping her voice as calm and professional as possible, the nurse said, "Full cardiac arrest."

In the waiting room, Linda hunched over in a chair, her face buried in trembling hands.

Chapter 7

COMMITTED

"I'll do it," said Scott. "I'll give her one year."

Patrick shook his head in disapproval. "Still stingy, I see."

"Sorry to disappoint you, but it'll have to do."

"Fine. Now shut up and listen to me. This is important." He moved close and stared into Scott's eyes. He spoke quickly. "Once you agree to do this, it's a done deal. It's locked in and can't be reversed. So I'm asking you: Are you *absolutely sure* this is what you want to do?"

"Yes. I'm absolutely sure."

Patrick stepped back and seemed to visibly relax.

"So what happens now?"

"Like I told you before, it's simpler than you think."

"Meaning what?"

"It's done."

"Just like that?"

"Just like that."

∿∿∿

"Defibrillator's charged," said one of the technicians.

The doctor pressed one of the paddles to the side of Megan's chest and the other on top. His finger rested on the trigger that would deliver a powerful electric shock to her heart, hopefully jump-starting it. Because of the tumor that continued to grow in her brain, he knew it would in all likelihood be a futile effort at resuscitation. But he had to try.

"Clear!" he cried, preparing to activate the defibrillator.

"Wait," said the nurse quietly. Then it became a shout.

"Wait!"

He froze. They all looked at her as she studied the monitors. "Heartbeat has returned! Pulse coming back... Blood pressure rising... Respiration has begun..." She looked expectantly at Drake.

"Are you sure?" he asked.

Her eyes were wide open in unabashed surprise. "I'm sure! All her vitals are coming back very strong."

Drake stared at her a moment, then lay the paddles down. "Cancel defibrillation," he said, and went to see the monitors for himself.

"What did you do?" said the nurse.

"Nothing," he said, as he studied a data readout. "I did nothing at all."

The nurse frowned. "This could be just a temporary reprieve. Her tumor hasn't gone anywhere."

"If her tumor hasn't gone anywhere, why are her readings so strong?"

"Could it have shifted position?"

"Impossible. That thing's wrapped around her nerves and arteries like a python."

They all watched him as he considered what to do next. Finally he said, "It wouldn't hurt to take a picture. Schedule an immediate CAT scan."

***

"Did it work?" Scott asked.

"It worked. Barely. We got her in just under the wire."

Scott was surprised to feel a vague disappointment. Patrick sensed it and said, "Now what's the matter?"

"I don't know... I guess I was expecting something more."

"Like what?"

"If I really did just prolong someone's life, you'd think there'd be a clap of thunder, or something."

Patrick smirked. "A clap of thunder. That's rich."

"Not even a pat on the back?"

"Get over yourself, Northwood."

Scott yawned. He felt incredibly sleepy.

"Tired?" said Patrick.

"Yeah."

"That's normal. What you need to do now is get your ass home. Because you're gonna sleep like there's no tomorrow." Patrick turned and began walking back down the trail.

Scott stifled another yawn. "So Megan's really okay?"

"Go home, Northwood."

Scott's mouth opened again in another huge yawn. "I plan to do just that. Come on, Jake. Let's go."

The doctor and the nurse stood side by side, staring at the results of the CAT scan on a computer monitor. Nurse Parker's surgical mask hung loosely from her neck. She looked shaken. Doctor Drake didn't say anything for a long moment as he continued to study the images. "There's been a mistake," he finally said. "A mix-up. This scan belongs to another patient."

"There's no mix-up," said the nurse. "That scan is Megan's."

"But that's not possible." He felt his mouth go dry. "Do you hear me? It's not possible!"

"Yes, Doctor, I hear you. And I couldn't agree with you more. It's as impossible as it gets."

It had been all Scott could do to keep his eyes open and the car on the road as he drove home. He managed to dump a can of dog food into Jake's dish before heading to the bedroom, where he collapsed, fully-clothed, onto the covers.

Linda sat in the waiting room, afraid to even breathe. She'd had no update on Megan's condition since Drake and his team descended in a controlled frenzy upon her room. For all she knew, the worst had happened, so she was trying to brace herself for the most horrible thing a parent could face—the death of a child. Any minute now, he was going to come out here with that look of superior intelligence on his face and tell her that her daughter was—

"...Mom?"

Linda opened her eyes at the sound of the voice. Megan stood in front of her wearing a robe over her hospital gown.

Speechless, Linda could only stare at the girl, wondering if the vision before her was real.

"Mom, are you okay?"

It was only then that she noticed the doctor and nurse on either side of Megan. Both were smiling. The vision was real. *Her daughter was alive!*

Still, a low-level panic clutched her stomach. Why was she up walking around? Shouldn't she be in bed? "What's happened? Are you okay?"

Megan's face lit up in a beautiful smile. "That's what's so crazy, Mom. I'm okay. In fact, the doctor says we can go home."

"Home? I don't understand."

"Megan insisted on coming out and telling you the news personally," Drake said.

"What news?"

"My tumor. It's gone."

"Gone? But—how can that be?"

"I honestly don't know, " he admitted. "What I do know is, the tumor has definitely disappeared. As far as I can determine, Megan's in perfect health."

Linda looked at her daughter. She did indeed seem as robust as ever. Linda rose to her feet.

"I thought... I really thought that... you were going to..." She gathered her daughter into her arms and sobbed with happy relief. Megan clung to her just as tightly. They held each other a long time.

Scott gradually awoke to November sunlight slanting cool

and pale through the bedroom window. He sat up and massaged a crick in his neck. From his wrinkled clothes and the muscles that felt like rubber, he figured he hadn't moved the entire time he slept. Which, according to his watch, had been almost 24 hours.

Jake sat at the foot of the bed.

"I'll bet you have to go out."

The dog bounded off and Scott took him outside. It was a cold, clear day. He filled his lungs with the chilled air and looked at the snow-covered Olympics glistening in the distance.

Famished, he made himself a big plate of scrambled eggs and bacon. After a hot shower and a change of clothes, he was ready to begin the day, even though it was already past noon.

He went into the living room and sat down in the giant leather chair to gather his thoughts, replaying the latest encounter with Patrick in his mind.

"*...A meteor storm? How did it happen...*"

"*...We can talk about all that later. ...Megan's dying as we speak. If you're going to help her, you need to do it now...*"

He looked down. "Okay, Jake, time to find out for sure if Patrick's full of it or not."

Scott picked up the phone and dialed a number. It rang several times before he heard Brenda's harried voice.

"Cedar Rock."

"Hi, Brenda. I was calling to see if you've heard anything about—"

"You and everyone else. Megan was released from the hospital! She's home with her mom. She'll be back at work tomorrow."

Back at work? He was too stunned to speak. He finally managed to ask, "Did, uh, anyone say how she recovered so fast?"

"Everyone's saying it's a miracle." Brenda's tone became a bit more snappish. "I'm thinking it'll be a miracle when I get some help in here." She hung up.

Scott replaced the phone in its cradle. "Holy shit," he whispered.

∿∿∿

The Range Rover zoomed into the dirt parking lot of Autumn Lake and lurched to a stop. He jumped out, lifted Jake to the ground and sped down the trail.

"Patrick!" called Scott. "Where are you?!"

No answer.

"Don't hide from me! I know you're out here. You said we would 'talk about all this' and I'm ready to talk! I want some answers and I want them now! Where are you?!"

He crisscrossed the trails for over an hour, but there was no Patrick. Only the solemn green silence of the forest.

∿∿∿

The next morning, a cold front moved in from the Pacific. A dense drizzle leaked steadily from leaden clouds. Scott loaded Jake into the car and drove to Cedar Rock Restaurant. He wasn't at all surprised to see the parking lot packed and a line of cars waiting to get in, even in this miserable weather. He had to take a space far down the street, then headed for the restaurant.

He had never seen the Cedar Rock so busy, with at least two dozen people waiting to be seated. Gus and an assistant cook sweated at the grill, clearly trying to keep up with orders. Everyone seemed in good spirits, with all the lively chatter forming a steady din. Scott found a spot where he could lean against the wall and settled in for the wait.

Something new spanned the wall across from him. It was a large hand-drawn poster soliciting donations to help defray Megan's medical expenses. The poster explained that, because she had no health insurance, she would be forced to pay thousands of dollars in medical bills out of her own pocket. There was contact information for a fund that had been set up at a local bank. In the meantime, cash gifts of any kind were welcome. On a chair beneath the poster was a freshly scrubbed busing bin marked "DONATIONS." It was close to being filled with ones, fives, tens and twenties, plus a few checks.

From where he stood, Scott could see Megan bustling about, taking orders and clearing tables. Every so often, a customer would stand and hug her, whispering a few heart-felt words in her ear. When a seat finally opened up at the counter, Brenda led Scott to a stool and handed him a menu. He waved it off.

"Just coffee and an order of link sausages to go," he said.

"Coming up." She filled his cup from a freshly brewed pot, moved to the order-up station, balanced several plates of food on her arms and hurried off.

Scott sat with his back to the counter so he could watch Megan work the tables and booths on the other side of the room. It was nothing less than astounding to think this was the same person he'd seen in the ICU three days before. She looked as vigorous as ever, moving with efficiency and grace among the tables. Her dark brown eyes shone with an inner glow that he hadn't noticed before.

She was in the midst of taking an order when, as if feeling his eyes on her, she looked up and stared directly at Scott. She excused herself from the table.

Walking toward him, she thought of the last time she had seen him—the day she went into the hospital. She remembered their conversation:

Then what did you come here for?

To tell you something.

Tell me what?

To just... be careful.

"Hello, stranger," she said.

"Hello, yourself."

Scott took a sip of coffee. "I heard you were sick."

"Yes. Very."

"I'm glad you're better."

"That makes two of us."

Scott glanced around at her adoring legions. "Looks like a

lot more than two are glad.”

“I had a dream about you. When I was in the hospital.”

“Sure it wasn’t a nightmare? I sometimes have that effect on people.”

“It wasn’t a nightmare. But it was... strange.”

“What happened?”

“I dreamed I was locked in this tiny room that was completely dark and stifling. I could hardly breathe. Then the room just seemed to melt away and suddenly I was in the middle of a forest. You were there. I remember there was a dog with you. You have a dog, don’t you? One who likes cheeseburgers?”

“I have a dog. Then what happened?”

“Nothing. You just stood there looking at me. Then I woke up.”

“Not much of a dream.”

“I had it yesterday morning. A couple hours later, I got to come home.”

He didn’t say anything in response. She smiled and pushed a strand of hair from her forehead. “So you see, it wasn’t a nightmare. It was a good dream.”

She turned to go back to the table of hungry customers.

“Megan.”

She stopped. “Yes?”

“The dog in your dream. What did he look like?”

“He was kind of cool-looking. Not very big. Dark brown hair. Kinda scruffy and bristly. Soulful eyes.”

“That sounds like Jake, all right. Only...”

“Only what?”

“You’ve never met Jake.”

“Well, then you must have described him to me.”

“I must have.”

She smiled and headed back to her customers.

～ ～ ～

With the restaurant so busy, it took a while before Brenda returned with the sausage order. Scott paid in cash at the counter and included a decent tip.

Leaving the restaurant, he saw that it was still drizzling. He came across Megan and her mother standing under the awning outside the front door. Linda was trying to hand a small white bag to Megan.

"Doctor Drake says you have to keep taking your pills."

"I don't see why. I feel fine."

Linda glared at her daughter in worried exasperation. "Megan, what is wrong with you? You came this close to meeting your maker. He says they'll help prevent a recurrence."

"Fine. If it makes you happy, I'll take the stupid pills." As Megan took the bag, she saw Scott and motioned him over.

"I want you to meet my mother, Linda. Mom, this is Scott, the guy I was telling you about. He doesn't have to work. He gets to screw around all day."

He smiled at her. "Nice to see you again."

Linda looked at him and remembered him standing over Megan in the hospital.

". . . If I truly can shave some time, say, a few months, or even a year, from my own existence in this world and give them to you, I'll do it..."

Had he really said that? Such an odd thing to say to her very sick daughter.

"Hello, Mr. Northwood."

"You two have met?" said Megan.

"Scott came to see you at the hospital."

Megan looked at him with curiosity. "Really? I didn't know. Somehow, that doesn't seem like..."

Scott finished her sentence. "Doesn't seem like something I would do? It isn't. Just think of it as a momentary lapse in my otherwise perfectly ordered life."

"I hope I wasn't too difficult that day," Linda said to him. "Everything's still kind of a blur."

"You had a lot on your mind."

He found himself captivated by her lopsided smile.

She glanced at Megan with those glistening, vulnerable

eyes. "You could say that."

"You must be happy to have your daughter back home." He realized how self-conscious his voice sounded, something that hadn't happened since he'd been in grade school.

"You have no idea!"

"So, Scott," said Megan, looking back and forth between him and her mother. "What are you doing for Thanksgiving?"

"I, uh, haven't even thought about it."

"Why don't you come spend it with us? Mom, would that be all right?"

"I don't see why not," Linda answered.

Scott suddenly felt panicky. Why was that, he wondered? "I... wouldn't want to intrude."

"You wouldn't be intruding," said Megan. "Every year, we invite all the strays to our place and have a feast. It's low-key but fun."

"Strays?"

"People who don't have any place else to go that day."

"Is that what you think my situation is?" he asked, a little hurt by her assumption.

"Well, what do you usually do on Thanksgiving?"

Each year he would pick up a fully prepared turkey dinner for two from Central Market. Jake and he would eat until they couldn't walk and then watch a DVD. He was usually asleep before nine.

"What can I bring?"

Megan and Linda laughed.

"Bring some wine," said Linda. "We'll take care of the rest."

Megan took out her order pad. "What's your email address? I'll send you directions."

"I don't have one."

"Then give me your cellphone number so I can call you with directions."

"Don't have one of those, either."

The two women exchanged looks. "I'm afraid I'm not very

good at sending smoke signals!" said Megan.

He laughed and offered his landline number. As she wrote it down, Brenda stuck her head out the door, shouting, "Megan! I could use a little help in here!"

"I've got to go. See you on Thanksgiving!"

She disappeared through the door. Scott suddenly felt awkward standing alone with Linda.

"I've got to get back to work, too," she said.

"What day is Thanksgiving this year?"

"I'm pretty sure it falls on a Thursday."

He cocked an eyebrow at her and she grinned back.

"Sorry. Couldn't resist. It's in two weeks."

"I'll be sure to mark it on my calendar. So... I guess I'll see you then."

"Good-bye, Scott."

He watched her walk to her car, which was double-parked in front of the crowded restaurant. She turned and smiled at him as she climbed in. He waved back and headed in the opposite direction to his own vehicle. The day wasn't nearly as gloomy anymore.

On the drive home, he ate half a sausage and handed the other half over to Jake.

He was lost in thought, as he chewed. "You know what, Jake?" he said. "I've never described what you look like to Megan."

From then on, the only sound in the car was the rhythmic swish of the wipers as the rain continued to fall.

A few days before Thanksgiving, Scott returned to the Cedar Rock. He took a seat in Megan's section. She saw him and marched over. Stopping in front of him, she glared. She did not look happy.

"Was it you?"

"Was it me, what?"

"I think you know what I'm talking about."

"I'm afraid I don't have a clue."

"Somebody made an anonymous donation to my bank fund," she said.

"I'm sure lots of people have—"

"For a hundred thousand dollars."

"Wow," he said. "That'll pay for a lot of aspirin."

"Very funny. Thing is, my medical bills won't come to near that amount. Plus I've received a ton of donations from other folks. Everyone's been very generous. So I've got a lot more money than I need."

"Must be nice to have such a loyal following," he said.

"So..." She leaned on the table and searched his eyes. "I'll ask you again. Was it you? If it was, there's no way I can accept that money."

Scott had spent enough years running a business to know exactly how to handle this. He looked her in the eye with all the sincerity he could muster and lied. "No. It wasn't me."

Her eyes narrowed. "I'm not sure if I believe you."

"I wrote a check to your fund for the amount of five hundred dollars, and that's all. I didn't make any anonymous donation."

She continued to stare at him.

"Look, Megan, I think you're a fine young woman, and I wish you the best in life and all that crap. But if you think for one minute I would just give that kind of money away, I recommend therapy. I have my own selfish retirement to worry about. And I intend to maintain a disgustingly comfortable lifestyle well into geezerhood."

She looked dubious, but had no choice but to accept his answer. "Okay. Then I guess I'll just have to keep trying to find out who it was. Thing is, you're the only person I know who has that kind of money."

"Don't be so sure. Just when you think you know a person, they can turn around and surprise you."

"No kidding. What can I get you?"

"Just coffee today."

She returned with a pot and filled his cup.

"Are you still planning on coming over for Thanksgiving?"

"Wouldn't miss it." As she started to walk away, he called out to her. "Megan, before you go, can I ask you something?"

The restaurant was slow enough that she could linger. "Sure. What's up?"

"Actually, it's, uh, about your mom."

"Really? What about my mother?" Her eyes were smiling.

"Is she, uh, seeing anybody? You know. Like, going out with someone? Hooked up? Spoken for? Dating anyone? Whatever it's called these days."

Megan assumed a disapproving frown. "Who wants to know?"

He was surprised at how flustered he suddenly felt. Here he was—the guy who'd kept a such a tight lid on his emotions that he couldn't even admit to ever having been in love; two brief meetings with Megan's mother, and he sounded like a bumbling fool. Betty's comment from that night came into his mind. Well, there didn't seem to be any glass in front of him when it came to Linda Hillis.

He could feel his cheeks turning red, which, in turn, made him more flustered, which in turn made him redder. "Look, I don't want you to get upset, but I think your mom's a very, uh, enticing woman—I guess is the word I'm looking for. She seems really nice, too. And, well, I thought, maybe—"

Her eyes went wide in mock horror. "You want to ask my mother out?!"

It took him all that time to realize she was teasing him. "Well, yeah. What of it?"

"You think she's *enticing?* How about, like, she's totally hot?"

"Well, yeah, she is, I guess. I mean, I don't want you to think that I—"

"Boy, are you ever blushing. I didn't think anyone could blush that much."

"Look. Maybe, uh, we should just forget the whole—"

"Stop." She smiled. "I think it's a great idea. And to answer your question, no, she's not seeing anyone." Her smile faded a little. "Actually... there is this one guy she's been seeing off and on for a couple of years. Jack Lofgren. But it's been a lot more off than on recently."

"Oh."

"I don't think she's seen him or even talked to him in months. I really think their relationship—if you could even call it that—is at an end. Plus he has some... issues."

"What kind of issues?"

"He's got a bit of a reputation as a ladies' man. I mean, he is good-looking. He's been married a few times. And he does like his cocktails."

"Sounds like a jolly good fellow. What does he do?"

"He's a commercial fisherman up in Alaska. Has his own boat. Comes down to Seattle during the off-season."

"Great. I'm in competition with a macho sea captain from the frozen north."

"But I seriously think it's over between them. And I've seen the way she looks at you."

"So there might be hope?"

"Could be. I say go ahead and ask her out. She just might say yes."

Megan turned and walked away, smiling to herself. Scott sat in the booth sipping his coffee, doing the same.

He spent a couple restless nights in the days leading up to Thanksgiving. To have met Megan was a gift. She was so full of life and mischief. He had zero regrets about what he had done for her. He would do it again in a heartbeat.

And now, on top of that, to have met Linda—another amazing gift. He couldn't remember ever feeling this way before. He tried to define the feeling, but his analytical mind seemed to be failing him. All he seemed capable of thinking about was that extraordinary moment in *The Wizard of Oz*, when Dorothy leaves Kansas in black and white, and then enters Oz, a riot of blazing colors.

Finally a verbal definition came to mind – *giddy!* Yes. That was it. He had never felt giddy before in his life. Such a strange, alien, *wonderful* feeling.

Chapter 8

THANKSGIVING

On Thanksgiving, Scott arrived at Linda's house a little after two. Under his field coat, he wore an open-collared blue dress shirt and a brown cashmere sport coat. He rang the doorbell while cradling three bottles of wine. Megan opened the door and smiled when she saw him.

"Hi, Scott. Thanks for coming."

"Thanks for inviting me."

"My, but don't you look pretty. I don't think I've ever seen you in anything but jeans and a flannel shirt."

"You look pretty fetching yourself."

Indeed she did. She wore a red silk blouse with a white skirt that accentuated her slender figure. Her subtle make-up brought out her striking dark eyes. She wore her hair up, which made her look older and more sophisticated than her twenty years.

She held the door wide. "Come on in. Let me help you with that wine so you can take your coat off." He handed the bottles to her.

They entered a small, comfortably furnished living room where a dozen people of all ages sipped cocktails. He recognized many of them as customers from the Cedar Rock. Also present was Greg, the old man from Harrison Hospital whom Scott had helped with the flower vases. They nodded at each other in greeting. A football game played on a television with the sound muted. Light jazz wafted from a sound system. The air was permeated with the smell of roasting turkey.

"Hey, everyone," said Megan. "This is Scott. Even though he's got a stick up his butt half the time, he's turned out to be one of my favorite customers."

"Greetings, fellow strays," said Scott.

After quick introductions, Megan pulled him by the arm. "Let's go say hi to Mom."

They went into the kitchen. Linda was leaning over the open oven, basting a turkey, her shapely backside facing them. Megan noticed his smile of appreciation and rolled her eyes. She loudly cleared her throat.

"Ahem. Mom. Scott's here."

"Oh." Linda set the baster down and closed the oven. She turned around, smiling her crooked smile. "Happy Thanksgiving," she said.

She was dressed in a black and gold dress with a low-cut neckline, with her hair falling to her shoulders in soft, shining brown waves. Scott thought she looked terrific.

"Same to you."

He noticed her half-finished martini perched on a nearby counter. She followed his gaze and said, "Would you like a drink?"

"A vodka tonic would be fine."

Linda stepped to the kitchen table, now converted into a temporary bar. As she mixed his drink, she said, "You know, to be honest, we weren't a hundred percent sure you were going to show up."

"Oh? Why not?"

She glanced up at him. "My daughter said you've lived alone a long time and are pretty set in your ways."

"She said that?" He gave Megan a sidelong look.

"I did not," she answered. "I said you were a stubborn, prematurely crotchety loner with too much time on your hands."

There was an awkward silence, then Scott smiled gamely. "Don't hold anything back on my account, Megan," he said. "Feel free to speak your mind."

Linda broke into laughter, and Megan gave him a quick

approving smile, as if to say, *Well done.*

⌒⌒⌒

Half an hour later, Scott sat on the couch next to Greg. The old man took a sip of his Scotch and water, and gestured at Megan who was talking with guests across room. His watery blue eyes glimmered as he said, "It's sure nice having her back. For a while there, I didn't think she was going to make it. No one did."

Scott looked Megan's way. "It looks like she pulled through just fine."

"Boy. Isn't that the truth. She is one lucky girl."

Scott smiled to himself and thought how surprised Greg would be to find out that luck had nothing to do with it. Scott continued staring at Megan, and felt something catch in his throat. To see her back in the full bloom of her young life, sassy and animated as ever, was an amazing feeling.

Greg downed the rest of his drink and stood up. "Excuse me while I go find the little boys' room."

Scott continued to stare unabashedly at Megan. As if suddenly aware of his eyes, she turned and looked at him. He didn't look away. They watched each other until she came over and sat beside him.

"Okay, here's the deal," she said. "It's my mother you're interested in. *Comprendo? Capiche?* My *mother.*"

"Don't flatter yourself, little girl. Even if we were the same age, you're not my type."

"Oh, really. And why aren't I your type?"

"You're way too ugly. And annoying. And then there's the bad breath. And the nose hairs. And the chronic flatulence. And the—"

"Very funny."

"I was just getting started."

"Well, you can stop right now."

He took a swallow of his drink. "Any luck tracking down the mysterious bank donor?"

"Nope. I've given up."

"So you're going to keep the money."

"Yep."

"What are you going to do with it? Hit the casinos?"

"Yeah, sure. I'm going to do three things with it. First, I'm going to pay off my medical bills. Then I'm going to give some to Mom—I've never had to pay rent here. She could use a little help." She fixed him with a radiant smile, and said, "And then I'm going to Europe!"

"Megan, that's fantastic!"

"So you think it's okay?"

"You sound like you're asking my permission or something. Of course, it's okay! Especially after everything you've been through."

"I'm glad you feel that way. Mom took a little convincing."

"Really? Why is that?"

"She's always been such a stickler about getting an education. Which I still fully intend to do. I've just put it on hold for a year or so, because of... what happened to me. I mean, you never know, right?"

"So your mom's okay with it."

"Once I explained to her how important it was to me, she came around pretty quickly."

"When are you going?"

"Right after the first of the year."

"It's going to be cold."

"Not much colder than here."

"I guess that's true. How long will you be gone?"

"That's what's so awesome—I have no idea!" She couldn't keep the excitement out of her voice. "I imagine I'll come home when the money runs out."

"Which country are you going to first?"

She rolled her eyes. "Jeez, you sound like my mother."

"Aw... please. Humor me."

"Well, first, I'm going to England. It seems the logical place to start, since I can at least speak the language. From there, I'm not sure yet. I'll figure it out as I go along."

Scott shook his head in wonderment. "I've gotta tell you—

I'm very impressed."

"About what?"

"You're extremely adventuresome, Megan. A lot more so than I was when I was your age."

"I doubt that."

"I'm afraid it's true."

She had never seen this wistful side of Scott. "Tell you what," she said. "How about I drop you a postcard now and then?"

He broke into a big smile. "I would love that. Let me give you my address." He pulled a pen from his coat and scribbled on a napkin. "The Brits have no idea what they're in for."

"The English and I will get along just fine."

Megan checked her watch. "We should be close to eating." She stood up. "I'm going to see if anyone needs a drink. Why don't you go check up on Mom—see if she needs any help."

"That's the best idea I've heard all day," said Scott, and winked at her.

⌒ ⌒⌒

The kitchen counters were covered with steaming bowls and platters of mashed potatoes, gravy, dressing, Brussels sprouts, green beans, salad, and cranberries. Linda was using a cooking thermometer to check the temperature of the turkey.

"Perfect," she said.

"Can I give you a hand with anything?"

"Oh, yes! You certainly can. I need to get this guy on that serving platter."

Wielding oversized tongs, together they hefted the sizzling turkey onto the platter. Scott admired the perfect smoothness of her arms as they did so.

"We need to let the bird rest before we eat," she said, looking pleased. "In the meantime, maybe you could pour some of that wine you brought."

"I'd be happy to." He picked up a corkscrew and began opening bottles. "Do you mind if I ask you a personal question?"

She smiled. "Ask anything you want. It doesn't mean I'll necessarily answer it."

"Megan's never mentioned her father. I'm curious—where is he?"

Her crooked smile vanished. Her eyes seemed to focus on something far away.

"Never mind," he said. "It's none of my business."

"No, it's okay. I don't mind telling you. You just caught me a little off guard." She glanced at the oven clock. "We've got a few minutes. I'm going to tell you a story. Is that okay?"

"Sure."

"Once upon a time, there was a girl growing up in a trailer park who was an only child. Her dad worked at the lumber mill. Her mom was a housewife. The girl got good grades at school, but she didn't have any money to go to college. Her saving grace was that she was good —and I mean *really* good—at soccer. So good, in fact, that she won a full-ride soccer scholarship to the University of Washington."

"Wow." Scott took a sip of his drink.

Linda leaned against the counter and took a swallow of her martini. "That first year of college was a dream come true for the girl. She was one of the best players on the team, and she loved going to school. She even fell in love with a boy. This girl was no dummy. She didn't want to jeopardize her fairy tale life, so she went on the pill. She got pregnant anyway..."

Scott stared at those defiant, wounded eyes.

"She would have had an abortion, but this was a pill baby, a little being whose spirit was so strong that... well, it just didn't seem right.

"She worked it out with the school so that she could continue taking classes but stop playing soccer until the baby was born and she could get back in shape. So she and the boy got married. After a lot of hard work, she was accepted back on the team. Everything was good again. So good, in fact, that in celebration, she and her husband went up to Stevens Pass to spend the day skiing. You see, she was also an excellent skier. And then, on the last run of the day, a young man on a snowboard ran into her. A compound fracture of the femur can ruin your whole day."

She paused to take a swallow of her martini before continuing. "She was removed from the team and forced to leave school. Not so long after that, the boy who was the father of her child went down to the market to buy a half-gallon of milk. He never came back."

"I'm sorry." It was all he could think to say.

She finished the last of her drink and set the stem glass down. "I'm not sorry at all. For anything. Well, except for that damned snowboarder, who didn't have a lick of insurance or a pot to piss in."

Scott set his own glass down. "Ms. Hillis, I was thinking."

She smiled. "About what, Mr. Northwood?"

"About, maybe, you and I could—"

Greg suddenly appeared. "I have been officially appointed by the hungry masses huddled in the next room to tell you that the smell of that turkey is driving everyone crazy! Are we going to be eating soon, or should we order a pizza instead?"

Linda laughed. "No pizzas! We're dishing it up right now. Grab a platter."

A big grin spread across Greg's face. "Now you're talking!" He grabbed a bowl of salad and headed out of the kitchen. Linda started to follow with a pot of mashed potatoes, but then stopped in the doorway. She glanced back at Scott, smiled, and winked.

"Hold that thought," she said.

⌒⌒⌒

People took their seats at the dining room table. Linda and Megan sat at the places of honor at either end. Scott held Linda's chair out for her and then gestured at the chair on her right.

"May I sit here, Ms. Hillis?"

"You may, Mr. Northwood."

Megan noticed this exchange from the other end of the table and allowed herself a quick smile.

Linda said in a voice for all to hear, "As those of you who have spent Thanksgiving with us in the past know, we don't say grace. We just dig in."

This was met with knowing chuckles as she continued. "But this year, I just wanted to say a couple of words... of thanks..." She looked at Megan. It was difficult for her to speak. Hot tears welled up and spilled over, but she continued as best she could. "I think it's pretty darn obvious what... I am so very thankful for..."

She stopped speaking, and Megan smiled at her mother through her own teary eyes.

"Hear, hear!" said Greg. Everyone burst into applause.

Megan raised her glass of wine. "Happy Thanksgiving, Mom."

The room soon filled with the buzz of conversation and the clatter of serving spoons as food was passed around and they all loaded up their plates. Scott was just about to shovel a forkful of mashed potatoes and gravy into his mouth when a loud, insistent car horn sounded outside the house. Unlike a rhythmic car alarm, this beeping was deliberate—and demanding.

Everyone tried to ignore it and keep eating, but the horn didn't stop. The sound became extremely annoying.

Linda slammed her fork down. "What in the world—?" She and Megan rose from the table, and hurried through the living room, out the front door to see who was making all the racket. Scott, Greg, and the rest followed.

Chapter 9

CAPTAIN JACK

Parked in the driveway was a huge black pickup truck. Its windows were so deeply tinted that whoever was behind the wheel couldn't be seen.

Scott noticed the truck had Alaska plates.

The honking ceased. Linda approached the vehicle, trying to peer through the darkened glass. "Who's in there?"

The door on the driver's side flew open. A man in an Armani tuxedo stepped to the ground. Average height, maybe in his early forties, he was solidly muscled and moved with the swagger of a much younger man. Under thick blonde hair, his ruddy, clean-shaven face broke into a huge smile.

"Hello, Linda!" he said.

So this must be Jack Lofgren, Scott thought, dismayed. He was cheered, however, to see that Linda did not look at all happy.

In a cold voice, she asked, "What in the world are you doing here?"

"I came to see you."

Scott watched her fold her arms over her chest. "You don't call for months. You don't answer your phone. Then, out of the blue, you show up on Thanksgiving? What the hell is wrong with you?"

"Nothing. As a matter of fact, everything is right with me."

"Have you been drinking?"

"I haven't had a drink in over three months."

"Ah! Forgive me if I say I find that hard to believe."

"I checked myself into the best rehab clinic money can

buy. That's where I've been the last ninety days. They don't let you use the phone."

He moved close to her, drinking her in as if she were the only other person in the world. He didn't even glance at the crowd behind her. "I wanted to make sure I was on the straight and narrow before I saw you."

This seemed to soften her a little. "Why are you wearing a tuxedo?"

"I wanted something appropriate for the occasion."

"What? Thanksgiving?"

"No. This occasion."

He reached into his pocket, pulled out a small black box and placed it in her hand. When she opened it, a large diamond ring sparkled in the fading light. Linda's eyes squinted in suspicion as she looked at it, and then at him.

"Okay, Jack, what's going on?"

He bent down on one knee. "What does it look like?"

Her mouth dropped open. "Oh, no," she whispered, clearly shocked.

He smiled. "Oh, yes." In a deep confident voice, he said, "Linda Hillis, will you marry me?"

She glanced at Megan as if seeking guidance, but the girl seemed to be in her own state of disbelief.

Greg nudged Scott. "If that don't beat all."

Scott didn't respond, but stood there watching Linda and Jack. He could barely believe this. He was aware of a feeling even more foreign than the emotion Linda had evoked in him: he felt as if his soul were being folded closed. And the pain this brought him was as shocking as it was excruciating.

Linda looked too stunned to speak. "Honey?" said Jack. "Hello? I'm asking you to be my wife."

Flustered, she said, "I... don't know what to say."

Jack looked hopeful. "So, at least it's not a no."

"Yes."

"Was that a yes?"

She quickly shook her head. "No! It's not a yes. It's not a

no. It's... I don't know what it is. I think I need to sit down."

Jack got to his feet. The air seemed to have gone out of him. Linda placed a hand on his arm. "Don't look so hurt. You have to realize this is the last thing in the world I expected. It's too much to take in. I can't give you an immediate answer. I'm going to need time to think about it. I hope you understand."

He smiled and said, "I do understand." He glanced at the other guests as if seeing them for the first time, then looked back at Linda. "I didn't mean to put you on the spot. But once I made the decision to ask you, I couldn't think about anything else."

She seemed both flattered and embarrassed by his earnest tone. "Look. We just sat down to dinner. You're welcome to join us, if you want."

"Are you sure? I wouldn't want to impose."

She laughed. "Impose? Gee, that's a good one! If this isn't an imposition, I don't know what is! But come inside and have something to eat. There's plenty of food." She held the box out to him. "In the meantime, you better hang on to this."

"No, you keep it for now. Just for safekeeping. I'm afraid I might lose it."

She turned and headed back to the house with Jack beside her.

Megan fell into step next to Scott. She gave him a quick disappointed shrug. He nodded in agreement.

⌒⌒⌒

Jack had shoved Scott's chair out of the way and pulled his own up next to Linda's. Eating with gusto from a plate piled high with food, he spoke between mouthfuls. "This year turned out to be the best season The Raging Guppy's ever had."

"What's The Raging Guppy?" asked Greg.

"That's the name of Jack's boat," said Linda, not looking up from her plate.

"We caught more salmon than in the last five years combined. The crew worked eighteen-hour shifts. We were all dead tired, but we kept at it until the hold was overflowing."

Scott's plate of food sat untouched in front of him. In his chair, pushed back from the table, he sat in silence as Jack told stories of life in Alaska. Scott drained the wine in his glass and refilled it.

Megan spoke up from the other end of the table. "Is that how you were able to afford the new truck? The last time I saw you, you were driving a ten-year-old Dodge Ram that looked like it *had* rolled down a hill. Oh. Wait. That's because it had rolled down a hill."

Jack jammed another forkful of turkey and gravy into his mouth. Chewing, he took his time answering her. When he finally did, he spoke with studied casualness, as if he had rehearsed this moment. "You mean the truck in the driveway? No, actually. I didn't have to pay for it."

"So you stole it?" said Megan.

"No, I didn't steal it. It's a perk written into my contract."

"What contract?" Linda asked.

Jack grinned. "The one I signed with The Most Dangerous Catch," he said.

The table went silent as everyone stopped eating. Finally Greg said, "I watch that show. Are you saying you're gonna be on it?"

"Yep."

Even Linda looked impressed. "How did that come about?"

"They got scouts in port up there who are always looking for new boats to feature. They checked us out and liked what they saw."

Everyone started asking questions at once. "When's it going to be on?" "How much are they paying you?" "Are you moving to Hollywood?" "Are you going to be rich and famous?"

Scott downed his wine in one gulp, then stood up and eased himself past Greg.

"Where you goin'?" said Greg.

"Little boys' room."

Scott found his way to the bathroom. After washing his hands, he stared at his reflection in the mirror. What in the hell was he doing here? What did he think was going to happen? He gave a self-deprecating laugh and turned away from the mirror.

Retrieving his coat from the living room closet, he heard a burst of laughter coming from the dining room. "Jack Lofgren, king of Alaska fishermen, regales his audience with tales of derring-do on the high seas," he whispered to the empty room.

Megan emerged from the dining room carrying a stack of dirty plates. When she saw him, she stopped. "Not sticking around for dessert?"

"I don't think so."

"Hang on a sec before you go."

She went into the kitchen, dumped the plates in the sink and came back. "I just wanted to say I'm sorry about this."

"No reason to apologize. You didn't know Yukon Jack was going to show up."

"I kind of expected things to go in another direction."

His smile was wistful. "Me, too."

Her voice took on a challenging tone. "Can't say I blame you for running out with your tail between your legs. That's some pretty stiff competition in there."

He wasn't about to take the bait. "See, Megan, that's the thing. I have no desire to get into a pissing contest with a swashbuckling sea captain from the Great White North. Which I guess goes to show that maybe you were right about something."

"What's that?"

"I am set in my ways. And you know what? I'm fine with it."

"So... you're just going to pick up your marbles and go home?"

"That's right."

"You're not even going to say good-bye to Mom?"

"Your mother seems a little preoccupied at the moment." He opened the front door and started to walk out.

"Scott. Wait."

"What?" He held onto the door but stopped moving.

"Is it still okay if I send you a postcard sometimes?"

He grinned. "I'd love it if you would. Have a great time in Europe, Megan. Have the best time of your life."

She grinned back. "You bet I will."

Scott headed out into the autumn darkness, closing the door behind him.

He was jarred awake by the telephone ringing. He glanced at the clock. It was a little before 10 p.m. He assumed it was Shelly calling to wish him a Happy Thanksgiving. Certainly no one else would call at this time.

He picked up the phone and said, "Hey, Sis."

"I didn't know you had a sister."

He recognized Linda's voice and sat up with his back against the pillow. "Up kind of late, aren't you?"

"It's not that late, is it?"

"How did you get this number?"

"From Megan. I hope it's okay."

"Actually, I'm glad you called," he said. "I didn't get a chance to thank you for your hospitality."

"You didn't stay very long."

"Well. Things got a little crowded for my taste, so I decided to leave."

"I probably would have done the same thing."

"The soon-to-be-rich-and-famous Jack Lofgren is quite a character."

"Hmm. No denying that."

"Is he enjoying the rest of his Thanksgiving?"

"I wouldn't know. I sent him to a hotel."

Scott was silent a couple of seconds. Then he said, "Have you given him an answer yet?" He hoped she would say— *You bet I did! I told him to get in his truck and take his diamond back to Alaska.*

"No."

He gave a quiet sigh. "Are you going to marry him?"

"To be honest, Scott, I'm a little confused right now. I don't know what I'm going to do. I mean, Jack and I have had our moments, both good and bad. At times, he can be so incredibly sweet. But then, other times..." Her voice trailed off.

Great, he thought. All this baggage turning up that he wasn't expecting. "Linda, why did you call me?"

She seemed to choose her words with care. "I'm not exactly sure. It just seems that any possibilities that may or may not exist between you and me never really got a chance. And I find that sad. I know we've only just met, but I was looking forward to getting to know you better. I still am, for that matter. But only if you're game."

He thought about what she was saying, but he couldn't help but recall that raw pain he'd felt at dinner, that extraordinary sadness he'd worked so hard to keep at bay. "I don't think that's such a good idea."

"Why not?"

"Maybe some things just aren't meant to be."

Her voice took on an edge. "Oh, please."

"What?"

"I've always hated that expression. What the hell is that supposed to mean, anyway? 'Some things just aren't meant to be.' Things are what you make them to be."

"Can I be totally honest with you?"

"I wouldn't have it any other way."

"Okay. Well, tonight, for a little while, I felt like I was in junior high school."

"Junior high—? What do you mean?"

"I felt like the computer geek trying to compete with the quarterback for the attention of the head cheerleader. It wasn't a very pleasant feeling."

"Are you serious?"

"Yes. I'm serious. And, yes, I was planning to ask you out. But now, like I said, it doesn't seem like such a good idea."

"Why not?"

"With Jack suddenly in the picture, everything's changed."

"Before he goes jumping to conclusions, maybe the computer geek—and by the way, I don't think he's a geek—should ask the cheerleader how she feels about things."

"I'm sorry, Linda. It's no use."

"Why is it no use?"

"This may sound like a strange thing to say but—I'm just not used to not being in control of situations."

There was a long silence. Then she said, "Gee, Scott. I wouldn't want you to change your life or anything. Sorry to bother you."

There was a click as she hung up. He stared at the receiver before placing it back in the cradle, thinking about the words he'd said. *Can I be totally honest with you?* What crap! He knew he hadn't been the least bit honest. Running away from Linda was something he had felt forced to do, but even he suspected the reason for that might have very little to do with Jack Lofgren.

So, he said to himself, if it wasn't about Jack or about high school or about some stupid competition, what was it about? He would swear up and down that he didn't have a clue, but even as he said these words to himself, he had the strong sense that the reason was right there inside him, if only he had the courage to find it.

～～～

He tried to resume his ordered, quiet life. As autumn deepened into winter, he spent the long dark days at home reading, channel surfing, listening to music, watching DVDs or just staring out the window at the Olympic Mountains. But now he felt a void, an aching hollowness to his peace of mind. He struggled to ignore the gnawing sensation of emptiness and tried to compartmentalize his feelings—something he had always been so good at. But that no longer seemed to be the case.

And then there was that thing Patrick had said to him. It

kept nibbling at the back of his mind. *You don't do anything except sit around on your ass.*

Yeah, well, so the hell what! It was his life and he could live it as he damn well pleased.

Christmas and New Year's came and went, barely making a ripple. He sent his yearly yuletide check to Shelly. In return, he received his annual gift from her—a box filled with socks, T-shirts and underwear, items he never got around to buying for himself until he could practically read a newspaper through the fabric. And he continued to look out his window, seeing not much of anything.

Chapter 10

MAX

Weeks passed. Rain or shine, the highlight of each day continued to be Scott's walk with Jake at Autumn Lake. During stormy weather, their daily ramble took on the trappings of a wilderness expedition. Depending on how cold and wet it was, Scott would dress in appropriate layers of cotton, fleece, wool, rubber, leather, and Teflon.

He always kept a supply of towels in the car for Jake, who loved the rain. He would splash through puddles with a kind of deranged glee. Afterward, Scott would wipe the mud from his paws and undercarriage before lifting him back into the car.

It was during just such a downpour that Scott ran into Patrick; he was standing in the middle of the trail. The driving rain dripped from his hair and coursed down his face, but he didn't seem to notice.

"Hello, Patrick." Scott wasn't exactly surprised to see him again. "Fancy meeting you here."

"There's a guy in Seattle needs your help," said Patrick. "We don't have much time."

Scott sighed. Same old Patrick. Abrupt to the point of rudeness.

"'Hello, Scott. I haven't seen you in a while. How is everything?' 'Not too bad. What brings you here?' 'I'm here because I never thanked you for what you did for Megan. You know, giving up a year of your life to a complete stranger and all.'"

Patrick's eyes widened in amusement. "Oh, wait, I get it. You're being sarcastic while scolding me for not being properly appreciative of what a wonderful human being you are. Well, you have definitely put me in my place. Please, oh please, forgive my insensitive behavior. How's that? Feel better now?"

Scott shook his head. Some things were never going to change. "What do you want?"

"Like I was sayin'. There's a guy in Seattle that's gonna get creamed by a runaway car."

"Who is he?"

"Name's Max Grabowsky. He's thirty-five. He's—"

"Wait," said Scott. "Don't tell me. He's an amazing person. Everyone loves him. He lights up the room the minute he walks in. He's spent his whole life rescuing puppies and giving alms to the blind."

Patrick smiled. "Gettin' a little touchy, aren't we? Max doesn't rescue puppies. What he *does* do is run a one-man charity that delivers meals to poverty-stricken kids who would otherwise go hungry. Works his butt off on a shoe-string budget. If Max croaks, let's just say that a lotta kids and their families are gonna end up in dire straits."

"What am I supposed to do about it?"

Patrick gave Scott his I'm-talking-to-an-idiot look. "What do you think?"

"Why should I get involved?"

"You did before."

Scott gave him a hard stare.

"What's the matter?" Patrick asked.

"I think I get it now."

"Get what?"

"Every time some half-way decent person is about to meet an untimely end, you're going to come and demand that I shave time off my life and give it to them. Is that how it works?"

"Like I told you," there was exasperation in Patrick's voice.

"I'm an Enabler. It's what I do. And no one's demanding that you do anything."

"Really?"

"All right. I admit sometimes I go a little overboard. I can't help it. I tend to get caught up in the situation."

"So where does it end? Do you plan on pestering the crap out of me every time you get a new Prospect?"

"You call it pestering. I call it persuading."

"I don't care what you call it, I don't like it."

"And yet, it works," Patrick retorted with a smug smile.

Scott was getting angry. "Well, it's not going to work anymore. You can badger me all you want, but I'm through playing this game." He shoved past Patrick and continued along the trail.

"You can't just walk away from this, you know," Patrick called out.

Scott detected a trace of panic. He didn't break stride. "Watch me."

Patrick began following at a fast walk. "Tell you what. I'll make you a deal."

"What kind of deal?"

"What if I promise to stop being so..." he seemed to be searching for the right word.

Scott was happy to help out. "Obnoxious."

"I was gonna say aggressive. Here's the deal. From now on, any time I want to bring a Prospect to your attention, I'll lay out the facts for you calmly and clearly—no hard sell. I'll ask you to take a serious look at the situation. Then you can decide if you want to get involved or not. Period."

"That's it?"

"That's it."

As Scott considered the offer, a thought came to him. "I get the impression that if I say no, you're not going away any time soon, and will probably do everything you can to make my life miserable. Right?"

"Whatever would make you think such a thing?" This was accompanied by a huge smile.

"I thought so. Tell you what. I'll agree to your so-called deal. But there's something I want in return."

"What?"

"You've been evading my questions from the start. I want some straight answers."

"What questions have I been evading?"

"Questions about you. I mean, who are you? Where did you come from? Why are you here doing these things? How in the world are you able to do them?"

"Okay, you got a point. I'll answer the best I can, but I may not be able to answer them all. Is that agreeable to you?

"It is."

"So we have a deal?"

"We do. And now, as per the terms of the deal, I've got a question for you."

"Sorry, but it's gonna have to wait."

"Why?"

"Because Max Grabowsky is running out of time. If you're gonna help him, we have to act now."

"When is this incident with the car supposed to take place?"

"In two hours."

"Two hours?! I'm confused. With Megan, I had time to get to know her and decide if I wanted to get involved or not. Why the short notice?"

"It's hard to explain. The situation of each Prospect is different. I just found out about Max myself." Patrick's voice became urgent. "Look, we don't have time to stand here and argue. If we leave right now, we can catch the next ferry to Seattle. Hopefully, we'll have enough time to help Max."

"But I still don't know if I—"

"Nobody's asking you to commit to anything right this second. We just need to get there and be ready to step in, if that's what you decide to do. I'll explain more on the way. So what's it gonna be?"

It took Scott only a couple of seconds to respond. "Let's go."

They hurried back toward the car. Scott grabbed a towel to wipe Jake's paws, but Patrick stopped him. "No time for that. And no time to drop your dog off. Unless you want to miss the ferry."

"Sorry, Jake," Scott said, lifting the dog into the back seat. "Looks like lunch'll be a little late today." The Range Rover sprayed muddy gravel as it sped out of the parking lot.

Max Grabowsky was having a good day. After completing his twice-weekly trips to high-end restaurants downtown, his van was nearly filled with a bounty of food: bags of salad greens, tureens of soups and stews, roasted meats and poultry tightly wrapped in foil. It had all been carefully refrigerated after having gone unsold the previous day.

Max started the van and headed toward Belltown.

Scott managed to hit all green lights through Poulsbo on State Route 305. As soon as they left the city limits, he kicked the speed back up—but only to 55. The limit was 50 miles per hour, and he didn't want to risk getting a ticket, which would make them miss the ferry.

"So?" said Scott.

"What?" said Patrick, perplexed.

"So explain to me why you had more advance warning about Megan than you do with Max Grabowsky."

"Like I said, every Prospect's situation is different. I don't always have all the specifics."

"What's that supposed to mean?"

"If someone's got a terminal disease, things tend to progress gradually, so there's more time to deal with it. But when something's unexpected, like an accident, the window of opportunity is much smaller."

"How much smaller?"

"Well, never more than twenty-four hours. Sometimes a lot less...just a couple hours."

"Like now?"

Patrick nodded. "Maybe that explains why I'm more aggressive at some times than others."

"You mean obnoxious."

"Whatever works."

They crossed the Agate Pass Bridge onto Bainbridge Island. It was eight miles to the ferry terminal.

Scott checked his watch. The boat left in ten minutes.

It was going to be close.

⌇⌇⌇⌇

It had begun as a lark. On weekends, Max used to hang out at a restaurant on Capitol Hill. At the end of lunch hour, he would watch, dumbfounded, as perfectly good, unsold food got dumped into garbage bags and taken out back to be tossed into dumpsters.

A very needy family of six lived right down Max's street. The father had lost his construction job, unemployment checks barely covered their rent, and the family had to depend on the local food bank. But donations were down, and those four kids were perpetually hungry.

Max talked with the restaurant manager and got permission to take some of that extra food to his neighbors.

What began as a simple desire to assist a struggling family soon took on a life of its own. Word of Max's generosity spread to a number of families who had fallen on hard times. Before long, he became the main source of food for hundreds of people—the vast majority of them children.

The number of restaurants willing to help out grew, and he would work with the managers to make sure the food didn't spoil. As far as the Seattle Health Department was concerned, he was in violation of several ordinances, but since no one complained or got sick, they left him alone.

Max's day job was as an Information Technology specialist. He liked it; the money was good and the work interesting. But gradually, he found himself spending more and more time making sure that "his people" had enough to eat.

His boss, a compassionate woman, allowed him flexible hours so he could make his pickups and deliveries. Before long, what had started as a lark evolved into something deeper. He realized that this food bank operation was what he wanted to do with his life. The downside was that it didn't pay any bills.

He peered out the rain-speckled windshield at his first stop in Belltown, the Rain City Bar and Grill. The trendy neighborhood was packed with upscale restaurants. In his first hesitant forays there in search of eateries willing to sign on, he hadn't expected any takers, but now the restaurateurs tried to outdo each other as to how much food they could donate.

He parked at the curb, hopping out and grabbing the wheeled dolly from the back. Pushing that ahead of him, he headed into the Rainy City.

〰〰〰

Scott's luck with traffic lights ran out on Bainbridge Island. As they approached the very first one, it turned yellow: he floored it and ended up running the red. The blip and whoop of a police siren sounded as flashing blue lights filled the rearview mirror.

"Oh, man!" he said, slapping the steering wheel. "Just what we need!"

He pulled over with the police car close behind, and reached for his wallet. Patrick put a hand on his arm to stop him. "Repeat everything I say to this cop."

"What?"

"Just do it."

He rolled down his window as the officer appeared, his Smokey the Bear hat draped in plastic to protect it from the rain.

"The reason I pulled you over, sir, is that you ran the red light back there at the intersection."

"I know, Officer, but it's just that we—I mean, I—really need to catch the next ferry."

"You and everyone else I stop. So I'll tell you what I tell everyone else—leave earlier next time. License and registration, please."

Patrick gave the policeman a hard stare.

"Why did you say you pulled us over, Officer?"

Scott repeated Patrick's words. "Why did you say you pulled us over, Officer?"

A faraway gaze appeared on the officer's face. He scratched his jaw as if perplexed by something.

"I, uh, you know... for the life of me, I can't remember." He laughed, embarrassed.

"It's because you want to escort us personally to the ferry. Right?"

"It's because you want to escort us personally to the ferry. Right?"

"Why... yes. I believe so..."

"Then we better hurry, don't you think?"

"Then we better hurry, don't you think?"

"Yes. You're right. We better hurry. Follow me."

The officer went back to his cruiser and climbed in. He left the blue lights going and turned on the siren, pulling in front of Scott and motioning for him to follow.

The cruiser accelerated to over 80 miles per hour, the Range Rover close behind.

Scott glanced at Patrick. "How in the world did you do that?"

"I've got a few tricks up my sleeve."

"I wish I'd known you when I was a teenager."

They arrived at the ferry terminal in moments. The cruiser pulled over at the entrance to the vehicle holding area. The officer turned off his lights and siren, and looked around as if he didn't know where he was.

"Cops," said Patrick with a dismissive shake of the head. "They're usually around when you don't need one."

Scott had cash ready for the ticket booth.

"You just made it," said the ticket taker.

The Range Rover moved into the holding area where the

ferry crew was loading the last car in line. A crew member saw him coming and waved him aboard. Seconds later the boat pulled away.

～～～

As Max finished up at his last Belltown restaurant, he realized he was having a record day. The cold, rainy weather had kept a lot of customers at home the previous night, so there were plenty of leftovers. Today's weather wasn't much better, so lunch crowds were small, resulting in even more spare food.

Max had one last stop to make—the Meat Wagon Express Restaurant on First Hill. He started the engine and pulled into traffic. The wet street hissed from the tires of passing cars.

～～～

Scott and Patrick remained in their car as the ferry lumbered across Puget Sound. They were parked next to the railing on a covered car deck where they had a view of the water. After the frantic rush to catch the boat, Scott found the enforced quiet of the crossing a little disorienting.

"I'm going to stretch my legs," he said. He got out of the car and walked to the railing. The cold marine air on his face felt good.

Patrick appeared at his side. The two stared out across the gun-metal gray waters of the Sound. "We've got a little bit of time. Let's hear some of your questions."

"How do you know when something is going to happen?" Scott continued to look at the water.

"It's hard to explain. It's like... a feeling comes over me."

"A feeling."

"Yeah. It's like, all of a sudden, I'll get this tingling sensation, and I know somebody in the vicinity is about to die. Someone who should get another chance. Then all the information about that person just appears in my head. What they look like. Where they live. The work they do. And how they're gonna die. And I'm supposed to do everything I can to prevent it." He turned to look at Scott. "That's where you come in."

"Lucky me. Are there others out there like me?"

"Yeah."

"How many?"

"Counting you, I handle eight others."

"Are they all here in Washington?"

"They're scattered around the western states."

"What about you?"

"What about me?"

"Do other Enablers exist?"

"They do."

"Where are they?"

Patrick shrugged. "I couldn't tell ya. Scattered around the world, I guess."

"How many are there"

"I don't know. A dozen, maybe."

"Is Patrick your real name?"

"Real enough."

"Hmm. Do you have a last name?"

He scowled in annoyance at the question. "It's not important. Saving Max Grabowsky is important."

"About saving Max Grabowsky... There's something I don't get."

"Yeah?"

"You say Max is going to get hit by a car, right?"

"Right."

"Think back to the meteor storm. When I asked you how that happened, you said something interesting."

"Did I?"

"You said meteors are dirt floating through space. That it was just physics."

"Yeah. So?"

"So my question is, why isn't saving Max just physics? Why can't you go to Seattle and shove Max out of the way of the car? Why do you need me?"

"It's hard to explain."

"Try."

"The meteor storm was just rocks burning up in the sky. Nobody was in danger. Nobody died. It was a light show put on for you so that you'd know I'm for real. But when it's a matter of life and death, it's a different story. Enablers aren't allowed to intervene directly, especially in a situation where the cause of death is a material event—like a car accident. The Implementer has to be the one to physically step in."

"But I don't even know this guy."

"You didn't really know Megan, either, and you came through for her."

Scott watched the Seattle skyline materialize through the rainy gloom. The ferry would dock soon. "I don't know, Patrick."

"What don't you know?"

"If—if I'm up for this."

"Why not?"

"Giving up more of my life for someone I never met? I don't know if I've got it in me."

"Think about Danny."

"What about him?"

"Remember the memorial service? All the people who were there? Max is like ten Dannys rolled into one. To a lot of folks, the guy's a goddamn saint. And he's going to be dead. Very soon. Unless you do something about it."

Scott considered the words as the city's mist-shrouded buildings loomed over them.

"We're gonna dock in a couple minutes," Patrick said. "So what's it gonna be? You gonna help Max or not?"

Scott pulled the collar of his coat up around his neck. He stared down at the cold gray water churning against the side of the ferry.

Another person besides Max Grabowsky had an appointment to keep on First Hill. But he was running late.

Emmett Fisher didn't care what his doctor said, he'd be damned if he was going to quit smoking. He'd smoked for fifty of his sixty-eight years and never had a serious illness. His father and his grandfather had both smoked like chimneys, and they'd lived into their eighties.

Emmett lingered in his bathrobe at the kitchen table with the newspaper, a chipped mug of black coffee in one hand and a cigarette in the other. He sucked on the Marlboro with conscious vehemence.

He'd had his annual physical the week before. After berating him for gaining fifteen pounds, the doctor listened to Emmett's chest and frowned at whatever he heard through the stethoscope. He'd given him an EKG on the spot. The readout was alarming. After much cajoling, he convinced Emmett to come back for an MRI.

According to his watch, the procedure was scheduled to take place in a little over an hour. This left him plenty of time to get dressed, drive to the hospital on First Hill, and find a parking spot.

It was only when he glanced at his watch a third time that Emmett noticed the second hand wasn't moving. The battery was dead.

He jumped up and scurried into the bedroom to check the bedside clock.

His appointment was in twenty-five minutes! And the hospital had a strict policy of charging for no-shows.

"Shit!" he said.

He threw on pants and a shirt, and dashed into the garage. Backing his deceased wife's twenty-year-old yellow Cadillac out into the driving rain without looking, he nearly hit a guy on a bicycle.

Skidding to a stop, the cyclist cried, "Hey! You almost ran me over!"

Emmett rolled down his window. "What kind of moron rides his bike in the rain?" he yelled back.

The cyclist lay his bike down and approached the vehicle

with balled fists. "You got a problem?"

Emmett grumbled under his breath, "Ah, go screw yourself." Then he rolled the window back up and gunned it toward First Hill.

The Meat Wagon Express Restaurant was so named because it always offered a meat special-of-the-day, served up quickly at a low price. Because of its proximity to Seattle's two largest hospitals, it did a brisk business. Ambulances, aka "meat wagons," regularly screamed by, and Max figured that must have factored into the christening of the restaurant.

Although the Meat Wagon was far from his other stops, he always came here because the manager donated so much unsold food. But parking near the busy hospitals was a terrible problem.

Max got around that by doing what he always did: turning the van's emergency flashers on and double-parking in front of the restaurant. Madison Avenue was one of Seattle's steepest streets, but at least he was pointed downhill. This made it easier for him to load the van from the rear doors.

He zipped up his coat, pulled the hood over his head, and stepped into the pouring rain. Grabbing the dolly from the back of the van, he dashed inside the restaurant.

Two lanes of cars at a time rolled off the ferry at a slow, steady pace. Because it had been last to board, the Range Rover would be one of the last to disembark.

Patrick drummed his fingers on the armrest. "Think they could unload this thing any slower?"

"How much time do we have?"

"Oh, man." Patrick let out a burst of air. "We are gonna be cutting it very, very close."

"I don't understand."

"What?"

"What do you mean by 'cutting it close'? I had the impression that, since we made the ferry, saving Max was a sure thing."

"What makes you think that?"

Scott was incredulous. "Gee, I don't know. Maybe it's because I just handed over a year of my life to some guy I've never met. And now, you say there's no guarantee we'll even get there in time? That he could still get killed?"

"Yeah. That's what I'm saying. Like it or not, you and Max are still subject to annoying little things like the laws of physics. Sometimes, all we can do is use the advance warning to try and change the outcome, and hope for the best."

Cars in front of them began moving forward.

"Hope for the best?! I still don't think—"

"Let's go!" said Patrick.

Scott put the car in gear and drove off into heavy rain.

The yellow Cadillac roared up to the entrance of a parking garage and stopped. Emmett Fisher squinted through the smoke from the cigarette in his mouth at the bright red neon sign that glowed FULL.

He punched the steering wheel. "Goddamn it!" This was the third garage he had tried. All of them were full.

The clock on the dashboard said he was now more than twenty minutes late.

He scanned Madison Avenue for a parking space.

There. On the other side of the street. A woman getting into her car.

"Now we're talkin'." If he could get parked and inside the hospital in the next few minutes, he knew he could talk his way into keeping his appointment.

He made a sudden wide U-turn in the middle of the block, generating a commotion of screeching brakes and honking horns. Ignoring the racket, he pulled up beside the car parked directly behind the woman and waited for her to leave. He had to stand on the brake since the Cadillac was facing downhill.

Inside the Meat Wagon, Max stacked the last containers of the day's special onto the dolly.

"Sure you don't need a hand with that, what with the rain and all?" asked the manager. Max had the feeling that Don had known hunger at some point in his life, because this was often his best stop.

"I'm fine, Don," Max smiled. "Thanks for this." He tipped the dolly back on its wheels. It was heavy, but he could manage. "I've never seen so much meatloaf, potatoes, and gravy in my life!"

"Try not to eat it all in one sitting."

Max laughed. "There's going to be a lot of happy tummies in Seattle tonight. See you next week."

He headed for the door.

Cars coming off the ferry dispersed slowly into the city, causing traffic to back up around Colman Dock. It rained so hard that Scott turned his windshield wipers on high.

"Which way?"

"Straight up the hill to Madison."

"Boy, it's really coming down."

Scott turned the Range Rover up the hill and came to an abrupt halt at the bottom of a column of brake lights. He could see a red traffic light in the distance.

"Shit." Patrick began drumming his fingers on the armrest once again.

Rain pounded on the car roof while they waited for the light to change.

"I've got a question," Scott said.

"What?"

"If we're too late... that is, if we don't make it to Max in time, do I get my year back?"

Patrick glared at him. "Of course, you get your year back!

Whatta you take me for, a thief?"

"Just asking."

"The light's green."

The line of cars crept up the hill.

Emmett seethed as he waited for the woman to vacate the parking space. He could see her face clearly in her side-view mirror: she was fixing her makeup.

What little patience Emmett possessed snapped. He rolled down his window, pitched the still smoking cigarette stub, and laid on the horn. Startled, the woman looked back at the idling Cadillac.

Emmett stuck his head out the window and shouted, "Come on, lady! I don't have all day! Enough with the makeup already! You're worse than my dead wife!"

The woman pursed her lips together and glared at him. Very slowly and deliberately, she held up her hand and extended the middle finger. So as to fully savor his aggravation, she held the gesture for a long moment, then resumed fixing her face.

"Screw you, lady! You hear me!? Screw you, you goddamn bi—Unngh!" Emmett clutched his chest with both hands. He was suddenly unable to speak because his heart had exploded.

His eyes bulged in confused surprise at this new and horrible sensation. Then his entire body convulsed; his back arched upward and his legs went completely rigid. His foot slipped off the brake and onto the gas pedal, jamming it to the floor.

With a roar of its powerful engine, the Cadillac lunged down the hill.

The Meat Wagon Express was six blocks away.

Max wedged the last containers of food into the back of the van wherever they would fit. He grinned at the size of the day's take—*a record haul!* If he kept racking up days like this, he'd have to get a bigger vehicle. He didn't have a clue how that would happen, but he'd have to give it some serious thought very soon.

⌃⌃⌃

Scott guided the Range Rover up Madison Avenue through a steady torrent of water.

Patrick was suddenly hyperalert. "Pull over!" he barked, his eyes darting up and down the street. "It's going to happen right around here!"

Scott pulled to the curb. "Could you be a little more specific?" he said, struggling to keep the ire out of his voice. "Because I need more to go on than—"

"Blue van!" Patrick gripped his forehead as if in sudden pain. "Look for a blue van!"

Scott peered out the window. "I can't see squat in this weather. How am I supposed to—wait!" He pointed down the block. "There!"

Down the hill on the other side of the street, barely visible in the gloom, was Max's double-parked van. A man in a hooded coat was attempting to wrestle a two-wheeled dolly into the back of the van, which was jammed to capacity with vats, bins, and boxes.

"That's him!" cried Patrick.

He and Scott hopped out and ran down the street. An approaching siren wailed in the distance.

"Hey, Mister!" Scott yelled. "You need to get out of the street! Hey, buddy!"

He got no reaction; his cry was lost in the wailing siren that grew louder by the second.

Patrick stopped and pointed up Madison Avenue. "Northwood!" he screamed.

Scott looked up the hill. Three blocks away, a yellow Cadillac was barreling toward them. It seemed to be going a hundred miles an hour.

Scott continued running toward the van. "Max! Get out

of the way!"

But once again the blaring siren blotted out the warning.

The Cadillac was suddenly at the top of the block rocketing toward the van.

Max finished loading the dolly and slammed the back doors closed.

Scott shrieked, "Look out!"

This time, Max heard him. He looked up and saw Scott sprinting across the street toward him. Out of the corner of his eye, he caught another blur of motion—something large and yellow, and moving very fast.

Max turned to see the speeding Cadillac closing on him from a hundred feet away, and he froze.

Without breaking stride, Scott dove through the air, knocking Max off his feet and onto the sidewalk just as the Cadillac smashed into the van.

The collision was like a bomb going off. The gas tanks of both vehicles exploded on impact. Fortunately for Scott and Max, the enormous forward momentum of the heavy car propelled both vehicles down the hill as if they'd been shot from a cannon. The two vehicles tumbled and spun together down the street, strewing fiery debris. Cars swerved crazily to get out of the way. With a final screech of metal on asphalt, the van and the Cadillac skidded to a halt at the bottom of the hill.

All traffic stopped. Workers poured from nearby buildings to gape at the scattered wreckage that lay smoking and sputtering in the rain.

Scott and Max lay sprawled on the sidewalk under the awning of the Meat Wagon. The owner charged out of the restaurant and knelt beside them. "Jeez! Are you guys okay?"

"Man, I don't know... ." Max was clearly shaken. "I think so." Lifting himself to a sitting position, he realized that, aside from a few bruises, he was otherwise unhurt.

"How about you?" the restaurant owner asked Scott.

"I'm okay," he said, running a trembling hand through his

hair. "Was that ever a close one."

"They don't get any closer." Don shook his head. "I saw the whole thing! I want you both to wait right here while I call an ambulance."

"I don't need an ambulance," said Max.

"It's just a precaution. Please! I'm telling you to stay put. I'll have someone bring out some blankets." The owner hurried inside the restaurant.

Max looked up at Scott, dazed. "What the hell just happened?"

"Runaway car."

"Wow." Max surveyed the array of damage scattered along the bottom of the hill. "So I'm thinking my van is totaled."

"More like vaporized."

He turned to Scott. "If you hadn't shoved me out of the way right when you did..."

Scott didn't respond, but, after a moment, he heard the profound sadness in Max's voice as he said, "All that food! Gone..."

Scott got to his feet. "That may be true, Max. But at least you're alive. I mean, come on. That's good, right?"

"How do you know my name?" A new expression came across Max's face.

"What?" Play dumb, Scott thought, trying to figure out how he was going to deal with this.

"I've never seen you before. How do you know my name?"

"I don't know," Scott answered. "The guy from the restaurant must have said it."

"No. He didn't."

"Are you sure? You hit the ground pretty hard, you know."

"I'm sure," said Max with conviction. "Who are you?"

Scott looked across the street where Patrick stood on the sidewalk watching him. "You know, on second thought, I think I will go to the hospital. Just as a precaution, like the man said."

"Why don't you wait for the ambulance?"

"I'm okay to walk. You can't spit in this part of town without hitting a hospital."

He turned and walked across the street.

"Who are you?" Max called after him, just as a swarm of restaurant employees came running toward him with blankets and first-aid equipment.

Scott and Patrick climbed back inside the Range Rover. Jake pressed up against the back of the driver's seat and began licking the back of Scott's neck. The dog had never done that before, and he laughed at the feel of Jake's rough, wet tongue.

"It's okay, boy," he said, pushing him away. "I'm fine. Everything's fine."

"Everything's fine, huh?" said Patrick. "You couldn't keep your trap shut and just walk away, could ya?"

His anger was confusing. "Hey! What's your problem? I just risked my life to save your Prospect. I think a little gratitude might be in—"

"I'll tell you what my problem is. You come diving out of nowhere to save Max, and then you call him by his name! He's never seen you before in his life."

"So? I don't see what the big—"

"Just think for a minute. Think about how that man is going to interpret what just happened."

"I still don't..."

"He might start thinking he's got a goddamn guardian angel looking out for him."

"Well, in a way, he does, right? And what's so terrible about that?"

"I'll tell you. It could make him reckless. I've seen it happen. And we don't need that."

Scott considered Patrick's words. "Maybe I see your point."

"No shit."

Sirens were still screaming as first responders raced to the scene.

"These streets are gonna be gridlocked any second," said

Patrick. "Let's get outta here."

"What about the other car?"

"You mean the Caddy?"

"Yes."

"What about it?"

"Shouldn't we check on it?"

"Why?"

"Whoever was driving it could still be alive and need help."

"Screw 'im."

"Excuse me?"

"I said, screw that prick! Trust me, the guy's an asshole. Or, I should say, *was* an asshole." Patrick laughed at his own joke.

Scott felt a wave of exhaustion wash over him. He could barely keep his eyes open.

"Tired?" said Patrick.

"Yeah," said Scott, holding back a yawn. "I remember feeling like this right after..." He tried and failed to stifle another.

Patrick completed his sentence. "Right after giving Megan her year. Comes with the territory. Think of it as a side effect."

"I hope I can drive."

"You're fine. You can sleep on the ferry. Now let's beat feet."

Scott started the engine, put the car in gear and headed toward the Seattle waterfront.

∿∿∿

The ferry's engines filled the air with a throbbing rumble as the boat shimmied and shuddered across the roiling gray waters of the Sound. Scott reclined his seat as far as it would go and fell into a sound sleep. Patrick sat beside him, his restless eyes watching passengers come and go from their cars. Many carried cups of coffee or containers of clam chowder from the galley. Jake sat in the back seat, staring calmly at Patrick.

Patrick scowled at the dog. "What're you lookin' at?"

Jake didn't blink. Just kept watching him.

A tiny smile creased the corners of Patrick's mouth. He reached back and roughly scratched the dog's ear. Jake closed his eyes and gave a quiet groan of pleasure.

Scott was still fast asleep when the boat docked at Bainbridge Island. As the cars began to roll ashore, a ferry worker saw that he was asleep and tapped on the window. Scott jerked awake and looked around to get his bearings. He glared at Patrick. "Why didn't you wake me up?"

Patrick just smiled as the ferry worker rolled his eyes at the cranky driver talking to thin air.

Although he was drowsy on the drive to Poulsbo, Scott was able to stay awake. It was getting dark but at least the rain had stopped.

"Where do you want to be dropped off?" he asked Patrick.

"Where do you think?"

"Autumn Lake?"

"Bingo, Einstein."

They drove the rest of the way in silence.

It was fully dark by the time Scott pulled into the park. He'd never been to Autumn Lake at night. Beyond the headlight beams, the surrounding forest disappeared into a deep and total blackness.

Scott put the car in park and turned to face Patrick. "So do you sleep, or what?"

"I wrap myself in a black cape and hang upside down from a tree."

"Wouldn't surprise me a bit."

Patrick opened the door and started to climb out.

"Wait a minute."

"What?"

"Before you go, I've got a question and I want a straight answer."

Patrick slammed the door in clear exasperation. "Fine. What's your question?"

"The meteor storm proved to me you're real. You really do exist in some way, shape, or form that I don't understand. And I have no choice but to accept it. I get that."

"Is this goin' somewhere?"

"My question is this: Why is it that I can see you, but to other people you don't exist?"

"Let me ask you a question: If Megan and Max knew what I did for them, do you think they would say I didn't exist?"

It was Scott's turn to be exasperated. "Of course not. Come on, you know what I mean."

"Yeah, I know what you mean. Matter of fact, I was wondering when you were gonna ask. This is where we get into the woo woo stuff. Are you ready? 'Cause here it comes: Just because a person can't see something, doesn't mean it doesn't exist."

Scott scowled. "Gee, thanks. That clears that up."

"Spare me the sarcasm. You asked me, and I'm tellin' you. Think about it, Northwood. What in hell is reality, anyway? Every creature experiences the same world in a totally different way. A person looking up at night sees stars and knows that they're suns like our sun. A squirrel looks up at the same sky and nothin' registers! He's focused on his own little squirrel world. Does that mean stars don't exist? Of course not. It just means the squirrel hasn't got the ability to perceive them."

"I'm not talking about squirrels. I'm asking about people."

"Same thing. Just a matter of degree."

"Meaning what?"

"Jeez! Everyone's ability to perceive what's around them is different. What's real to one person might not be real to somebody else." A sardonic grin crossed Patrick's face. "Lucky that you've been blessed with the ability to see me."

"Some might call that a curse."

Patrick's grin widened. "I guess that depends on how you perceive it." He climbed out of the car and shut the door. Scott watched him walk toward the trailhead and vanish into the woods.

Recovering from his ordeal in Seattle, Scott slept late the next morning, so it was mid-afternoon before he and Jake got around to their walk. The rain held off, but the trail was still muddy from the previous day's drenching. Jake splashed happily through the puddles. Scott looked for Patrick, but there was no sign of him.

As he toweled Jake's feet off in the parking lot, Scott murmured, "Isn't it funny how Patrick manages to show up only when he wants something."

Chapter 11

The Raging Guppy

That night, Scott watched the national news while he ate dinner. The program was almost over, which was fine with him. The top news stories were usually so depressing that he preferred the lighthearted segments at the end of the broadcast.

Settling into his chair with his plate on his lap, he took a swallow of wine, then sliced into a pork chop. The news anchor launched into a teaser for the show's final segment.

"And finally this evening, do guardian angels really exist?"

Black and white footage appeared of Scott's flying tackle of Max Grabowsky a micro-second before the van was obliterated by the Caddy. The brief video was speeded up and jerky, but the images were clear enough.

Scott began to cough.

"Coming up," intoned the anchor. "A story about a man whose life is saved by a complete stranger who comes out of nowhere, and then just as quickly disappears."

A commercial came on as Scott continued to hack. He went to the kitchen, poured a glass of water, and drank until his throat cleared.

When he'd caught his breath, he returned to the living room and sat back down.

"And now," the anchor was saying, "from our affiliate station in Seattle, Washington, we'd like to show you something that can only be described as amazing. Yesterday, the security camera of a bank captured this footage of a collision between a parked van and a runaway car that occurred in front of a nearby restaurant. Watch what happens just before they hit."

The jerky video was shown in its entirety. The force of Scott's tackle knocked both men out of view of the camera.

"Now," the anchor said, "we'll show it to you again in slow motion so you can see just how close this was."

The video was played frame by frame. Even in slow motion, Scott was running so fast that his face was a blur. In the frame right after the tackle, his feet had just cleared the van's bumper. In the next frame, the front end of the Cadillac appeared. In the frame after that, the Cadillac struck the van. Two frames later, both vehicles exploded into fireballs, which were immediately hurled off camera by the momentum of the Cadillac.

"The name of the man who was shoved out of the way of the runaway car is Max Grabowsky," said the anchor. "This is what he had to say."

An interview with Max by a local television reporter that must have been shot shortly after the collision began to play.

"I had just finished loading up my van when a guy shouts 'Look out!' I look up and see a car big as a tank coming right at me. I just froze. The next thing I know, I'm lying on the ground. The guy's on top of me and my van's completely demolished."

"Did you know this man?" asked the reporter.

"I never saw him before in my life."

"Did he say anything to you?"

"Things are still a little fuzzy. I think he said something about that being a close one. And something about how I should be happy to be alive."

"Then what happened?"

"Then he just walked away."

"Without telling you his name?"

"Yeah. But that isn't the weird part."

"What weird part is that?"

"He knew my name."

"How do you think he knew your name?"

"I have no idea."

"It sounds like you may have a guardian angel watching over you."

"I never believed in that stuff. Now I don't know what to believe. It's a miracle I'm even alive."

"Anything more you'd like to add?"

"Yes, there is. If the person who shoved me out of the way happens to be watching this, I just want to say that I was pretty out of it so I didn't have the chance to say thank you. I'm saying it now." Tears appeared in his eyes. "Whoever you are, man, thank you... for saving my life."

The television cut back to the news anchor. His eyes were also glistening with moisture.

"Mr. Grabowsky is well known to the poor of Seattle. He regularly distributes food to needy families, and in many cases he's their main source. Now, because Max is without a van, he worries that they won't get the meals they've come to depend on him for. A fund has been set up to help him buy a replacement vehicle. You can visit our website for details. And now, from all of us here in New York, good night."

The nightly news theme began to play, and the broadcast ended on a grainy freeze-frame of what could be seen of Scott's face. It was blurry and indistinct, but some of his facial features could be made out.

Scott hit the mute button as a commercial came on. He sat very still while staring at the screen, then spoke out loud. "You're welcome, Max."

About to turn off the television, a promo came on screen with an image that stopped Scott in his tracks: a man with a chiseled face wrapped in a fur-lined parka standing in a heroic pose in the wheelhouse of a fishing vessel as rain and wind beat against the window.

Jack Lofgren.

Scott turned the sound back on and heard the gravelly voice of an announcer: "Tonight. *On The Most Dangerous Catch*. Captain Jack and the crew of The Raging Guppy battle freezing rain and twenty foot waves as they try to break their own record for salmon."

Jack opened a window and shouted through the tempest at his crew. "Let's get those lines out! I'm ready to do some fishin'!"

The scene cut to crewmembers staggering like drunks about the deck of the wind-lashed boat, struggling to deploy heavy-gauge fishing lines.

"Tonight at ten. Followed by America's hottest new reality show, *One Night Stand.*"

A good-looking, hard-partying young couple was shown downing shots of tequila in a boisterous bar.

"Will she? Or won't she?" said the announcer.

Cut to the same guy next morning in boxer shorts looking very hung over, knocking on a bathroom door.

"Did they? Or didn't they?" said the announcer.

"Tiffany? Are you okay?"

He was answered by the sound of retching coming from the other side of the door.

Scott shook his head and turned off the television.

⌇⌇⌇

Later that night, with Jake asleep beside him, Scott lay in bed reading. He set the book on the floor, flipped off the light and attempted to go to sleep. After tossing and turning for most of an hour, he turned the light back on and sat up.

The clock on the nightstand read 10:20.

He grabbed the remote from the nightstand, turned on the TV and quickly found *The Most Dangerous Catch.*

The crew was howling in jubilation as they winched aboard a line of wriggling salmon. Jack was standing at the helm of The Raging Guppy, grinning as he watched them work. He was shouting to be heard above the wind and the churning waves. "Are we catching some fish or what?!"

The sudden noise woke Jake, who jerked his head around and glared at Scott.

"Sorry." He lowered the volume, and Jake let his head fall back to the mattress.

Scott watched as Lofgren and his crew hauled in line after line of fish while battling the high seas and freezing weather of the North Pacific.

When the hold was full, the crew collapsed onto their bunks, and Jack Lofgren steered the boat back to land while voicing a rambling commentary about the hardships and rewards of life as a fisherman in Alaska.

As The Raging Guppy entered the harbor of a large coastal fishing town, Lofgren, looking tired but happy, guided his vessel through calm waters toward a boat slip.

There, waiting on the wharf, was Linda.

Scott felt like his heart was trying to jump out of his chest. She wore a white fur-lined parka over jeans and knee-high boots, and her face had a ruddy glow. She looked great.

He watched as she waved at Jack, and he waved back. "There's nothing like getting home to a good woman after being out here for days on end." His voice sounded too loud to Scott; of course, everything about Jack Lofgren seemed too loud. Yet he kept listening as the man went on. "Linda and me aren't married yet, but I know she'll come around eventually."

Jack's segment came to an end, and another one began, with a different boat and a different captain, and Scott turned off the TV. It took him a long while to get to sleep. He couldn't stop thinking that no matter what issues he was dealing with—or possibly *not* dealing with—he'd been a fool to let her slip from his life. That void in his life had a name, he thought with a sad smile, and the name was Linda.

Chapter 12

JASON

As the gray days of winter crept by, Scott kept to his daily routine—except for the times Patrick would show up with a new "Prospect situation" for him to consider.

One day in late January, Patrick approached him about a boy from Mercer Island. Jason Epstein had been born with a natural musical ability so great that his piano teacher was convinced he was a second Mozart. He had arrived in this world with a small hole in the left atrium of his heart, and in his twelve years of life, the boy had undergone numerous operations to correct this dangerous condition. Unfortunately, each fix was temporary; the older Jason got and the bigger he grew, the bigger the hole became. And this made it increasingly difficult to repair. It was only through his doctors' Herculean efforts that the hole stayed patched well enough for his heart to keep pumping blood.

But now his surgeons had exhausted their bag of tricks. The hole had grown too large. No patch would hold.

They predicted Jason's heart would give out by the end of the week.

~~~

"That's what's so messed up," said Patrick as he finished making his case to Scott. They walked side by side on one of the trails while Jake padded behind them. "This kid is the real deal. If he could keep on living, even until he was just twenty, I'll bet you he would create music that would blow the world away." He paused for effect and said, "Emphasis
~~~

on *if he could keep living.*"

"Yeah, I get it."

"Just so you do."

Scott stared at the ground as he walked. "You said Jason was twelve years old."

"Correct."

"And you'd like him to make it to at least twenty."

"Yup."

"Do the math, Patrick. At the minimum, you're asking me for eight years."

"So?"

Scott stopped walking. "*So?* That's all you have to say?"

"If people had a choice between you or a young Beethoven, who do you think they'd pick? Who do you think they *should* pick?"

"This isn't a popularity contest. This is my life we're talking about."

"Oh, gee. That's right. This is all about Scott Northwood's fantastic, incredible, highly accomplished life. Oh. Wait. Let's make that his trivial, worthless, self-centered waste of a life."

Scott tried to stem his anger. "Are you done?"

"I'm done. For now."

"Let me ask you something; do Jason's parents love him?"

"Are you kiddin' me? They love the shit outta that kid! Not to mention he's their only child."

"Okay, so if they love him so much, why don't they give him some of *their* time?"

"Oh, believe me, they would if they could."

"Then why don't you enable them and leave me out of it?"

"I can't. It doesn't work that way."

"Well, it should work that way! Why does it have to be me?"

Patrick rolled his eyes. "We've been over this, Einstein. Think back to what you were willing to do for Danny, a guy you hardly knew—*extend his life at the expense of your own.* That's the reason I can enable you. The ability to transfer time from one life to another has to come from a motive that's completely unselfish."

"Are you saying that a mother who's willing to give up her life for her child is selfish?"

"It's exactly what I'm sayin'."

"That's one of the craziest things I—"

"No, think about it. A lot of people would happily trade places to save a loved one. Why? Because they can't bear to part with them. It would make *them* feel a whole lot better if *they* were the ones to croak."

Scott couldn't believe what he was hearing. "You are one cynical bastard, Patrick."

"Hey, don't get me wrong. Wanting to sacrifice your life for your kid is a noble thing. But it's also instinct. A mother's desire for her precious baby to survive is almost always stronger than her own need for self-preservation."

Scott tried to give the words serious thought, though he was finding it hard to do.

"I can tell you're not convinced," said Patrick. "Look at it this way. Just for a minute, suppose there's a terminally ill kid who lives down the street from the Epsteins. Let's say Mrs. Epstein doesn't know this kid, has never met this family. But one day she hears the sad news that he's at death's door. Got the picture? Okay. Then let me ask you this: Even if she could, do you really think Mrs. Epstein would hand over a chunk of time from her own life to save a kid who's a complete stranger? Seriously? Naah. Not gonna happen. And if you think otherwise, then have I got some deals for you. I got bridges for sale, passenger ships, railroads, space shuttles, you name it."

Scott hated to admit it, but Patrick had a point.

"Do you get what I'm sayin' here, Northwood?" he continued. "In order for Implementing to work, you can't be related to the Prospect. You can't even be particularly close to them. In fact, it's best if you don't know them at all. I think you'd agree that it's pretty hard to get any more unselfish than that."

Scott's anger deflated as quickly as it had appeared. "You just made me realize something," he said. He resumed walking, and Patrick fell in beside him.

"Yeah? What?"

"A minute ago, you said my life was worthless and self-centered. But now you pointed out how I'm doing unselfish acts for perfect strangers. That doesn't sound so worthless to me! Does it?"

"You're only doing it 'cause I was able to get under your skin."

"Don't be too sure about that."

"Getting back to Jason," said Patrick.

"Yeah. 'Getting back to Jason'. Let me ask you something."

"What?" said Patrick, sounding annoyed once again.

"Remember when you told me there were eight other Implementers? The ones you said were scattered through the western states?"

"Yeah. But what's that got to do with—"

"Judging from my experience with you, it seems that the main purpose of Enablers is to extract as much time as possible from us unworthy Implementers and transfer it to more deserving folks who are about to die. Right?"

"I don't see what any of this has to do with Jason. Whose pulse, by the way, is getting weaker as we speak."

"I'll take your evasion of the question for a yes. Now. About Jason. I'm going to give him a year."

"What?!" Patrick was incredulous. His brow furrowed in anger. "A year?! For someone like Jason? That's about the stingiest—"

"Shut up and let me finish—or Jason won't get one second of my life!"

Patrick managed to stay silent.

"I have an idea," said Scott. "I'll give Jason one year. If you don't think that's enough, go make your case to your other Implementers. See if they're willing to each chip in some of their own time—say, a year apiece. If they are, who knows? Jason could end up getting even more than eight years of additional life. And the good thing for us is that it lets us spread the damage. No one gets intimidated into giving up an outrageous chunk of time."

Patrick pinched his lip in thought. "That's never been done."

Although Scott was careful not to show it, he was both pleased and relieved that Patrick seemed intrigued by the idea. "Has anyone ever tried?"

Instead of answering, Patrick turned and disappeared down the path.

"Hey!" Scott shouted after him. "If it works, maybe the other Implementers and I could unionize!"

In a Seattle hospital that night, Jason Epstein dreamed he was standing beside a lake in the middle of a forest. The day was cool and overcast. Everything around him was completely still. No leaves rustled in the motionless air, and there wasn't the slightest ripple on the surface of the water. The lake shone like a dull gray mirror.

The totality of silence was unsettling. An eerie sense of foreboding permeated the woods. Standing at the water's edge, Jason had never felt so lost and alone.

He was startled by a thrashing noise in the nearby undergrowth. It sounded like a large animal was clawing its way through the tangle of bushes toward him.

Jason backed away, preparing to dive into the lake to escape whatever was coming.

The thrashing got closer and louder, heading directly for him. Just as he was ready to leap out of the way, a medium-sized brown dog burst from the shrubbery. The dog shook itself, looked around and saw Jason. The dog's tail started to wag slowly back and forth, and Jason gave a big sigh of relief. He tip-toed toward the dog and got down on one knee.

"Hi, boy. What are you doing way out here by yourself?"

As if in answer, there was more friendly tail wagging. Jason reached out and scratched his ear, and the dog tilted his head and grunted with pleasure.

Jason became aware of someone else's presence. A trim, middle-aged man with hair the color of copper and silver stood at the edge of the undergrowth, watching him. He was wearing jeans, a flannel shirt, and a faded green field coat.

"Is this your dog, mister?" said Jason. "He seems to be lost."

The man turned and walked into the forest.

"Hey, wait a minute!" Jason got to his feet and followed.

"Mister, what about your dog?" The boy glanced back at the spot he had just left.

The brown dog was gone.

Jason hesitated, then kept walking in the direction of the man, who had now been swallowed up by the dense forest.

Jason felt a wave of panic rise in his chest.

"Hello? Is anybody out there?"

He moved faster through the thick green undergrowth.

"Can anyone hear me?" The thought of being left out here all alone was overwhelming.

He broke into a run and stumbled into a clearing where the man and the dog stood side-by-side.

For some reason, Jason felt comforted by the sight of them. His sense of foreboding began to lift.

"There you are," he said. "For a minute, I thought you were trying to ditch me." Getting no answer, he went on. "I like your dog. What's his name?"

The man still didn't answer him. In fact, they looked as if they were in a trance of some kind.

A tone-like vibration, barely audible, tickled the air.

Jason cocked his head to one side. "What's that sound?"

It was coming from directly behind him.

He turned around to listen.

The tone was a little louder now. Carried on a delicate breeze, it sifted through the wall of trees. It sounded as if someone were pressing the key of a giant pipe organ a mile away.

Jason turned back around to ask what it was, when he abruptly stopped talking.

Eight more people were now standing in the clearing.

Startled, Jason took an involuntary step backward. Yet he didn't feel threatened by them. They looked like regular people you'd pass on the street. Men. Women. Young. Old. They wore shorts and T-shirts. Slacks and polo shirts. Skirts and blouses. One man had on a suit and tie.

They all looked at Jason with the same trance-like gaze. Strange as the situation was, he still wasn't frightened. If anything, he found the presence of these people reassuring.

The tone-like vibration grew louder.

Jason turned around to listen.

It was stronger now, clearer. And it was followed by other tones that blended together and built on each other, creating an ethereal, haunting melody that filtered through the swaying boughs of the trees.

He had never heard anything like it.

As the melody expanded and deepened, the tones became richer, more complex. The music was filled with tragedy and sorrow, with heartbreak and lamentation.

It stirred the very soul.

Even though he was only twelve, the young man was overcome with emotion. Tears ran down his face as he turned back to the others. "Can you hear it?" he asked.

But they were gone, including the man and his dog.

Jason didn't mind. He no longer felt lonely or afraid. He turned back to listen as the music came from every direction, filling the forest with its poignant melody.

He closed his eyes, letting it flood over and through him.

Then a familiar voice came from far away. *"Jason..."*

He stirred in his sleep.

"Jason, can you hear me?"

Groggy, he opened his eyes and looked around. It took him a moment to realize where he was. A hospital room. His eyes were wet from the tears that had streamed down his face in the dream—and also, apparently, in reality.

His parents were sitting on either side of the bed. They each clasped one of his hands in theirs.

"Mom...? Dad...?"

"Yes, Jason," said his mother. "We're right here."

He noticed that their cheeks were wet. They, too, were crying.

"What's wrong?" he asked, becoming fully awake. "Are you sad?"

"No, Jason," said his mother. "In fact, we're very, very happy."

"Why?"

"The doctor just finished running some tests," said his father. "He says... he says you're going to be all right. He doesn't know why. He doesn't understand it. He said that your body spontaneously generated tissue over the hole in your heart. It healed itself. Jason, you're going to be okay. Do you understand?"

"Yes," said Jason. "I understand." Then his face clouded. "But... did he say for how long?"

"Yes," said his mother. "He said, 'for years to come'." There were more happy tears. "For years to come..."

Chapter 13

OLIVIA

It was with shock and embarrassment that Scott finally admitted to himself that he enjoyed watching reality TV shows. It had started with *The Most Dangerous Catch*. At first, he had watched every episode in hopes of catching a glimpse of Linda, or hearing Jack make some reference to her. To see her on the show and imagine what might have been was a form of weekly torture that Scott felt obligated to endure for making the mistake of walking away from her. In the meantime, he rooted for Captain Jack to screw up.

But then Scott found himself getting caught up in the lives of the other captains and crews profiled on the program. From the safety and comfort of home, it was great fun to watch them battle the high seas—and sometimes each other. During commercials, there were trailers and teasers for other shows. Some of them piqued his interest and he started watching those, too.

Except for the news, Scott had never watched much television. But reality TV opened up whole new worlds. It allowed him to vicariously experience things that he personally would never do. It also helped distract him from the grim fact that, every time he extended the life of one of Patrick's Prospects, his own existence was being shortened.

～ ～ ～

It was on a soggy day in mid-March that Patrick once again intercepted Scott on the trail. This time, it was about a thirty-five-year-old woman with advanced breast cancer who had only days to live. Her name was Olivia Johansen.

Over a span of several years, Olivia and her husband, Kevin, had adopted eight severely handicapped children who had been abandoned by their natural parents. The ailments of these kids ranged from severe retardation to quadriplegia. Even though the Johansens had two healthy kids of their own, the idea of these damaged children being left to the mercy of the state broke their hearts. They had taken on the adoptions simply because it was the right thing to do.

As word of the Johansen family filtered through the Seattle community, reporters came calling. Olivia and Kevin were both quite shy and would never have sought the attention of the media. At first, they did all they could to avoid the spotlight. But their incredible generosity had struck a chord with a large and growing number of people, and so the Johansens allowed their story to be told.

Several good and unexpected things occurred as a result of the publicity. For one, they became a source of hope and inspiration to other families caring for disabled children. Second, charitable donations begin trickling in, which went a long way to help pay their sizeable bills. But it was only when they learned that there had been a considerable spike in the adoption rate of unwanted children—a boost attributed directly to them—that Olivia and Kevin finally became comfortable with the attention.

Then Olivia got sick with a fast-moving and particularly vicious form of breast cancer. And now she was near death.

There was no question that this would spell the end of their happy extended family. It wasn't a matter of money. Kevin worked full time as an anesthesiologist and made an excellent salary. That and the charitable donations enabled them to stay financially afloat. But if any family truly needed a stay-at-home mom, it was the Johansens. All the children were under the age of eighteen, which made for a lively and sometimes volatile household. Olivia was the glue that held them together. It would be impossible for Kevin to work full time and still handle all the special needs.

The hard fact was that when Olivia died, the family would have to be split up.

When Patrick finished laying out the details, he waited to hear what Scott had to say. After a minute or so, he said, "Well?"

"Well what?"

"What's it gonna be?"

Scott spoke in measured tones. "I'm thinking I'll give her a year."

"It's always a year with you," said Patrick, his voice edged with disapproval. "Your generosity is overwhelming."

"Knock it off, Patrick."

"I'm not gonna knock it off. You are so useless, it's incredible."

"Once again, you're starting to annoy me."

"Good."

Scott scowled. "Let's take a time out here and tally up all that I've done for your Prospects so far: Megan Hillis—one year. Max Grabowsky—one year. Jason Epstein—one year. Not to mention the eight additional years he got."

"Not from you."

"Yes, but instigated by me. And now, Olivia Johansen— one year. That adds up to four years of my life, Patrick. Gone forever."

"You make it sound like some catastrophic loss for mankind."

"It is catastrophic—for me!"

"And how many handicapped kids have you adopted recently?"

Scott came to an abrupt halt on the trail. Patrick really knew how to press his buttons, and boy did he seem to enjoy doing it!

"Goddamn you, Patrick! That's not fair and you know it. And stop being so obnoxious. That was part of our deal, remember?"

"Now that I think of it, Northwood," Patrick sneered, "I know why I like coming down so hard on you."

"Enlighten me. Please."

"Because you and me both know you've still got a buttload of years left! And they can be put to excellent use. But getting any more than a year at a time outta you is impossible. It's like that syphilis guy rolling the rock up that hill! So, yeah, you're right. A deal's a deal. But that doesn't mean I have to like it!"

"You mean Sisyphus."

"Huh?"

"Never mind. All I'm saying is, at the rate I'm going, I'll be lucky if I'm still around in twenty years."

"Oh! Poor baby."

They resumed walking and Scott took it as an opportunity to rethink some of the things Patrick had said about Olivia. She did sound like an amazing woman. Was he making this decision too quickly? Was he being too stingy? Should he give her more time?

An idea hit him.

"Look. About Olivia. Is there any way we can revisit her situation down the road?"

"What do you mean 'revisit'?"

"Bear with me, I'm still working this out. Say, around this time next year, you give me an update on how things are going with her. Maybe by then, they'll have enough help from friends and relatives to keep their family together."

"But what if they don't? And they're still in the same jam?"

"*Then* I'll decide whether to tack on more time or not. Is there any rule that says I can't do that?"

Patrick looked thoughtful a moment. "No," he said. "There isn't. You can go back and give somebody as much time as you want. In fact, that would be great."

"Why is that, Patrick? You're not exactly the warm and caring type. What's in it for you?"

"Like I keep tellin' ya, Northwood, I'm just doin' my job."

"Yeah? Well, I'm not so sure if I buy that."

Patrick gave a laugh. "Like I'm really concerned with what you think. So you gonna help Olivia or not?"

"I said I'd help her and I will. Just one more question."

"Ask away."

"What about Jake?"

At the sound of his name, Jake, who had been padding along in front of them, stopped and glanced back at Scott.

"Your mutt? What about him?"

"Can I use any of my time to extend his life?"

Scott heard the snicker in Patrick's voice as he said, "Uh, that would be a no."

"Why not?"

"Transferring time between people and animals doesn't work. Period."

"Are you sure?"

"This isn't the first time I've been asked that question. I've checked into it. So, yeah, I'm sure. That's just the way it is."

Scott watched the dog as he made his way up the trail, and felt a sharp pang of sadness in his chest for the day when he wouldn't be around anymore. "I don't suppose you can tell me how long he's got?"

"Not a clue. So can we do this already?"

Scott's voice became a sigh as he said, "Okay. Let's get it done."

"Well, then. You know the drill." The two men halted on the trail and turned to face each other.

"Are you *absolutely sure* this is what you want to do?"

"Yes. I'm absolutely sure."

"Okay, that'll do it," said Patrick, his voice clipped and businesslike. He turned and hurried back down the trail, saying, "I suggest you go home and get ready for dreamland."

As he disappeared, Scott felt the familiar, eerie sensation of sudden sleepiness tugging at his brain. He yawned and smiled down at Jake.

"Can't say I didn't try, old bean. Come on, let's go home."

Early next morning, in the dimly lit room of a Seattle hospital, Olivia Johansen opened her eyes to see her husband dozing in a chair next to the bed. She reached out and laid her hand on his. He woke with a start, looked at her and smiled.

"Hi," she said.

"Hi." Kevin moved close and took both of her hands. "How're you feeling?"

"Okay, I guess... I was having the strangest dream."

"What about?"

"There was this man in a forest... out in the middle of nowhere, walking his dog. The sun was going down. He started walking past me like he didn't see me, as if I wasn't even there. Then I felt this overwhelming urge to talk to him. So I did."

"What did you say?"

"I told him it was going to be dark soon, and he and his dog should get home."

"What did he say?"

"He gave me the most intense look. And he said, 'You need to do the same thing.' Then he just smiled and kept on walking. And I woke up."

Kevin stared at her. Tears welled in his eyes. Alarmed, she said, "Kevin, what is it? Why are you crying?"

"I had a dream, too."

"What was it?"

"I dreamt... I dreamt, Olivia, that you were healthy again. Completely cured. Only..." Kevin managed to hold back his tears. "Only my dream is real."

"I don't understand. What are you talking about?"

"Olivia. Listen carefully. Your cancer, it's gone."

"What do you mean?"

It was all he could do to maintain his composure. "I mean it's gone. Disappeared. Overnight."

"But... how can that be?"

"I don't know. The doctors don't know. They're completely baffled."

"Are you saying... I can come home? To you? To the kids?"

"Yes, Olivia. You can come home."

They broke down in each other's arms, tears of happiness and relief flowing down their faces.

When Scott watched the local news that evening, a brief segment about Olivia Johansen aired. It showed Kevin pushing her out of the hospital in a wheelchair as a reporter described her amazing overnight recovery. When they got to the car, Olivia—looking shockingly healthy—stood and gave a big smile and a wave to a group of clapping, cheering nurses and doctors. Kevin opened the car door for her. Olivia climbed in, followed by her husband. The vehicle disappeared into Seattle traffic.

When the segment ended, Scott turned off the television and sat there, smiling to himself.

As he mused on Olivia's happy turn of events, it occurred to him that there hadn't been any more of the Max Grabowsky-type "material events". Patrick had said they rarely came up, which pleased Scott. He was glad to have helped Max evade a violent death, but it had been the most harrowing day of his life and he had no desire to repeat it. Doling out chunks of time to the terminally ill was about all he could handle.

He heard a moist clucking noise. Jake stood in the doorway of the kitchen licking his lips, having just finished his supper. He gave a deep, satisfied belch.

"Good appetite," said Scott.

After a walk with Jake one blustery day in April, Scott decided to pick up his mail. Because ninety-nine percent of it consisted of bills and junk mail, he saw no reason to check it every day. Usually a week or more would go by before he'd bother to retrieve it from the mailbox outside the gate to his house.

As he sat in the idling Range Rover sorting through it, he came across a colorful card. When he looked more closely, his face lit up in happy surprise.

"Check it out, Jake. A postcard from Megan!"

The photo was of the London skyline at sunset. On the other side, written in tiny feminine handwriting, was a miniature whirlwind of a note:

> *Dear Scott,*
> *Greetings from Jollye Olde Englande. Been here since first week of January. Never even made it out of London. What an incredible place! A lot has happened. Taking graphic design classes at London Art Institute during day. Working as barmaid at night. Had raging toothache. Went to British dentist. He was so sweet and gentle. Long story short we are madly in love! More later. Cheerio for now!*
> *Megan*

Scott tucked the card into a coat pocket and put the Range Rover in gear. He couldn't stop smiling as he drove down his driveway.

That night, as he tried getting to sleep, his mind was alive with imagined scenes of Megan's happy new life in London. He'd been smiling pretty much nonstop since receiving the postcard.

Right now, because of him, of what he did, a young woman was in Europe having the adventure of her life.

A person who would otherwise be gone...

A shudder passed through him and his smile faded. The arrival of Megan's card caused the reality of what he'd been doing to hit home. By voluntarily shortening his own lifespan, he was allowing these others—Megan, Max, Jason, and Olivia—to keep going, to continue doing the things they were meant to do, to fulfill their purpose in life, whatever that might be.

Something occurred to Scott that made him sit up in bed.

What if *this* was *his* purpose in life? Maybe, at the end of the day, when all was said and done, *this was what he was meant to do.*

And if that was the case, was it really so terrible?

He lay there and another thought bubbled to the surface. There was something about Megan's situation that had been subconsciously bothering him, and now he knew what it was.

All the people Scott had helped so far would, in turn, go on to make a profound difference for good in the lives of many others. At least, this was the case that Patrick had made for them.

All except Megan.

Sure, she was kind, charismatic, and smart. And she had the knack for making people around her feel special. But he had trouble visualizing her doing much more than that. The more he thought about it, the more mystified he felt. Why had Patrick brought her to his attention?

And then another thought occurred to him: In November, Megan's year would be up.

He didn't know what he was going to do about that. As he settled back down onto the pillow, he decided he would cross that bridge when he came to it.

Chapter 14

ALFRED

Fifty miles north on San Juan Island, Alfred James Hersom the Fourth woke up in his customized bed. It had been built on a revolving platform, programmed to follow each morning's sunrise so as to take maximum advantage of the stunning views from the cavernous master bedroom of his waterfront mansion.

It was going to be one of those glorious mid-spring days in the Northwest, clear and crisp. The sky burned electric blue, which turned the waters of the Sound a deep and vibrant cobalt.

But none of this registered with Alfred. In fact, very little rose to the surface of his consciousness. The incredible luck of being born into one of the oldest, richest families in America enabled him to live whatever kind of life he wanted. Early on, he had decided to spend his days being as free from strife, pain, and discomfort as possible. In this endeavor, he had been wildly successful.

Until today.

He padded into the ornate bathroom made entirely of pink-veined Florentine marble and stepped into a shower the size of a walk-in closet. Water jetted from twelve solid gold faucets at a pre-programmed temperature. As he lathered his pudgy 43-year-old body, he thought he really should cut back on the rich foods he was so fond of and start some kind of exercise regimen. "Any kind of exercise at all would be beneficial," his doctor had urged. "Particularly because you are the least active person I've ever met."

Alfred made a firm pledge to himself: he would bite the bullet and start exercising that very morning. Well, after breakfast, anyway. Or maybe it would be better to wait until just before bedtime, then it would tire him out and he'd sleep better. Then again, tomorrow was just as good as today. But he was definitely going to start soon.

After rinsing off, he stepped out of the shower, and the faucets automatically shut off. He dried himself with a bath towel made of the thickest, whitest, softest Egyptian cotton money could buy. As he let the towel drop to the floor, the stroke hit.

It was the strangest sensation. There was no pain and no fear, just a feeling of nearly every muscle in his body abruptly ceasing to work. He sank to the floor like a giant marionette whose strings had been snipped.

Though his body was completely paralyzed, his mind seemed fine. After a brief bout of mild shock and confusion, he was able to think quite clearly. It was only after he had lain on the marble floor for several minutes, unable to move even a finger that he fully grasped what had happened.

Then the fear began.

Scott spent the beautiful morning in bed being lazy. He took his time reading the paper and drinking coffee. Every so often he gazed out the window at the Olympic Mountains. The air was telescopically clear, which made the mountains appear so close that he felt he could reach out and scoop a handful of snow from the ridgeline.

After showering and dressing, he made a bigger breakfast than usual. By the time he and Jake had eaten, it was after one o'clock. On their daily walk, Scott noticed how the forest was well into its springtime transformation. The skeletal browns and grays of winter were disappearing beneath tangles of unruly new foliage.

They hadn't been on the trail long when he heard laughter coming toward them. There was a sinister quality to it.

They came to an abrupt stop and waited uneasily.

Patrick came around a corner.

Scott had never heard the man laugh before, and the sound was unsettling, even menacing. He couldn't begin to imagine what would appeal to the man's sense of mirth.

"What's so funny?" he asked.

Patrick struggled to get himself under control. "A new situation just came up and... and..." He started to laugh again.

"Just so I'm clear," Scott said. "You've got a new Prospect—who I assume is close to dying. And you're laughing about it?"

"Yeah, I am," said Patrick, again breaking into hard-edged peals of laughter. "This next one's a special case! I think you're gonna like it."

"Why?"

"Let me fill you in. The person's name is Alfred James Hersom the Fourth. Ever hear of him?"

It took Scott a moment. "Are you talking about the Hersom family?"

"Bingo. They go all the way back to the Revolutionary War. Own a ton of choice real estate. I'm talkin' entire city blocks of Manhattan. Not to mention huge interests in oil, tobacco, shipping, technology, manufacturing, the arms industry. You name it—they got their fingers in every financial pie. There's whole generations of Hersoms never worked a day in their lives."

"Must be nice."

"Yeah. And Alfred, my new Prospect, is the poster child for inherited wealth going to waste. He's the most spoiled, arrogant, entitled son of a bitch you could imagine."

"How much money does he have?"

"How does three billion sound?"

Scott whistled.

"Yeah. Dude's got mansions all over the world. A fleet of private jets, yachts... More art than most museums. I could go on and on."

"Please don't."

"Okay, but check this out: He's never given a dime to charity."

"You sure?" Scott looked incredulous.

"Scout's honor. And here's his excuse: the free market regulates everything—including charities—for the better, period."

"Sounds like quite a guy."

"I told you you'd like this one."

"Yeah. But... why are you—?"

"Way ahead of you: If Alfred is such an epically selfish prick, why am I bringing his situation to you?"

"Exactly."

"He had a massive stroke early this morning. At his mansion in the San Juans. House cleaners found him and he got airlifted to Harborview. Dude's in critical condition, as in paralyzed from the eyebrows down. And any minute now, he's going to experience a series of organ failures. I'm afraid poor Alfred is not long for this world."

"I still don't see what you want with me. I say good riddance."

"Well, normally you'd be right. But here's the kicker. Even though Alfred's body is totally incapacitated, his mental abilities are fine. Sharp as a tack. And lying on his bathroom floor all morning, scared shitless, he had a lot of time to think. Take a guess about what?"

"He doesn't want to die?"

"Bingo. The jerkoff had an epiphany like you wouldn't believe. His brain was screaming so loud, 'Don't let me die! Please! I'll do anything! I'll give every last dollar to charity! I promise! Please don't let me die! I'm begging you! Please! Please!' Man, it was unbelievable."

"I think I see where this is heading."

"He's literally dying to make a deal with anything or anybody he can to save his ass. And if Alfred, by some miracle," Patrick winked at Scott, "pulls through, he promises he'll immediately set up a foundation and give all his money to charity. That's where you come in."

"Oh, come on! Do you really expect me to hand over a chunk of my life to a jerk like that?"

Patrick smiled. "Hear me out. Alfred's so frantic to live that he didn't specify *how long*. So it wouldn't take so much a chunk of your life as a nugget. Or even a pebble, maybe."

"But what if he doesn't hold up his end and decides to keep his money?"

"I've seen enough deathbed promises to have a pretty good idea which ones are real and which aren't. Trust me. This one's the real deal. Alfred's had the living shit scared out of him. If he survives, he'll get those documents drawn up and executed as soon as he can."

"How long will that take?"

"Maybe a week. Two at the most." Patrick smiled. "And what do you wanna bet that, as soon as the paperwork's signed, our buddy Alfred's gonna have another massive stroke. Only this time, it'll be one he maybe doesn't recover from."

Scott was appalled at the deviousness of the plan. "Man, that is cold!"

Patrick's smile broadened. "Ain't it, though."

Scott couldn't keep from breaking into an involuntary grin. "I mean, really cold."

"Yep. I couldn't agree more. Time's a wastin', Northwood. Douchebag's gonna croak any minute. Are you in, or are you out?"

Scott let out a laugh. "I am so in."

"I knew it. You got a little bit of the dark side in you after all. All right, let's do this." Patrick attempted to look seriously into Scott's eyes. "Are you... *absolutely sure* that this... that this... is what you... you... *oh, crap!*" They both dissolved in laughter before he could finish.

It took a couple more tries to get through the brief but necessary ritual without laughing. When they did, Alfred James Hersom the Fourth's life had been successfully extended by fourteen days.

Scott alternately yawned and laughed as he walked back

to his car. He was both pleased and disgusted with himself by what he had done.

Mostly he was pleased.

As it turned out, it took only six days for Alfred to have the documents drawn up and signed. At the last minute, having no desire to end up penniless, he reneged somewhat on his end of the deal by inserting a clause that allowed him to keep 100 million dollars. He was determined to make the necessary sacrifices in order to survive the rest of his life on what amounted to pocket change.

Two weeks to the day after his miraculous recovery, Alfred took an afternoon nap. While he slept, he had a vivid dream of being lost in a darkened forest in which sinister laughter reverberated through the trees.

When he woke up, he lay in bed attempting to decipher the meaning of such a strange dream. The more he thought about it, the more it seemed that the dream was really a nightmare.

As he lay there, an enormous blood clot that had amassed in one of his legs broke loose. It traveled up his carotid artery to the base of his cranium where it stuck fast, shutting off the flow of blood and oxygen to his brain as effectively as shoving a cork into a bottle. Thus Alfred James Hersom the Fourth expired.

Except for the presence of a few distant relatives hoping for an inheritance windfall, and a pastor who said a few words because he was paid to do so, no one else showed up at Alfred's funeral. And because his new will stipulated that—in the event of his death—the hundred million he had set aside would be rolled into the rest of his charitable foundation, no windfall was forthcoming.

Chapter 15

A DRIVE IN THE COUNTRY

Summertime in the Pacific Northwest is nothing short of magical. The forests become a silent, slow motion explosion of every shade of green imaginable. As much as Scott liked gloomy weather, even he would admit to welcoming the arrival of long days filled with sunlight and warmth.

On a warm evening in late July, he settled into bed to watch *The Most Dangerous Catch*. A soft breeze flowed in through the open windows. The air was fragrant with the scent of wild berries ripening in the woods.

Jack Lofgren and his crew, after a particularly successful week of fishing, were headed back into port. They looked tired and dirty, but happy. It was a calm, clear day in Alaska as The Raging Guppy motored slowly into the harbor.

Then Jack did something unusual. He passed the word that he wanted his entire crew to gather inside the wheelhouse. After they'd all squeezed into the cramped space, he produced a bottle of twenty-year-aged single malt scotch. He was in an unusually good mood, no doubt because of the excellent haul of fish. But there seemed to be something more to it.

"Is everyone here?" he asked.

The crew grunted in unison.

Jack looked serious. "Good. I have an important announcement to make."

He clasped the shoulder of the crewman nearest him, who was a man nicknamed Road Block. Thickset, scarred, and grizzled, he was the biggest man there. Pushing 60, he was also the oldest. Every one of the hard years he'd spent scraping a living from the North Pacific seemed to be carved into his face.

Jack looked solemn as he spoke. "Road Block here has decided to have a sex-change operation."

The men exploded in raucous guffaws.

"I can't wait to see you in a skirt, Road Block," said Benny, one of the younger crewmembers.

Road Block glared at him from under his tattered baseball cap and answered in a voice resembling a cement mixer. "And I can't wait to get you ashore and crack a few ribs, wise ass."

"Ooo, how did you know I like it rough?" said Benny. The fishermen nudged each other and laughed some more.

"Okay, knock it off," said Jack. "What I wanted to tell you guys is that Megan—my girlfriend Linda's only kid—is getting hitched next week in London, England!"

Scott felt himself tense.

Jack handed a stack of paper cups to Road Block, who took one and passed the stack until they all had a cup.

"His name is Jonathan Coatsworth." As Jack spoke, he poured a generous shot into each cup. "He's a dentist. He said that when me and Linda get married, I can have all my dental work done for free. But I'd have to travel to England to get it!"

The crew laughed.

"Linda and me have been invited to attend the nuptials." Jack poured the last of the bottle into his own cup. Scott noticed the amount was at least twice what the others had received. "We'll be leaving in a couple of weeks for the British Isles. So I'd like to propose a toast: To Megan, my future step-daughter!"

The crew shouted as one, "To Megan!" and they all downed their shots.

Scott turned off the television. He was surprised and confused by the emotions that flooded through him. There were shock and anger, disappointment and hurt. He also experienced an acute sense of feeling left out of something that, by all rights, he should have been invited to.

If it hadn't been for him, there wouldn't even be a wedding.

He knew it was irrational and childish to think this way, but he couldn't help it.

He was still upset when he turned off the light an hour later, which meant he didn't sleep very well that night. Which meant Jake didn't get much sleep either. Which meant they both were uncharacteristically grumpy for much of the next day.

It took some mental wrangling, but Scott eventually got his thoughts and emotions sorted out enough to come to terms with what had happened. He suspected that Megan might even want him at the wedding. But he also realized that by not inviting him, she did, in fact, do the right and compassionate thing. Her mom was going to be there and it was obvious that Linda didn't want to see him. And of course Captain Jack would be there as well. It was a no-brainer—Scott's presence was a bad idea for all concerned.

Megan was only trying to spare his feelings.

And yes, she was able to have this wonderful celebration only because of his unselfish gesture, but, he told himself for perhaps the hundredth time, she had no way of knowing that. She never would. And he needed to accept that, once and for all.

He had taken all of it much too personally, he knew. As Patrick would say, *Get over yourself, Northwood.*

After thinking long and hard about it, he knew what he had to do; he needed to stop torturing himself with thoughts of Linda. He had to do everything he possibly could to forget about her and move on with his life, such as it was.

As the long, warm days of summer passed uneventfully by, Scott became increasingly nervous. Patrick hadn't approached him in months—not since that blustery spring day when he had transferred two weeks of his life to Alfred Hersom. The unexpected three billion dollar charitable foundation that Alfred left behind had been big news at the time, and had apparently inspired several other idle billionaires to set up their own foundations. Even Scott had to admit it hadn't been a bad tradeoff.

He figured Patrick had been busy with his other Implementers that summer, but he knew it was just a matter of time until he showed up. And that made Scott uneasy.

On a crisp, breezy day in early October, he was heading home from Autumn Lake when, on impulse, he decided to drive through the country. He'd been feeling restless the last few weeks as fall tightened its grip on western Washington. A change of venue, even a temporary one, seemed like a good idea.

After a couple of hours of aimless driving, he found himself on a narrow stretch of rural road deep in the hinterlands of South Kitsap County. He was pleased to realize that he had no idea where he was. It was nice to let his mind wander as the countryside slid by. Jake was perched happily in the passenger seat.

In the months that had passed since Jack and his crew toasted Megan on TV, Scott had kept on watching the show, but now he changed the channel if a segment featuring The Raging Guppy came on. Hard as he'd tried, he had been only marginally successful at purging all thoughts of Linda from his mind, and he had no desire to view anything that would remind him of her.

The country road came to an abrupt end at a stop sign on a busy street, bringing him back into civilization. As he wondered which direction to turn, a man walking a large Akita came toward the Range Rover from the right. The Akita saw Jake in the car and, with a snarl, lunged at him, causing Jake to lean trembling against Scott.

"Whew! Okay, then," said Scott, "left it is."

After the turn, he drove about another half mile before stopping at a major intersection. As he looked around to get his bearings, he was surprised to see that he was on the outskirts of Bremerton. A twinge of hunger reminded him that he and Jake hadn't eaten since breakfast. They'd been on the road since ten o'clock, and it was now almost two.

He spied a grocery store about a hundred yards down the boulevard. He pulled into the parking lot, went inside, and found his way to the deli in the back. For two o'clock on a weekday afternoon, the place wasn't busy. In fact, he was the only customer.

He ordered a turkey and cheddar cheese sandwich for himself, and slices of ham and roast beef for Jake. Grabbing a bottle of ale from the cooler, he headed to the checkout counter.

There was only one cashier working, a woman, whose head was turned away from him as she stared outside at the deep October blue of the sky.

Scott placed the bottle on the counter with a soft thud to get her attention. She turned to look at him as he set down the sandwich and sliced meat.

"Scott?!"

He found himself looking into those sensitive, fawn-colored eyes. *"Linda?!"*

She smiled. "Hello."

He was too stunned to do anything but stammer, "What—What are you doing here?"

"I work here." Her demeanor was friendly enough.

"No, I mean, why aren't you—I mean... I don't know what I mean."

"You thought I was still up in Alaska?"

"Well, yeah. I've been watching the show and—"

"You mean to tell me Scott Northwood watches *The Most Dangerous Catch?*" Her eyebrows arched in amusement.

"I'm afraid so."

"You don't strike me as the type of person who would like it."

"To be honest, I didn't. At first. But after a while, it kind of grows on you."

He couldn't believe he was standing here talking to her. It felt like a dream.

"I've heard it can have that effect on people." Linda frowned in confusion. "So... if you've been watching the show, then you'd know that Jack and I split up when we were in England."

Scott noticed she grimaced when saying the name Jack. "I... missed a couple of episodes, so, no, I didn't know that."

Linda was silent as she rang up his sandwich and beer.

He wondered what in the world had happened in England. "If you don't mind my asking, how was Megan's wedding?"

Linda didn't answer for a moment as she placed the items in a bag. When she finally spoke, her voice was brittle with hostility. "Megan's wedding. Hmmm. Let's see. How should I put it? Wait, I know. It was awful! Horrible! Disastrous! Does that answer your question? That'll be twelve dollars and forty-seven cents." Tears appeared in her eyes.

Scott took his time pulling a twenty out of his wallet as he searched for something to say. He laid the money on the counter and said, "I'm sorry, Linda. I had no idea. If you don't want to talk about it, I—"

"It's okay," she said. A mixture of sadness and weariness replaced the hostility in her tone as she pulled herself to-gether. "I'll tell you what happened. You've been so kind to Megan. You have a right to know." She yanked a Kleen-ex from a box next to the cash register and dried her eyes. "Jack started drinking again. In Alaska. At first, it was just a few nips. A shot here. A cocktail there. By the time we got to London, he was hammered pretty much all the time. That was it for me. I promised myself that, right after the wedding, we would go our separate ways."

"I'm sorry to hear that."

She gave a harsh laugh as she handed him change. "Don't be. And it gets better. Or worse, would be more accurate. I didn't find out until we got there that the TV show is quite the hit in Britain. Turns out Jack was a minor celebrity and didn't even know it. It also turns out that the mother of one of the bridesmaids is a huge fan of the show—and of Jack in particular. Plus she's relatively young. And good-looking. And divorced. And likes to drink."

"Uh oh."

"Yeah. So we're all at the chapel, waiting for the wedding to begin, and Jack is nowhere to be found. Neither is the bridesmaid's mother."

"Oh, no."

"Oh, yes. The wedding and the reception go on as planned. Still no Jack. And he's not answering his cellphone. Eventually, I make it back to our hotel—where I find them passed out in bed together."

"Wow... What did you do?"

"Murder crossed my mind, but he's not worth being locked up for. I am so glad I didn't marry that bastard! That is one sorry leopard who's never going to change his spots."

"And now you're back in Bremerton."

"And now I'm back in Bremerton. My boss let me have my old job back."

"Where are you living?"

"Same house. I considered selling it when I moved to Alaska, but I just had a feeling... So I rented it out instead and, boy, am I ever glad I did!"

"Sounds like you're doing okay."

"I'm doing just fine." The flat way she said this made him think the opposite was true.

He couldn't think of anything to say. Just as the silence was becoming awkward, a harried young mother with two small boys in tow came up behind him pushing a basket of groceries. One of the boys began grabbing items from the candy display. The other one crawled into the space underneath the basket.

"Trevor, put that back! Nate, get out from there!"

"I probably should get going," said Scott. "It was nice running into you, Linda."

She gave him a quick, sad, lopsided smile. "Same here." She turned away and began scanning the mother's groceries.

He picked up his sack and headed out the door. He sat in his car, his heart pounding. "Jake, you're never going to believe who I just ran into..."

In the coming weeks, he agonized over whether to call her or not. The last time they'd talked was when she'd phoned him on Thanksgiving night and he'd behaved like a childish, self-centered ass. *I'm just not used to not being in control of situations,* he'd told her. *Gee, Scott. I wouldn't want you to change your life or anything,* she'd replied.

She probably wanted nothing to do with him.

In any event, he decided he would no longer avoid watching Raging Guppy segments of *The Most Dangerous Catch.* In fact, he was looking forward to it. He was curious to have a look at Captain Jack Lofgren after what Linda had told him.

His patience was finally rewarded one night as the show opened with The Raging Guppy materializing out of the misty dawn gloom of Dutch Harbor, Alaska. The vessel was motoring away from the main dock, heading for the fishing grounds of the North Pacific. Scott had seen the show enough times to know that the boat's speed was faster than what was considered prudent for the sheltered waters of the bay.

As he expected, Jack Lofgren manned the wheelhouse. But there was something different about him. He wasn't his usual energetic, arrogant self. When the camera moved in for a close-up, Scott could see why: Lofgren's eyes were glazed and bloodshot. He looked as if he'd been up all night.

Benny bustled into the wheelhouse and gave Jack a goofy grin. "How was your weekend, Skipper?"

"My weekend was just great," Jack answered, a curious note of defiance in his voice. "Me and some women I met who are up here on a cruise partied till dawn for three nights."

Benny eyed him warily. "Sounds like fun."

Jack grinned and winked, which only made him look worse. "You have no idea."

As Benny left the wheelhouse and moved forward on the ship, the camera followed his movements through the window. When it panned back to Jack, he was shoving a small flask into the pocket of his coat. He pushed forward on the throttle, noticeably increasing the speed of the vessel.

"Yes, sir," he said to the camera. "I am so glad I'm no longer with that (bleeping) bitch. Ever since she left, my life has been one long party that just won't—"

The door to the wheelhouse banged open. Road Block filled the entrance. "Jack, you need to slow the Guppy down."

Jack glared at him. "What for?"

"Because we're going faster than the posted limit and visibility sucks. You know as well as me there's shoals out here that aren't very well marked. And, what with an ebb tide to boot, I don't think—"

"No! You don't think, Road Block!" snarled Jack. "Your job is to leave the thinking to me. I've been sailing these waters twenty years and I know every—"

A horrendous, grinding crunch drowned out his words. Both men fought to keep their balance as The Raging Guppy shuddered to a stop. The cameraman must have fallen down, because there were a bunch of quick jumbled shots before the camera managed to focus back on Road Block.

"Good job, Jack! You've run us aground!" He stomped out of the wheelhouse, shouting, "All hands on deck! I mean now!"

The rest of show went on to document the hole that had been ripped out of the bottom of The Raging Guppy, and how the crew was forced to abandon ship. As the angry fishermen climbed into lifeboats, Benny said, "Six minutes from shore to shipwreck. That's gotta be a record for the shortest fishing season of any boat in the history of Alaska!"

"Shut the (bleep) up," Roadblock yelled at the man.

The final scene showed Jack being escorted aboard a Coast Guard cutter where he would undergo testing for drugs and alcohol. In the background, only the roof of the wheelhouse was visible above the waterline.

Scott laughed as he turned off the television. He sat there a moment debating with himself, Should he call her? What in the world was stopping him? He grabbed the portable phone and punched in a number. "What the hell, Jake," he said to his dog. "I don't think she'd mind. This is too good not to share."

Linda picked up after two rings. "Hello?"

Scott thought he could hear suppressed mirth in her voice.

"I hope I'm not bothering you, but I just had to call."

"Is this Scott?" Laughter began to bubble out of her. "Did you watch the show?"

"I did. I'm thinking maybe they should change the name of The Raging Guppy to something like the Grounded Grouper."

She was laughing harder now. "I can't believe it! He didn't even make it out of Dutch Harbor!"

"At the end, maybe they should have flashed the words 'Episode *Not* To Be Continued...'"

They both laughed some more. When it finally subsided, Linda, trying to be serious, said, "You know, I was raised to believe that it's not polite to laugh at the misfortune of others."

They managed to stay silent for a full three seconds before breaking into another fit of laughter. When they finally settled down, Scott said, "I never heard you laugh before. It's such a nice sound."

"I guess I haven't had a whole lot to laugh about lately."

"I suppose not."

"But seeing Jack wreck his boat? That'll do it every time."

They chuckled again, but then her voice became pensive. "We can laugh about it. But unfortunately, that whole crew is out of a job now, thanks to Jack. I know a lot of those guys. They're good folks. I feel bad for them."

"Well, try to look on the bright side. If something like that had happened out on the open ocean, they could have lost a lot more than their jobs."

"Yes, I suppose that's true."

His voice took on a more serious tone. "Linda. Do you mind if I ask you something?"

Her voice was suddenly guarded. "Go ahead."

"Now that Megan is married and living on the other side of the globe, have you thought about what you're going to do?"

"I have, actually. She and Jonathan want me to come live in England with them."

Scott felt his heart shift. He struggled to keep his voice matter-of-fact. "Sounds exciting. Are you ready to live in a foreign country?"

"You're asking that about someone who lived in Alaska?"

Scott couldn't help but smile. "What would you do in England?"

"Jonathan's practice is going really well, to the point that he's even offered me a job. I would live with him and Megan, for a while at least, until I got my bearings and found my own place."

"So, basically, what you're saying is, you're being forced to choose between Bremerton and London."

"Yeah! It's a tough call, I know." She sounded as if she were smiling.

"Are you going to take them up on it?"

Hesitancy came into her voice. "I honestly don't know. But I have to admit, it's pretty tempting."

He didn't say anything in return.

"Hello? Scott? Are you still there?"

"I'm still here."

"What do you think I should do?"

He was silent a moment. Then he said, "I think you should do whatever makes you happy. You certainly deserve it."

"That's a nice thing to say."

"Listen, I've gotta run. It's been good talking to you."

"Same here. Good bye."

"G'night."

He turned off the phone and set it on the nightstand, then lay there, hands behind his head, staring at the ceiling.

Running into her at the market had been the most wonderful surprise. And now, after hearing her voice again, hearing her laugh, he was shocked by the intensity of his emotions. It felt like his veins were charged with electricity.

And here she was about to disappear again.

Probably for good this time.

He lay there, wondering if he should do something, or if it was better to leave it alone. A new thought came into his head, and he jerked upright, his eyes wide open in the darkness.

What in hell was wrong with him? Of course, he was going to do something about it! Ever since he was fourteen, he had been living in a vacuum, going through the motions, eating three meals a day, sleeping alone every night, feeling absolutely nothing. But at that moment, two weeks before, when he'd accidentally run into Linda at the store, his black and white world had broken alive. Sure, the new Technicolor world would include some regret and quite a lot of sadness, but it also held the kind of ecstatic hope he'd never allowed himself to feel. No, he realized, with a sudden and long-overdue burst of insight; with the kind of hope he'd *always* had up until the day his parents had been killed.

How stupid he had been, he acknowledged to himself. In all these years since that terrible event, he'd been too fearful to really feel anything, too terrified of going through one more big loss. And losing Linda again would be a huge loss, because he knew with complete certainty that he was head-over-heels in love with Linda Hillis, that he'd been in love with her from the moment he had first seen her, standing near Megan's hospital bed.

By the time the light of dawn was fingering through the sky, he had made up his mind about exactly what he was going to do. And, despite having had just about no sleep, he felt energized by the power of his new resolve. The world he knew had been transformed.

He sprang out of bed and fired up the coffee pot. Soon, he and Jake were off on their walk at Autumn Lake. It was a beautiful October day. The colors of the forest were sharp, the air bracing. He found himself praying that he wouldn't run into Patrick, and, happily, that prayer was answered.

After returning home, he deposited Jake on the couch. This was one trip he would make alone, he decided. By the time he left moments later, the dog was snoring with abandon.

Scott headed south toward Bremerton. He had no idea what Linda's hours were at the market, but that didn't matter. He would drive directly to her house. If she wasn't home, he would wait for her to show up.

It was afternoon when he got there. He knocked at the door, but she wasn't home from work yet, so he sat in the rocking chair on her porch to wait. As he rocked gently back and forth, he wondered what her reaction would be. Linda was hardly an open book. In fact, he had no idea what she really thought of him.

In times gone by, he knew these thoughts would have stopped him. But now there was no choice. He would wait for her even if it were forever.

What he *hadn't* planned on was falling asleep.

He heard her calling to him from far away in the blackness.

"...Scott..."

Her voice was loud in his ear as she shook him awake.

"Scott! Wake up!"

He jolted upright in the rocking chair. For a panicked moment, sitting on the darkened porch, he had no idea where he was. Then he saw her standing over him and the panic ratcheted up a notch. He hadn't counted on feeling this discombobulated when he faced her.

She was still wearing her fleece pullover from work. The nametag read 'Linda' in a bold, flowing script. She looked tired, and didn't seem exactly thrilled to see him.

"Jeez," he said, massaging the crick in his neck. "What time is it?"

"It's eight o'clock. What are you doing here?"

He got unsteadily to his feet. He had a cramp in one leg. "I must have fallen asleep."

"No kidding. But that doesn't answer my question."

He rubbed the sleep from his face, struggling to collect his thoughts. "There's something I, uh, wanted to tell you. To talk to you about."

"Can't it wait? I've had a long, crappy day and I'm tired."

This was not the conversation he had envisioned.

"It won't take long."

She sighed, folded her arms across her chest, and leaned against the railing. "Fine. So talk."

He realized he was very cold. "Can we at least go inside? It's a little chilly out here."

"I'd prefer we stay on the porch. What do you want?"

He pulled the collar of his coat up and jammed his hands into the pockets. "Do you remember last night when I told you that you should do whatever makes you happy? That you deserve it?"

She shrugged. "Yes, I remember. What about it?"

"Well, the reason I'm here is, I'd like to rephrase that."

"What do you mean, 'rephrase'?"

"I don't think you should go to England."

"Oh, really."

"Yes. Really. I think you should stay here."

"Is that a fact."

"Yes."

"Then tell me: Why in the world should I stay here?"

"Because *I* can make you happy."

This seemed to take her by surprise. "What are you say-ing, exactly?"

"Linda. What I'm saying is... I'm in love with you."

She stared at him without expression.

"You're it for me, Linda. I've never felt like this about any-one. I've known it from the moment I first laid eyes on you, back at Harrison Hospital when Megan was sick. Only, I didn't *know* that I knew it, until last night... hearing your voice, picturing you when you laughed..."

She closed her eyes and gave a longer sigh, one that was tired and wary.

"It's awfully quiet out here," he said, hearing how nervous he sounded.

Linda opened her eyes. "Scott, we've been through this al-ready."

He looked at her in surprise. "No. We haven't."

"I guess what I'm saying is, *I've* been through it."

"I don't understand."

"Don't you remember?"

He could hear the terrible pain in her voice.

"Last Thanksgiving? When you told me that 'some things just weren't meant to be'?"

"Yes. I remember." He could hardly believe how stupid he had been, but he went on. "And I remember you said that 'things were what you *made* them to be'."

"You also said you didn't like not being in control of situ-ations."

"I did say that. But I can explain. There's more to it than—"

"Believe me, Scott, when I tell you that no one's going to control me ever again."

"Linda, I don't want to control you."

She was shaking her head from side to side. "We don't know each other at all."

He ventured a friendly smile. "I think we do a little, ac-tually. More than you think. And I would certainly like to know you better."

"It's too late. I've already made up my mind. I'm going to live in England."

He was stunned. "But—last night... you said you didn't know what you were going to do."

"Well, that was last night."

"What's so different about today?"

"I'll tell you what's different. It's amazing, really, the effect that one especially horrible day at work can have on a person. The morning cashier called in sick, so I had to pull a double-shift. Then the night cashier was going to be late, so I had to work an additional two hours. I've been on my feet eighteen hours straight. And you know what? Today wasn't really that different from a lot of days." She rubbed her right thigh. "God, my leg is so sore... I'm sorry if I sound like a whiner but—"

"Linda, you're not a whiner."

Physical exhaustion gave her voice a ragged edge. "The fact is, Scott, I need a break. I mean a really serious break. From my job. From here. From men. From that whole fiasco with Jack..."

He could see that she was struggling to keep the tears out of her voice. "And I miss having my daughter around. So, yeah, the idea of living in England is looking pretty good to me right now."

She seemed spent as she stared at the ground.

He was petrified by the thought that he might never see her again. *This can't be happening.* "Please," he begged, "will you at least think about what I said?"

"I don't need to think about it. I'm sorry, Scott."

Without looking at him, she turned, unlocked the door and went inside. He heard the deadbolt click. A lamp went on behind the living room curtain.

He remained standing on the porch for several minutes, staring at the light through the curtain, feeling the cold, empty shell of his life closing back over him. Then he got in his car and drove away.

Chapter 16

THE SHREDDER

When he arrived home, Jake was there to greet him at the door.

"Hey, boy. You must be hungry. Let's get you some dinner."

Scott tossed his coat on a chair and went into the kitchen.

Jake seemed to sense that something was wrong. He ate without his usual gusto, now and then casting a worried glance at Scott, who sat at the kitchen table with a full goblet of wine in front of him.

When the dog finished eating, Scott downed the wine in one long drink, and took him outside to do his business.

The night was clear and cold, and the dark bulk of the Olympics formed an ebony silhouette against the star-filled sky.

"*. . . Linda. I'm in love with you.*"

"*. . . I've made up my mind. I'm going to live in England.*"

He had never experienced pain like this. It felt as if his insides had been yanked out.

Back in the house, he refilled the goblet. "What do you say we call it a day, Jake. I'm pretty beat."

They went to the bedroom, where he stretched out on the bed and propped some pillows up behind him. Jake jumped up and lay next to him.

Downing half the wine, he set it on the nightstand. He picked up the remote, turned on the TV, and flipped quickly through the stations, hoping to run across something, anything, to take his mind off the last two hours. He clicked past a celebrity chef. A dancing contest. A home remodel. A sit-com.

He gulped the rest of his wine, then resumed the erratic channel-surfing. A news show, a singing contest. He landed on a movie, a teen comedy from the eighties. Mildly entertaining, it held his attention for a few minutes. But as soon as it cut to a commercial, he began working the remote again. He came across a channel on which a man with silver hair dressed in a dark blue suit appeared to be hosting some kind of true crime show.

". . . as we return now to the History Channel's *Hired Killers of the Mob: America's Most Notorious Hit Men.*" The narrator looked like a retired prosecutor. Lean of body and face. No-nonsense style. Cynical eyes.

"Our next segment features a hit man who will go down in the annals of law enforcement as one of the most prolific and cold-blooded murderers ever to work for the Mafia."

Ah, who cared? He again aimed the remote at the TV. Then a mug shot appeared on the screen.

"Meet Patrizio Moretti, also known as 'The Shredder.'"

Scott froze. He was staring into eyes that were like bottomless pools of liquid obsidian.

It was Patrick.

The host continued. "Moretti, an only child, was born in the Bronx to immigrants from southern Italy." Photos of a young Patrick appeared. "As a boy, he attended public schools, where he received excellent grades. According to those who knew him at the time, he went to church regularly with his parents, even becoming an altar boy."

In spite of the wine he had drunk, Scott's head cleared.

More photos appeared. "When he was fourteen, Moretti's parents were killed in a car wreck. He was sent to live with relatives who resided in a different neighborhood. Moretti didn't get along with his new family and, while still in his teens, took to cutting class and hanging out in Little Italy, where he fell in with a rough crowd. He soon dropped out of school altogether, preferring to educate himself in the ways of the street."

Too shocked to move or think, Scott lay there, watching as the show launched into a detailed reenactment of Patrick's life.

As a young man, he had made a conscious decision to become a criminal. And, he turned out to be quite good at it. Before long, he attracted the attention of Louie Malatesta, patriarch of the Malatesta crime family. Based in New York City, the Malatesta empire stretched across the entire Eastern Seaboard. Its tentacles even extended west to Chicago, Denver, and other big cities.

Malatesta saw in Moretti certain qualities that, if properly cultivated, could be put to good use—the term "good" being relative. The young man possessed large measures of intelligence, cunning, and ruthlessness—a potentially lethal blend of traits that, at least in Malatesta's experience, were found in successful hit men.

Malatesta's timing for enlisting a talented new enforcer couldn't have been better. A vicious gang war had just erupted between the Malatestas and a rival family named Lucchesi over control of turf claimed by both.

Moretti's preferred method of execution was a single blast to the body at close range from a sawed-off shotgun. He never aimed above the neck because that would obliterate the head and make identification of the body problematic. A consummate professional, he did everything possible to eliminate the correct target.

To minimize the possibility that his victims might survive, Moretti took steps to enhance his weapon. He used custom-made, high-powered shotgun shells packed with flechettes. These were tiny, razor-sharp steel projectiles that produced a much larger spread pattern than standard buckshot loads. When fired at close range, they essentially shredded the body. Hence the nickname.

Patrizio Moretti's new career was off and running.

From the beginning, he insisted on working alone. That way, there were never any witnesses to his actions. Before long, he became quite skilled at his craft, and built a reputation for never botching a job.

Whenever a serious adversary of the Malatesta family needed to be eliminated with no mistakes and the outcome assured, it was The Shredder who got the call. According to the narrator, Moretti was proud that he drew the most difficult assignments.

As for dealing with any personal qualms about the cold-blooded taking of human life, it was rumored that he strongly believed that the targeted persons were exceptionally despicable people who deserved to be whacked a hundred times over. Besides, if he didn't do it, somebody else certainly would.

Patrizio Moretti had found the perfect job. He was doing something at which he excelled; he liked working on his own; the hours were reasonable; the pay was fantastic; and it was never, ever boring.

The Shredder was happy with his lot in life.

Then came the day when things went wrong, the day on which he made a couple of minor mistakes for which he would end up paying dearly. Thinking about it later, the announcer reported, he would realize that, over the years, he had grown cocky in his work. This overconfidence caused what should have been a routine assignment to turn into a disaster.

The Shredder's undoing began when an over-the-hill, mid-level wise guy named Antonio Galli decided to take over the heroin trade in New York City. This wasn't the most brilliant business plan, since that enterprise had long been dominated by the Malatesta family.

For those who knew him, Antonio's interior lights were of low wattage. Yet he had made a career out of hatching and pulling off reckless, boneheaded schemes. His friends were frankly surprised that he had survived so long.

Thousands of Louie Malatesta's customers were functioning addicts who had bought from the family for decades. Louie always took the income from his extensive and lucrative drug trade for granted. It was his bread and butter. So when he learned Antonio had undercut his prices, and that his former clientele were lining up to buy from Galli, he was furious. He made the call to Patrizio.

The second Antonio heard that The Shredder was looking for him, he fled town.

Unfortunately for Antonio, he hadn't covered his tracks very well. He had a daughter who lived with her husband in an upscale suburb of Dallas, Texas. A subsequent check of phone records turned up a flurry of calls between Antonio's number and Texas just before he disappeared.

As the reenactment continued, the narrator made it clear that the details of what happened next came to light in a series of statements to police made later by Moretti himself.

He had flown to Dallas, and spent several days watching the house. Every morning at 7:35, Antonio's daughter and her husband pulled out of their garage in a gold Cadillac. While they were gone, Moretti, using high-powered binoculars, caught glimpses of someone moving around inside the house. Whoever that person was, he never went outside.

It could only be Antonio.

Moretti was ready to make his move.

One morning, as soon as the daughter and husband were gone, Moretti walked toward the house. Though it was a warm day, he wore a charcoal Burberry overcoat, with a bulge under one side. He eased open a gate that led to the side of the house, stepped through and closed it behind him. He crept down a flagstone path that led to a side door. Easily picking the lock, he removed the shotgun from its custom-made holster on the side of his hip and slipped into the house.

With the weapon at the ready and his ears straining, he padded from room to room.

A clink of metal on ceramic came from the rear of the house.

He made his way in that direction and found Antonio, his back to Moretti, standing in his bathrobe at the counter pouring a cup of coffee with his right hand. Antonio's left arm was in front of him where Moretti couldn't see it.

Moving silently, The Shredder came forward, the ugly snout of the sawed-off shotgun pointed at the center of Antonio's back.

Moretti realized a micro-second too late that the coffee maker had a stainless steel surface just reflective enough to alert the man to his presence.

Without turning around, in a flash of movement Antonio hurled the full pot of coffee over his shoulder at Moretti, simultaneously lunging for the kitchen door.

Moretti ducked, and the coffee pot just missed his head, smashing into the refrigerator behind him. Antonio meanwhile was out the door and sprinting across the wide lawn toward a gate in the fence.

Moretti charged after him, cursing under his breath. It was the first time in his career he had been caught off-guard.

The backyard was large and Antonio had a good head start, but Moretti was faster than the older man and gained rapidly on him.

Antonio's open bathrobe flapped crazily as the two men raced across the grass. Moretti's overcoat did the same. His breath came in jagged rasps as he closed to within ten feet of his target.

It was then Moretti noticed something odd about the man. He was running strangely, hunched over with both arms in front of him, as if he were holding something he was trying to protect.

No matter. Antonio was almost to the gate. Moretti couldn't let him get away. He brought the weapon up, aimed as best he could while in full stride, and fired.

The explosion reverberated like thunder through the quiet neighborhood. Flechettes sliced through Antonio's body like hot scalpels through butter. The entire front of his torso erupted in a stringy red fountain of shredded organs. He collapsed in a pile of mangled flesh not twenty feet from the gate.

A woman who had been watering plants on the back porch of the house next door screamed.

Job completed, Moretti turned and started to run back to his car, but he stopped. Out of the corner of his eye, he'd caught an unusual movement that made him look back at the body.

Something wriggled on the lawn next to what was left of Antonio. A soft mewling came from it.

The woman continued to scream. Moretti paid no attention to her as he walked to the body. The woman dropped her watering can and ran screaming inside.

Moretti stared at the ground. The shotgun fell from his hand. He dropped to his knees on grass that was now slick and red. He reached down and gently picked up the squirming form. Its terrified wail was barely audible.

Moretti stared at the baby girl in his arms, no more than a couple months old. She was swaddled in what had been a small pink blanket, but was now a scrap of blood-soaked cloth.

The lower third of her tiny body was missing.

Her cries weakened, then stopped altogether. She became still in Moretti's arms. He didn't move. Just continued to hold her while kneeling on the grass next to Antonio.

That was how the SWAT team found him minutes later when they charged onto the property. He offered no resistance as he was shoved to the ground, handcuffed, and hustled away.

Forensic evidence obtained from him and his shotgun proved that he had been the killer in 19 separate execution-style slayings across the country dating back a couple of decades. It implicated him as the prime suspect in over a dozen more.

Because only two of the murders had been committed within the borders of Texas, those were the only crimes for which Moretti could be prosecuted in that state. The attorney general assured shocked and angry citizens that, because of the preponderance of the evidence and the swift nature of Texas justice, he would almost certainly get the death penalty.

But as the prosecution began putting together its case, Moretti, in his first courtroom appearance, stunned everyone by giving a full confession for the killing of the baby girl and announcing that he had no intention of mounting any kind of legal defense. Curiously, as for Antonio Galli and the rest of his victims, he refused to answer any questions.

Moretti's fate was decided in record time.

As *Hired Killers of the Mob: America's Most Notorious Hit Men* drew to a close, the camera moved in tight on the mug shot of Patrick. The host's voice took on a tone that was grim yet gloating. "Six months after his confession, Patrizio 'The Shredder' Moretti was escorted into the execution chamber of the State Penitentiary in Huntsville, Texas. There, on a sunny October day in 1980, he was strapped onto a table, given last rites by the prison chaplain, and put to death by lethal injec—"

"*What!?*" screamed Scott. Jake jumped up out of a dead sleep beside him and started barking.

The camera cut back to the host. "Thank you for watching," he said. "Please join us next time when we profile another—"

Scott turned off the TV and lay very still, too much in shock to move. He suddenly catapulted out of bed, threw his clothes on and stomped into the living where he grabbed his coat out of the closet and headed out the door.

Jake padded into the living room and over to the window. He looked out in time to see gravel spray from under the wheels of the Range Rover as Scott tore off into the night.

He sped all the way down the dark quiet road to Autumn Lake, where he came to a sliding halt in the parking lot, high beams aimed at the trail. He jumped out, slammed the door and moved up the path at a fast clip.

"Where are you?" he shouted. "I know you're out there, Patrick! Come on and show your face! I've got something to say to you!"

Silence. Darkness.

He got as far as the illumination from the headlights would allow. Beyond that, the trail vanished into the deep blackness of the woods.

"Patrick! Where the hell are you!? Come out where I can— ow!" Scott tripped over a tree root. He got up and hurried back to the car. Grabbing a flashlight from the glove box, he flicked it on, and marched back up the trail, where he continued calling out to the night-shrouded forest.

"Come on, Patrizio. Yeah. That's right. Newsflash. I know who you are, Mr. Moretti! Or do you prefer to go by The Shredder?"

Darkness. Silence.

After he had gone about a half mile, Scott noticed that the flashlight beam was dimming. "Shit," he muttered. He couldn't remember the last time he'd changed the batteries. Or if he had ever changed them.

He stopped and shouted into the night. "Come on, Patrizio! I've got a question for you. Just one little question, okay? See, I'm confused about something. I just found out that you killed a whole slew of people in your life. And you probably would have kept on doing it, except for one minor hitch—*you were caught and executed in 1980!* So my question for you, Patrizio, is this—What is going on?!"

Scott pointed the flashlight into the woods. The blackness of the forest acted like a blotter, absorbing most of the sickly beam.

"Quit hiding like a coward!"

A voice came from close behind. "Hello, Northwood."

Scott whirled and trained the light on Patrick. He was standing in the middle of the trail about ten feet away. There was a casual malevolence in his voice as he said, "I can do without the insults."

The shadowy glow of the flashlight caused his face to look even more intimidating than usual. Scott took a breath and forced himself to calm down.

"Fine. Whatever."

Patrick's expression softened into one of cynical amusement. "So, once again, you want to know what the hell is going on."

"That's right."

Patrick nodded to himself as if he'd known this was coming. "It's time I filled you in on a few things."

"No kidding."

"Sounds like you saw that TV show starring yours truly."

"So you know about that."

"It's been around a few years now. Another one of my Implementers came across it and told me about it. All these cable stations. They make a show about every little thing, then broadcast it to death. I figured it was only a matter of time before you saw it."

"Remember when you proved to me you were real?" said Scott. "That I wasn't losing my mind? Ever since, I've been trying to figure out what you were. Were you an angel? A spiritual being of some kind? A manifestation of energy from another dimension? Imagine my surprise when I find out that, all this time, I've been dealing with the ghost of a cold-blooded murderer!" He gave a coarse laugh. "Some angel. It's more like the devil in disguise."

"Easy, Northwood. Like they say, there's two sides to every story. You gonna hear me out or not?"

"Do you deny that you were a hit man for the mob?"

A sudden vehemence entered Patrick's voice. "Hell, no—I'm not denying it! In fact, I'm goddamn proud of it! I was the best there was!"

Scott took an involuntary step back. This was about the last response he'd expected.

"Let me ask you something, Northwood. Did it ever occur to you that if somebody's done something bad enough to get himself targeted by the mob, he might actually deserve it? Because that was my experience. I did the world a favor by ridding it of human cockroaches. Every last one of 'em needed exterminating. And—who knows?—maybe in the grand scheme of things, I was acting as a force for the public good."

"And the baby girl? Did she need exterminating, too?"

Patrick looked down. Then, in little more than a whisper, he said, "When I was young, I was an altar boy. I actually *liked* going to church. I took it seriously. Hard to believe, huh?"

His voice trailed off, but when he resumed talking, the vehemence returned, although not as sharply.

"Everything changed after my folks died. I was sent to live with my aunt and uncle—alcoholics who had four boys older, bigger, and meaner than me. A couple of them were sadistic bastards. I can't even begin to tell you some of the things they... Anyway. I decided there was no God. I moved on. I became The Shredder. I never gave a second thought to any of the scumbags I croaked. Not one. Until the day I made the hit on Antonio Galli." His voice grew husky with emotion. "When I saw what I'd done to that tiny..."

Again, his voice trailed off. The black forest surrounding them was completely hushed, as if holding its breath. The flashlight beam was now very weak.

When he resumed speaking, his voice was calm. "I guess what I'm saying is, I never really lost the moral sensibility, I guess you'd call it, that I had as a boy. It's like it just went into hibernation.

"After they locked me up, I had time to think. Stuff I never thought about before. Life and death. Good and evil. Heaven and hell.

"So while I'm sitting in that cell, a sermon I heard when I was a boy pops into my brain outta nowhere. It was about where your soul, or spirit, or energy—whatever you wanna call it—goes after you die. It went something like this: the priest asked us where we thought the souls of Adolph Hitler and Oskar Schindler went after they died. Hitler killed millions of people, whereas Schindler risked his own life to save the lives of thousands. Did they end up in the same place? Or did they end up in different places? Of course, the preacher told us that Schindler's soul went to heaven. And Hitler's went straight to hell, where it would burn for all eternity. And of course, we all agreed with him. End of story.

"But the more I thought about it, I realized it wasn't that simple. What if the atheists are right, and there isn't any afterlife? If that's true, then all the religions are wrong. And it doesn't matter what we believe, 'cause when we die— poof!—we'll stop existing. Not a thing we can do about it.

"So then I thought, what if the atheists got it wrong? What if there is some kind of life after death, what if we do have souls? And if that turns out to be the case, then what about Hitler's soul and Schindler's? Either they went to different places, or they went to the same place. If they ended up in the same place, then it doesn't matter if you live a good life or an evil one, because the outcome'll be exactly the same. But that can't be true, right? Because then nothing would make any sense at all.

"So my instincts, my moral sensibilities, told me that if there really was an afterlife, there was no possible way that Hitler and Schindler could end up at the same place! And that led me to something else that suddenly seemed plain as day. How you live your life determines where you're going next. This made me a little nervous because my execution date was coming up fast, and I hadn't exactly lived the life of an angel."

Patrick smirked, as if recalling some wild escapades. But then he became serious again.

"I'm gonna be honest with you. It didn't just make me nervous, it scared the livin' shit outta me! My eternal soul was at stake. I knew it was going to end up someplace horrible. And that terrified me! It was at that point I figured I needed to try and make some kind of a deal to cover my bases."

"What kind of deal?"

"Basically, I promised I'd do whatever it took, and I mean

anything, to keep my soul from going anywhere near where Hitler's ended up.

"What I'm saying is that I was truly remorseful. A more repentant son of a bitch never lived. By the time the priest gave me my last rites, I was a changed person. Then they injected the happy juice into my veins."

"And you died?"

"And I went to sleep. That was it. There was no sense of time. I woke up out here at Autumn Lake—a long way from Texas. There are gaps in what I remember. I have no idea how—or why—I ended up in a jerkwater town where it rains all the time. More stuff goes on in New York in one minute than it does here in a hundred years. Be that as it goddamn may, when I got here, I knew I had a job to do." An unmistakable note of derision entered his voice as he said, "And so here I am, being an Enabler."

His disdain surprised Scott. "Huh. You don't seem real happy about it."

"Wanna know the truth?"

"Definitely."

"It sucks."

"Why?"

"Hey! You think it's fun dealing with a bunch of whining Implementers? You think I like spending all my time badgering you people into shortening your smug little lives? It's a lot of work. And it's a pain in the ass."

An idea came to Scott. "...Maybe you're going about it the wrong way."

"You think you could do better?"

"I'm just saying that, instead of constantly threatening to make the lives of your Implementers miserable, you could do something different."

"Like what?"

"Like try appealing to their better nature."

"Ha! Fat chance. When it comes down to it, people are selfish."

"Maybe. Maybe not. But some people might consider it a

privilege to do what you're doing. They might go about it in a different way and get better results."

Patrick looked at Scott like he was off his rocker. "What're you sayin', exactly? That one man's penance could be another man's privilege?"

"I guess that is what I'm saying."

Patrick gave a harsh laugh. "You're demented, Northwood."

"Hey, nobody's ruled that out completely yet. So answer my question. What are you? An angel? A devil? A ghost? What?"

"Think of me as a cosmic errand boy being held in limbo against my will."

"But it has to be a lot better than the alternative, right?"

"I don't have a choice except to assume it is."

"How long are you supposed to keep doing this?"

Patrick snorted. "That's what's buggin' the hell outta me—I have no idea! It might be a hundred years! Who freakin' knows? I've been doing this a long time now and I'm sick of it. All right, enough with the questions already. You asked me what the hell was going on. I told you what I know. So are we through here?"

"Yeah. We're through."

The flashlight died, plunging the two into total darkness.

"Great." Scott banged it against the palm of his hand a couple of times but to no avail. He suddenly noticed how cold it was.

Patrick's voice was annoyingly gleeful as it knifed through the blackness. "You know, a person could freeze to death out here."

"It's pretty chilly, all right."

"So how you gonna get back to your car, Einstein?"

Scott struggled to keep the fear out of his voice. "Good question."

"It would be a shame if one of my Implementers died of hypothermia."

"I couldn't agree more. Think you can help me out here,

Patrick?"

No response. Scott waited until the silence became unbearable. "Hello? Patrick? Are you there?"

Laughter suddenly rang out. "Come on, Einstein. Follow my voice. And I promise not to lead you off a cliff."

Although his heart was pounding, Scott forced himself to sound as casual as possible. "Anyone ever told you you've got a mean streak?"

Patrick laughed again and started singing. "Fly me to the moon, let me play among the stars..."

He sang loudly and surprisingly well. Scott followed the sound of his voice through the dark forest.

"...Let me see what spring is like on Jupiter and Mars..."

It was three in the morning by the time Scott pulled up in front of his house. He'd left a light on in the living room, and he saw Jake silhouetted in the window. When Scott went inside, the dog's tail wagged crazily.

"Hey, boy," he said, kneeling down to scratch behind Jake's ear. "I'm glad to see you, too."

When Scott stood up, he could barely keep his eyes open. He couldn't remember ever being this tired. He made his way back to the bedroom, got undressed and crawled into bed. He could feel sleep rushing toward him like a silent black tidal wave.

But just before he nodded off, his analytical mind concluded that—between the lack of sleep from the previous night, his disastrous soul-baring encounter with Linda earlier that evening, and hearing Patrick's wild story—this had to have been the longest, crappiest, most exhausting day of his life.

Chapter 17

JULIE

Bam! Bam! Bam! Someone banging loudly on the front door jarred Scott awake.

"What the—?"

He squinted at the bedside clock: A little after six in the morning. He'd been asleep for only a couple of hours.

Bam! Bam! Bam! Bam! Bam!

"Who in the world—?" He pulled on his robe, stamped to the front door and threw it open.

Patrick.

In a loud voice, Scott said, "What the hell is the matter with you!? Do you know what time—"

"We need to go." Patrick said, his brusqueness firing on all cylinders.

"What are you talking about? Go where?"

"There's gonna be an accident. If we wanna help her, we need to leave right now!"

Scott closed his eyes and pressed his palms into them. "This is ridiculous. I haven't had any sleep." He took his hands from his face and glared at Patrick. "Why didn't you mention this last night? If you had, I could at least have tried to prepare for—"

"I already explained it to you once, Einstein!" Patrick spoke sharply and fast, hardly taking a breath. "This is a material event! Like what happened with Max Grabowsky. I get very little warning—which means you get very little warning. If we're hoping to change the outcome, you have to physically be there. Things can unfold fast, so we have to act fast."

"Who is this person?"

"I'll fill you in in the car."

"What if I say no and go back to bed?"

"You could do that." Patrick reached over and began ringing the doorbell nonstop. "But I don't think you'd get much sleep."

"Fine. You win. As always." Scott stomped back to the bedroom. "Let me at least get some clothes on."

Patrick took his thumb off the doorbell and called after him, "Make it snappy!"

Linda was awakened out of a deep sleep by the ringing of her telephone. Disoriented, she sat up in bed and looked around. It was still dark outside. She glanced at the clock.

Quarter after six in the morning.

She thought for a fleeting moment it might be Scott. In a strange way, she kind of hoped it was. She'd been pretty harsh with him the night before and had gone to bed feeling bad about it. Sure, she had been exhausted and in a bad mood, but that was no excuse for her to have treated him that way. It took a lot of courage for him to show up at her door and say those things.

She picked up the phone. "Hello?"

It wasn't Scott. An English accent. "Linda. It's Jonathan, calling from England. I apologize if I've awakened you."

She felt a tightening in her chest.

"That's all right, Jonathan. What is it?"

For all of her son-in-law's British reserve, his voice cracked as he said, "It's Megan. I'm afraid... I'm afraid she's in hospital."

Linda closed her eyes, the cold, familiar dread sweeping through her body.

The Range Rover barreled down deserted pre-dawn

streets. The air was brittle and cold. Fitful winds gusted through the trees on either side of the road. It was going to be a blustery November day.

"So where am I going?" said Scott.

"For now, head in the direction of Quilcene. As we get closer, I'll be able to pinpoint her location."

"What's her story?"

"Her name's Julie Hamilton. Thirty-eight. Never married. Professor of Geology at the University of Oregon. For the last two years, she's done research on a new way of getting carbon dioxide out of the air and pumping it into the earth."

Scott was impressed. "Wow. You're talking about global warming, right?"

Patrick shrugged. "I guess. All I know is that it would be a good thing if she continues her work. Right now, she's on her way to Port Townsend for a conference with other specialists in her field. She likes to drive at night, which is why she's passing through so early."

"Let me guess—a head-on collision with a drunk driving home after a night at the casino."

"I have to get a lot closer before I know what's supposed to happen to her. Meanwhile, you need to tell me how much time you're willing to give her."

This triggered several minutes of haggling, resulting in Scott's committing to give Julie Hamilton his usual one year of additional life. After that, the two rode in mutually cranky silence.

Scott sped west across the Hood Canal Bridge. On either side of the floating span, powerful winds whipped the water into a frothy gray soup and buffeted the car so violently that he kept his hands gripped on the wheel. Light from the rising sun behind caused the snow-covered Olympic mountain range in front of him to burn a bright and iridescent pink against an intensely blue sky.

The sleepy town of Quilcene was located along the fiord-like Hood Canal, which bordered much of the eastern edge of the Olympic Peninsula. Normally about a thirty-minute drive from Poulsbo, Scott figured they'd arrive much sooner with the sparse early morning traffic.

As they approached the outskirts of Quilcene, Patrick became even more irritable. "We're running out of time. Can't you go any faster?"

Scott's response was just as cross. "I'm already going twenty miles over the limit. I'm just worried about how much time we would lose if I get pulled over by a—"

He was interrupted by the sound of a police siren behind him.

Scott looked at the flashing blue lights filling his rearview mirror. "Well, here we go again. Feel better, Patrick?"

The Range Rover rolled to a stop on the shoulder. Patrick said, "When he gets here, I want you to ask him why he pulled you over."

"Going to do your memory trick again?"

"You better believe it."

In his side-view mirror, Scott watched the officer approach. He didn't look friendly. As his beefy face filled the window frame, he barked "License and registration."

"Why did you pull me over, Officer?"

The question seemed to confuse the officer. "What?"

"Why did you pull me over?"

The officer didn't say anything but rubbed his face in befuddlement. Finally he said, "I, ah, I honestly don't remember, sir." Overcome with embarrassment, he said, "I apologize for the inconvenience. Have a nice day, sir."

The officer tipped his Smokey the Bear hat and walked back to his cruiser.

Scott watched in his mirror as the officer climbed back into his cruiser, turned off the flashing lights and made a U-turn.

Scott shook his head in wonder and muttered to Patrick, "You must be a scream at parties."

"I hate cops," said Patrick.

"Gee. I wonder why."

"Go."

He floored it.

A couple miles south of Quilcene, the road entered the Olympic National Forest. Trees here were so tall and densely packed that when there was a long straight stretch of road, it felt as if the car were skimming along the bottom of a deep, leafy green canyon.

As they entered one of these straightaways, Patrick became agitated. "We're close. It's supposed to happen right around here. She's driving a brown Honda SUV..."

"There!" cried Scott. "I see her!" He pointed down the road at a brown vehicle coming toward them from the opposite direction. It was a little over a mile away.

There were no other cars behind it.

Scott checked his rearview mirror.

No cars there, either.

He expelled a sigh of relief and said, "We did it. We beat the other car here. There's not going to be a head-on collision."

But Patrick remained on edge. "This doesn't feel right."

Scott realized that his hands were sore from gripping the wheel so tightly. He allowed himself to relax.

"Loosen up, Patrick. Julie Hamilton's going to be fine. All we have to do now is get her attention. Flag her down or something. The tiniest change in her movements will be enough to disrupt the timing so that—"

"It's not a car that's gonna hit her!" Patrick shouted. "It's a tree!"

"—What?"

"Look!"

Patrick pointed up at the trees bordering the road between the two cars just as a powerful gust of wind blasted through. A hundred giant firs twisted and swayed in a crazy dance.

One of them, a hundred-foot western hemlock, danced more than the rest. With a loud rippling crack, it toppled over onto the road. The Honda was directly beneath it. It happened so swiftly that Julie had no time to react.

"Oh, shit!" wailed Scott. "Oh, no!"

He and Patrick watched in horror as the tree smashed onto the car with a loud, sickening crunch of splintering wood and twisting metal.

"No!" Scott punched the accelerator to the floor and screeched to a halt near the fallen tree. He leaped out and ran toward it.

Patrick stayed inside the Range Rover.

"Julie!" cried Scott. He scrambled through the tangle of broken branches toward the wreckage. "Julie Hamilton! Can you hear me?! Say something if you can hear me!"

Silence.

Scott clawed his way to the SUV that was now just a pile of crumpled metal. There! An arm sticking out from under the tree trunk.

The arm wasn't moving.

Scott reached down and took hold of her hand.

"Julie. If you can hear me, if you're alive, squeeze my hand."

Her hand didn't move. It was warm and wet to the touch.

Scott withdrew his arm and looked down.

His hand was covered with blood.

⌒ ⌒ ⌒

Scott and Patrick rode in silence. Near Quilcene, they came across a string of police cars, ambulances, and fire trucks racing the other way, lights blazing and sirens screaming.

Neither man looked at them as they streaked past.

⌒ ⌒ ⌒

They pulled into the parking lot of Autumn Lake and stopped. Not a word had been uttered the entire way back. Now they sat unmoving, staring ahead while the engine idled.

Finally Patrick opened the door and climbed out. Holding

the door open, he turned to Scott and snapped, "If you'd listened to me and not dicked around this morning, we woulda got there in time."

"Now just hold on a minute! Are you saying that what happened is *my* fault?!"

"Who else's fault would it be! If we'd left two minutes earlier... even sixty seconds, we woulda stopped her before she reached that tree."

"Excuse me, but it was you who led me to believe she was going to be hit by another car. If you'd said anything about a falling tree, I'd have gotten there faster."

"I never said it was going to be another car. You just assumed that. Like I told you before, I don't know exactly what's gonna happen till just before it happens."

Scott shook his head from side to side and ran his hand over his face in frustration. In a tired voice, he said, "I can't keep doing this, Patrick. It's too much. It's too crazy. I feel like I'm losing my mind. What do I have to do to make this stop?"

"It'll stop when it stops."

"I'm through with this. Close the door. I need to get home."

Patrick made no move to leave. "Before you go, I got a newsflash for you."

"Now what?" said Scott. He'd reached the very end of his rope.

"It's Megan."

"What about her?"

"Remember last November? When you gave her another year of life?"

"Of course I remember."

"Her time's almost up. Her tumor's back."

As Scott took that in, he felt heavier in his seat. He didn't speak for several seconds. Then, in a quiet voice, he said, "How long has she got?"

"Two days. Three at the most."

Scott closed his eyes. He knew this moment would come,

but hadn't wanted to think about it. In fact, he'd managed to block it out of his mind for the last few months. But now, it was here. And the question burned in his mind: *What was he going to do about it?*

He opened his eyes and looked at Patrick, who stood watching him. Scott's voice was flat as he asked, "Anything else?"

"Matter of fact, there is," said Patrick. "She's pregnant. And guess what? It's gonna be a girl."

The two stared at each other. "Have a nice day," he said, closing the door and walking toward the trailhead. As he entered the forest, Scott heard him singing.

"When the moon hits your eye, like a big pizza pie, that's amore..."

His voice faded into the trees.

Scott pulled into his driveway, shut off the engine, and sat completely still. He felt like he was at the bottom of the ocean with the massive weight of water pressing in from all sides.

Something caught his eye—Jake, holding vigil at the window next to the front door.

It was only eleven o'clock in the morning, but to Scott it felt like well after midnight.

He entered the house, and Jake came to him, sniffing the blood encrusted on his hand. The dog looked into Scott's eyes with a worried expression.

"It's okay, boy," he said. "I'm okay. Let me take a quick shower. Then I'll get you some breakfast."

He stood in the shower as if in a trance, watching the dried blood liquefy in the hot soapy water and swirl down the drain. Suddenly his body was wracked by sobs that seemed to come out of nowhere. They were so deep and convulsive that they caused him to double over, but they stopped as quickly as they had come.

Tears still on his cheeks, he rinsed the last of the blood off his body and reached for a towel.

Chapter 18

THE DEAL

After putting on clean clothes, Scott fed Jake and made a pot of coffee.

Though thoroughly exhausted, he had not been able to sleep. Instead, he spent the rest of the day roaming from room to room, thinking about everything that had happened in the past year—particularly the last few days. He had no idea what he was supposed to do about any of it.

That afternoon, he lay on the living room rug, gazing out at the Olympic Mountains, trying very hard to make sense of things.

By the end of the day, he had made up his mind. He knew what he had to do.

"We haven't been for our walk yet today, Jake," he said, standing up. "What do you say?"

The dog's ears pricked up at the magic word, and he scrambled to his feet.

On the drive to Autumn Lake, Scott reached out to Jake in the passenger seat and gave his scruffy brown neck a scratch.

"Want to know something, you old mutt?" he said. "When it comes right down to it, you're my best friend."

The pale November light was slowly draining from the late afternoon sky when Scott and Jake arrived at the parking lot. The air was clear and cold, and the wind had stopped. The darkening forest was completely still.

Scott led Jake down a path that ended at the edge of the shallow lake. He found a moss-covered log to sit on. It wasn't long before he heard someone approaching. He went on staring at the lake as Patrick came to a halt beside the log.

"Didn't expect to see you back so soon." Patrick's East Coast accent sounded particularly abrasive.

"I've been thinking."

"Good for you, Einstein. What have you been—"

"I want to make a deal."

Patrick's eyebrows shot up in genuine surprise. "No shit. A deal, huh?"

"I figured since you made one, I'd try and do the same."

"Fair enough. What kind of deal?"

"Before I answer that, I have a question."

"Always with the questions. What now?"

"It has to do with Linda, Megan, and her daughter."

"You mean Megan's daughter who isn't born yet."

"Yeah. I assume you'd like to see Megan live long enough so that her baby is born."

"Now why would you assume that?"

"Because you think it would make up for taking the life of that little girl in Texas."

For a fleeting moment, something soft appeared in Patrick's eyes. "It could be you assume right. So?"

"So my question is this: when she's born—that is, *if* she's born—will this baby have to depend on me to give her time like I do to Megan, just to stay alive?"

"If Megan lives long enough to give birth, her daughter will be on her own path. So to answer your question—no. You're off the hook."

Scott nodded. "Good. That makes what I want to do a lot simpler."

"Which is?"

"Before I get into that, I want to be *absolutely sure* we're on the same page about something."

"What?"

"About how much time I have left. When all this start-ed, you told me I was slated to live into my nineties. I'm fifty-three now. Erring on the side of caution, let's call it ninety. So then, doing the math, ninety minus fifty-three equals thirty-seven years. Subtracting the years I gave to Megan, Max, Jason and Olivia, I've got about thirty-three years left to live, or give away, or a combination of both. Is that correct?"

"Yeah."

Scott let out a breath and nodded. "Just so we're clear on that. Here's my offer: Except for a small number of years yet to be determined, I want to give all the time I have left to Megan."

Patrick's mouth dropped open. "Did I hear you right? *All* of it to Megan?"

"You heard me right."

"But—why?"

Scott didn't answer right away as his gaze drifted over the lake before him. Finally he spoke. "I've been thinking. About a lot of things."

"So I gather."

"Linda has made it oh-so-clear she wants nothing to do with me. As much as it pains me to know that, I accept it. But the thing is... *I love her.* I always will. And so I would like to do something... *nice* for her. Something important. God knows the woman has gone through enough crap in her life. She's never had a break. Well, I'd like to give her one. I'd like to give her the happiness of being with her daughter and granddaughter for as long as possible."

Patrick was having trouble coming to grips with Scott's proposition. "Lemme see if I got this straight: making her happy means more to you than *your own life?*"

"That's right."

"But—she'll never even know what you did for her!"

"That's not important."

Patrick gave a low whistle. "Man. I thought I'd seen it all. But *this* takes the freakin' cake."

Scott turned to Patrick. "So. That's my offer. Interested?"

"I'm interested," Patrick said, the shock already gone from his face. "You are aware, of course, that if you do this, it's not reversible. None of that time can ever be transferred back to you."

"Yes, I know that."

"Just makin' sure." Patrick's face creased in suspicion. "So what do you want in return?"

"Two things."

"Here we go."

"It's not as bad as you think. I said I wanted to keep a small amount of time yet to be determined."

"Yeah. Determined how?"

"Whatever time Jake has left to live, I want the same for myself." Scott swallowed hard. "And no more."

Patrick was incredulous. "You're sayin' you only want to live as long as your *dog?!*"

Scott's smile was grim. "That's what I said, Einstein."

They both looked at Jake, who was sniffing and pawing at a rodent hole.

"He's not exactly a spring chicken."

"I think he's got a few good years left in him."

Jake sauntered over, sat on the ground next to Scott and stared up at him. Scott reached out to scratch the dog's ear, then turned and looked at Patrick. "And no tricks."

"What're you talkin' about?"

"I don't want Jake getting shoved in front of a car, or pushed off a cliff. He gets to live out his normal lifespan, whatever that would be."

"I would never pull a stunt like that."

"Yeah, tell that to Alfred James Hersom, the Fourth!"

"Hey, that was different and you know it. And don't forget we were both in on it."

"I didn't forget. I'm just saying, no tricks this time."

"You don't have to worry. I, uh, I happen to like that mutt

of yours."

Scott looked surprised.

Patrick cleared his throat. "What's the other thing?"

Scott hesitated a moment before answering. "This is where it gets a little dicey. I want you to erase my memory."

"Excuse me?"

"Not all of it. Just the parts that have to do with me being an Implementer."

Patrick ran his hand over his jaw. He looked troubled. "Man, I don't know..."

"Is that going to be a problem?" Scott started to rise. "Because if it is, then I don't think we can—"

"Whoa! Hang on, hang on. I didn't say I couldn't do it. It's just... Nobody's ever asked for anything like that before. Lemme think on it a minute..."

"Are you saying you can do it?"

"It's a pretty tall order..."

"Answer the question," said Scott, exasperated. "Can you do it or not?"

"Yeah. Yeah, I can do it."

"Okay, then." Scott sat back down. "Those are the terms. Are they acceptable to you?"

"Yeah," Patrick nodded, "I'm good with it."

"I told you you'd like it. Now, just so we're crystal clear about what's going to happen: I want you to wipe out all my memories of my dealings with you. And I want you to disappear from my life."

Patrick feigned a wounded expression. "Jeez! You really know how to hurt a person's feelings."

Scott ignored his derision. "I don't want to have any knowledge at all that I'm... I'm going to die right after Jake. And I don't want to remember anything about making this deal."

"What about people you've met because of me, like Megan? And Linda? The people at Cedar Rock Restaurant? It could be pretty awkward for you, to say the least, if you run into them and say you don't know them."

"I've already considered that. I don't need people thinking I'm crazy, though at this point they'd probably be right. Leave those memories intact. Understood?"

"Yeah, I get it."

"So," said Scott with finality. "Do we have a deal?"

"Yeah, we have a deal." Patrick extended his hand. Scott looked at it a moment, then extended his own. They shook.

"Okay," said Patrick. "It's done."

"Congratulations."

"For what?"

"I'd say that's a pretty good haul for an Enabler."

"Yeah," agreed Patrick. "It is..." An odd look crossed his face.

"What?"

"It's just that... nobody's ever done anything like this before. I feel like I just robbed a bank."

As the reality of what he'd done began to sink in, Scott answered with a melancholy smile. "Something tells me you'll get over it."

Then, his voice strangely earnest, Patrick said, "Listen. If it makes you feel any better, here's somethin' to think about. Suppose—and I mean just suppose—Megan's daughter grows up to do somethin' really great."

"Like what?"

"Like—I don't know. The cancer's gonna do Megan in eventually, right? So maybe that gets stuck in her daughter's craw. Or one of her grandkid's craws. Makes one of 'em want to grow up to be a doctor. Or a scientist. Someone who goes on to discover the cure."

Scott laughed at the absurdity of the thought. "Yeah, right."

A strange and mirthful light in his Patrick's eyes. "Hey, could happen, right? I mean, who knows?"

Scott's smile was tolerant at best. "Sure. Whatever."

"So," Patrick said. "When you want this memory thing to kick in?"

"The sooner the better."

Patrick nodded. "No problem."

"What happens now?"

"What happens now? Just go home. You'll sleep like you've never slept. And when you wake up tomorrow, it'll be a brand new world."

Scott stood up. "I guess that's it then."

"Yeah. I guess that's it."

It was getting dark, but there was still enough light to make out the path.

"Come on, Jake. Let's go home."

The dog shook himself, and fell into step. Leaving Patrick sitting alone on the moss-covered log, Scott and Jake headed down the trail.

The second she'd gotten off the phone with Jonathan, Linda dressed, packed, and drove to the airport, boarding the first available nonstop from Seattle to London. From Heathrow, she took a cab directly to Royal Marsden Hospital and Cancer Centre in London.

The journey took its stressful and exhausting toll. Looking as if she'd just escaped from being held hostage in a hostile country, she stood at the foot of her daughter's hospital bed with Megan's British oncologist, Doctor Maurice Brewer. He was a large man in his fifties with thick gray hair.

Megan lay propped up by pillows, eyes open and alert. Jonathan sat in a chair next to her, holding her hand. He still wore his white dentist's coat from the day before when he'd gotten the call that she had lost consciousness in their neighborhood market.

Linda, struggling to keep her voice calm, said to Dr. Brewer, ". . . You're telling me that yesterday, my daughter was near death—but today... she's fine?"

The man answered with restrained awe. "Frankly, I've never seen anything like it. Last night, I thought Megan had less than twenty-four hours to live. This morning, she came out of her coma and asked for water. We immediately gave her another MRI, which revealed no trace of the tumor. It's completely gone! I exchanged emails with Doctor Drake, her physician in the States. Apparently, something similar happened about this time last year."

It struck Linda that it wasn't "about" this time last year. *It was exactly the same day.*

"Megan's vital signs are strong," the doctor added. "In fact, everything looks quite normal. She can go home any time. I suggest keeping her quiet for a day or two. See that she gets plenty of rest."

Jonathan grinned at his wife.

"What do you say, love?" said Jonathan. "Are you ready to go home?"

"I'd like nothing better," she said. "I'm really sorry, Mom, that you came all this way—" She stopped and gave a wry laugh. "I was going to say 'for nothing.'"

Linda smiled through tears of relief. "I can't tell you how glad I am that I made this trip 'for nothing'!"

"Anyway, since you're here, I hope you'll stay for a few days, at least."

Are you kidding me?! "I can't think of anything I'd rather do."

⌒⌒⌒

When Scott woke up late the next morning, he was lying in the same position as when he went to bed. It was the best night's sleep he'd had in a long time, deep and dreamless. As he sat up and stretched, he felt different somehow. It was only after he got up and started moving around that he was able to identify this strange new sensation.

He felt good! Rested. Refreshed. Invigorated. In fact, this was the best he'd felt in months—if not years.

There was an actual spring in his step, as if the force of gravity had been cut in half. Try as he might, he couldn't put his finger on *why* he felt this way. No doubt a great night's sleep was part of it. But there was something more. He couldn't shake the feeling that he'd been living under a giant shadow for a long time and now the shadow had lifted. There was light everywhere.

He felt giddy. And for no apparent reason.

Yet he sensed that there was more to it than just his buoyant mood, that, somehow, there was more going on around him than met his eye.

And that bothered him.

For about sixty seconds.

Then he told himself to stop analyzing everything to death for once. Just relax and accept it. Which is exactly what he did.

He soon realized that he was famished, and set about making an oversized breakfast, including extra portions of bacon and sausage for Jake. By the time he'd finished eating and loading his dishes into the dishwasher, it was early afternoon.

Jake stood in the doorway of the kitchen watching him. He seemed to sense Scott's improved frame of mind. It met with profound canine approval.

"Whatta ya say, Jake? Ready to go for a walk?"

As they headed to the car, Scott discovered that he was looking forward to the rest of the day—something he couldn't remember feeling for quite a while.

Nights in London in the late fall were cold and gloomy, which only made the small, comfortable flat Megan and Jonathan shared that much more welcoming. After a long hot shower, she was glad to curl up on the couch in her own living room, wearing her flannel pajamas and robe, and to sip tea with her mother. Jonathan was taking his own much-needed shower.

"Aren't you tired, Mom? I mean, between that long flight from Seattle and jet lag, I know I would be."

"No, I'm okay. But I think I've been running on adrenaline nonstop." Linda's eyes didn't leave her daughter as she sipped her tea. "What am I going to do with you, Megan?"

"What do you mean?"

"These annual brushes with death are really starting to annoy me."

"I suppose it is getting a little old!"

They smiled at their gallows humor.

In a quieter voice, Megan said, "I'm sorry."

"Sorry? For what?"

"For putting you through the wringer. Again."

"Oh, honey! Don't be ridiculous. You have nothing to be sorry about. I'm just glad you're still kicking."

"Boy! Me too."

They stared at each other for a quiet moment. Then Linda said, "I can't get over the fact that these... 'episodes' happened exactly one year apart. I mean, what in the world..."

"I know. Pretty weird."

"Do you remember anything? From being in the coma?"

Megan gave a big sigh as she thought back. "All I remember is stopping by the market two days ago to pick up a half-gallon of milk and a dozen eggs. And then waking up in the hospital this morning. Hardly anything in between."

"Megan, what do you mean by 'hardly'?"

"Well. I do remember something, actually... A dream—if you could even call it that."

"What did you dream?"

"This may sound strange, but I dreamt about Scott Northwood. You remember the guy who—"

"*Of course* I remember Scott Northwood," said Linda with a little too much intensity, which caught Megan's attention. "What happened in the dream?"

"Not much, really. I was locked in a dark, tiny room. I couldn't breathe. It was horrible. Then the room kind of melted away, and I was in the middle of a forest. Scott was standing there, looking at me... I remember feeling safe."

"How strange."

"... Mom, there's more. I never told you this, but I had *the exact same dream a year ago.* Just before I woke up at Harborview."

Linda gasped. "Why didn't you tell me?"

"I don't know. I guess I was worried you might think I had some weird crush on an older man."

"Oh, no, Megan. I never would have thought that. But the dreams are odd. I wonder if they're supposed to mean something."

Megan's eyes turned dark, as if she had been thinking the same thing. "Maybe so."

They each took a swallow of tea. "So," Megan said pointedly, "speaking of Scott, do you ever run into him?"

"Well," Linda said, "as a matter of fact, I did run into him recently."

Megan gave her a knowing smile. "No kidding. What happened?"

Linda knew better than to try keeping a secret like this from her daughter. Sooner or later it would come out. She told Megan about Scott wandering into the Food King Market. And that he'd called her right after watching The Raging Guppy sink on television. How they shared a good laugh over it.

She finished the last of her tea and set the cup down. Then she took a deep breath and told her daughter about coming home from work to find him asleep on the front porch. About how he'd told her he...

Megan's jaw dropped. "He told you he was in love with you?!"

"Yes. He did."

Megan's eyes bore into Linda's. "What did you say?"

Linda dreaded answering her daughter's question, but there was no point in lying. Megan would know it if she did. "I told him that, after what I'd just been through with Jack, I needed to take a break from men."

"'A break from men'? You're comparing Scott to Jack?"

"I also told him I was making some changes in my life. That I was moving here to England. So I could be closer to you."

"'Closer to me'? I wouldn't exactly call that a big change,

Mom, seeing as how I've been living at home with you, like, forever."

"Well... at the time, it seemed like the right thing to—"

"What did he say?"

"He asked me if... if I would at least think about it."

"And what did you tell him?"

"I told him I'd already thought about it. That I'd made my decision. And then I sent him on his way."

"...And then you sent him on his way," repeated Megan. She closed her eyes and shook her head slowly from side to side. "I can't believe this."

"What?"

"Mother, what in the world is wrong with you?!" Megan never addressed her as "Mother" unless she was angry or really upset about something. Right now she was both.

"Nothing's wrong with me. Why are you—"

"How can you be so blind?! You and Scott would make the most amazing couple! You two would be brilliant together. Can you not see that?"

Linda suddenly felt flustered, angry at being told something that, deep down, she may have suspected all along but had been afraid to admit to herself. "Aren't you forgetting something?" she said.

"What? What am I forgetting?"

"That it's *my* life, Megan. That means you don't get to have a say in what I do or don't do."

"Oh, Mother, you are so wrong."

"Excuse me?"

"I do get to have a say in it."

"And what gives you—"

"I'll tell you what gives me the right. Take a good look at me, Mother. I'm the poster child for second chances. Not everyone gets them. Not by a long shot. But if I've learned anything the last couple of years, it's that second chances— and sometimes even third chances—really do happen. I believe in them with all my heart. And if one comes along, you've got to chase after it and grab it with both hands! Then pull it close and hang on with every last bit of strength!"

Megan stopped to catch her breath. Both of them seemed surprised at the passion of her words.

She continued in a quieter voice. "We get so few chances for happiness in this life. You have been unhappy for so long, Mom, so long that you don't remember what it's like to feel good. And I want you to feel good."

Linda felt her eyes tear up.

"Scott is a good man," Megan said. "Better than Jack could ever hope to be. Believe me, this I know."

Linda was silent a moment. Then she said, "Can I be... totally honest with you?"

"Sure, Mom."

"This is hard to admit, but the thing I don't understand is... what could he possibly see in a divorced single mom working as a checker in a rundown grocery store? I mean, he's wealthy. He doesn't have to work. He can go anywhere, do anything he wants."

The girl was touched by her mother's candor. Tears came to her eyes as she spoke. "Oh, Mom. You're so much more than that. You're smart. You're strong. You're kind. And there's something else."

"What?"

"I was there in the parking lot of the Cedar Rock that day. I saw the way he looked at you. I know he would be willing to give you another chance. So just take it, Mom. Please. I love you and I want you to be happy. God knows you deserve it. Okay?"

Linda smiled through her tears at her daughter. Her voice dropped to a whisper. "Okay."

A mischievous glint appeared in Megan's eyes. "You know, if you wanted, you could even show up unannounced on his doorstep, like he did with you."

"Oh! I would never do that. Besides, I don't even know where he lives."

"I do."

"You have Scott's address?"

"Before I left for Europe, I asked if I could drop him a postcard. He said yes. So I've got it if you want it."

"I don't know. I'd have to think about that…"

"So, Mom, you have to promise me you'll call him as soon as you get home. Okay?"

"I promise."

Their eyes hot with tears, mother and daughter embraced.

～～～

The previous day's cold blue skies had been replaced by a heavy drizzle that draped the trails of Autumn Lake in a shadowy gloom. Scott buttoned his coat up to his neck, shoved his hands inside the warm, roomy pockets, and kept walking. Jake padded along at his side.

Not one to let a good mood go unspoiled, Scott soon found himself thinking about his last encounter with Linda. His steps slowed as he recalled how painfully clear she had made it that her rejection was final. He would just have to put her out of his mind for once and for all, and get on with his life.

By facing reality and resolutely telling himself that it was over with Linda—before it had ever even begun—he had hoped to start feeling better. But the pain still cut too deep. He realized it was an ache that would be with him until he drew his last breath. But, he acknowledged, at least, after more than fifty years, he knew what love felt like. Surely that meant something.

As they passed a fork in the trail, Jake came to a sudden stop. His ears stood up and he huffed at something on the other path.

"What is it, boy?" Scott peered in the same direction, looking for a deer or a squirrel.

But there was nothing.

Jake huffed louder, and his tail started wagging.

"What in the world are you looking at?"

Paying no attention to Scott, Jake gave out low playful growls, his tail wagging even harder.

"Goofy dog! There's nothing there."

Mystified by Jake's behavior, Scott put the leash on him and pulled him away from whatever was causing him to act so strangely.

When Scott returned to his car, he felt somewhat heartened, but he couldn't shake the sensation that he'd just woken up from a horrible nightmare, one he had absolutely no memory of. Well, he thought, there was no use driving himself crazy. He finished toweling Jake off and hoisted him onto the passenger seat.

As he drove home, Scott struggled, with moderate success, to keep from thinking about Linda. Then an old saying popped into his head: *"Sometimes the best place to forget a woman is in the arms of another woman."*

He found himself wondering how Betty was doing in Scottsdale, and toyed with the idea of calling her. He could find out if she was seeing anyone and, if not, offer to fly her up for a visit; or even better, he could fly to Arizona. It wasn't a thought that brought as much excitement as he had hoped it would; in fact, the feeling in the pit of his stomach might better be described as desperation. But, he told himself, a blast of desert air would be welcome in the dead of a Northwest winter. He knew it was a rationalization, but he couldn't imagine going on this way. He had to force himself to do *something*, and this was the only thing he could think of.

~ ~ ~

Linda had been able to convince her boss to give her seven days of emergency leave. She wanted to be absolutely sure that Megan was completely healthy before making the long flight home.

By the third day of her visit, she, Megan and Jonathan had settled into a routine. They'd have breakfast together in the morning. Then, when Jonathan headed off to work, Megan and Linda would plan their day, which would be nothing more strenuous than seeing a film or visiting a museum. Then back home for a quiet dinner with Jonathan.

Linda and Jonathan took Dr. Brewer's instructions seriously. They made sure Megan got plenty of rest. She went in for one more hospital checkup, confirming that the tumor was indeed gone.

This morning, Jonathan drained his coffee and pushed back from the table. He took his dishes to the sink and picked up his coat from the back of his chair. "Well, I'm off." He leaned down and kissed Megan on the lips, then stood and turned to Linda. "I can't tell you how grateful I am that you came all this way."

Linda smiled. "It's what mothers do."

"Rest assured I'm going to reimburse you for the cost of this trip."

"Oh, Jonathan, don't be ridiculous!"

"I'm afraid I have to insist, so you don't have a choice in the matter. I trust you ladies will try and stay out of trouble today?"

"Don't worry," said Linda. "I'll keep an eye on her."

Jonathan smiled. "Said the wild woman from Alaska."

After he left, Megan poured them both more coffee from the carafe on the table. "I'm going to miss you when you head back to the States."

Linda stirred in the cream. "So, it's 'the States' now, is it?"

"Excuse me?"

"You're starting to speak like a Brit."

"You think so?"

"Well, I suppose it was bound to happen."

Megan laughed. "Are you okay with it?"

"Of course. Why?"

"Just checking." Megan smiled. "Because if you think *I* speak like a Brit, just wait till your grandchild starts talking!"

Linda choked on her swallow of coffee. "My *what?!*"

Megan grinned. "You heard me."

"Oh my God! Megan, why didn't you tell me!"

"We only found out last week. And then this... episode happened. I wanted to make sure I was in the clear before I told you."

Linda went over and hugged her daughter around the neck. "Oh, that's wonderful news!"

In an exaggerated English accent, Megan said, "Yes, Mum. I rathuh think it is, too."

∽∽∽

As Scott spent the rest of the day making his rounds, there was one place in particular he made it a point to stop by.

He entered Danny's tavern and took a seat at the bar. He ordered a Danny's Pale Ale from Pam, who had stepped in to run the business.

Barbara was bustling from table to table. When she saw him, she gave a little squeal and rushed over. Scott happily submitted to her big-armed bear hug.

Even though it was unusually cold out—not the best weather for drinking ale—the place was busy. He took this as a sign that Danny's Tavern was going make it just fine. He drained the last of his ale. On his way out the door, he gave Pam a hug.

As he climbed into his car, he decided on impulse to take himself to a late lunch on the Poulsbo waterfront. After glancing at his watch, he realized it would be more of an early dinner, but what the hell. He hadn't been back to the Viking Broiler since Betty had left. Since he was going to call her, he figured it would be okay to go back to the restaurant which he had once vowed never to return to.

He sat in a booth enjoying a cheeseburger and reading the newspaper. As he flipped past the obituaries to get to the comics page, something caught his eye: the death notice for Julie Hamilton, accompanied by a color photograph.

Scott stared at the image of an attractive, serious-looking woman of 38. Her eyes, dark and glistening, stared back at him.

Something compelled him to read her obituary. Julie Hamilton's career as a Professor of Geology at the University of Oregon was summarized in a few short paragraphs. There was a brief mention of her research on new procedures to combat global warming. While traveling to give a presentation at a conference in Port Townsend, her life was cut short by a freak accident. She had never married and there were no siblings; she was survived by her parents.

He was still gazing at her picture when the waitress appeared at his table. "Are you doing okay over here?" she asked.

Startled, he looked up. "Uh, yeah. Everything's great, thanks."

The young waitress glanced at the newspaper to see what he was so engrossed in and frowned. "That's that poor woman who was killed last week. It was on the news. It's so sad."

"It's tragic. She had so much going for her."

"Did you know her?"

"What makes you ask that?"

"The way you were looking at her picture. I thought maybe you knew her."

He looked at the photo again. "No. I didn't. But... it's weird. She seems familiar to me, somehow."

"Can I get you anything else?"

"No, thanks. Just the check, please."

He turned to the comics, but found he couldn't concentrate. He didn't know the woman, but something was making him wish he had. The waitress returned with the check.

"Think we'll get snow?"

Scott dug in his wallet for cash. "It sure seems cold enough. Is it supposed to?"

"On last night's news, the weather lady said a big storm is brewing out in the Pacific. She wasn't sure if it was heading up into Canada or coming in our direction, but we'll know by tomorrow."

"Hm! I guess we'll just have to wait and see."

"I love the snow. I hope we get a ton of it!"

Scott shook his head. "I'm not a big fan myself."

On his way home, he stopped by Central Market. As usual, Mike was working in the produce section.

"Hello, stranger," he said, cutting a wedge from an apple and handing it to Scott. "Where've you been?"

"I've been around." He took a bite of the wedge. Mike usually fed him samples of great produce.

"You haven't been in here for a while."

"Yes, I have."

"I haven't seen you."

"That's because I always talk to the checkers first to find out if you're working or not. I time my shopping so I can avoid you!"

"I can't tell you how cheerful that makes me, knowing my presence offends you!"

They both laughed.

"These are good. Got any more?"

"Fresh shipment just came in. How many do you want?"

"I'll take four."

Mike never hesitated to open up a case of fresh produce for Scott to taste. He returned from the back room and handed Scott the bag of apples.

"There better not be any bites taken out of these."

"Well, I did accidentally drop a couple of them. They rolled around on the floor a while. I hope that's okay."

"I don't mind a little grit. It makes for good roughage."

"So what's on your agenda this week?"

"I was thinking it'd be nice to take a break from this weather and go someplace warm."

"Yeah, you and me both! Unfortunately, I still have to work for a living."

"At least it keeps you out of trouble."

"What if I don't want to keep out of trouble?"

"Thanks for the apples."

When Scott got home, he fed Jake an early dinner, poured a glass of wine, and took it into the living room. He stood at the window watching a vast bank of leaden clouds descending over the Olympic Mountains. It definitely looked like some interesting weather was coming.

He went over to the leather chair and sat down. Placing

his glass on the coffee table, he began rummaging through a drawer of an end table. When he found what he was looking for—a slightly tattered address book—he paged through it until he came to Betty's number. He started to reach for the receiver, but couldn't bring himself to do it for several minutes. "Oh, hell," he finally spat out, and forced his hand to pick up the phone and dial.

On the fourth ring, a woman answered.

"Hello?"

"Hello, Betty?"

"Yes?"

"It's Scott Northwood."

"Scott Northwood!" she said, sounding friendly and surprised. "As I live and breathe!"

"Keep living and keep breathing."

"How the hell are you?"

"I'm fine. I just thought I'd call and see how you're doing."

"I'm doing great! It's nice to hear your voice."

"Good to hear yours, too."

The next day at 2 p.m., Linda's flight from London touched down at SeaTac Airport. She slept for much of the eleven-hour trip, and got off the plane feeling rested.

As she left the International Arrivals terminal to retrieve her car, she was shocked at how cold it was. Pulling her coat tight around her, she put her head down and walked fast.

By the time she turned down her street, light snow flurries were spinning through the air. The sky had become a low, solid mass of clouds that pressed down on the earth like a slab of gray granite.

Getting out of the car, she looked up at the glowering clouds and sighed. Well, she thought, it was early December, which meant short days, long nights, and harsh weather.

But the weather was not going to dampen her mood. She grabbed her luggage and went into the house. She turned up the heat, cranked up her sound system, and started to unpack; then put some chicken noodle soup on the stove with the burner on low. By the time she finished unpacking, the soup was ready, and ten minutes later she was taking a long hot shower.

From the time she got off the plane to pulling on clean jeans and a sweatshirt after her shower, she was thinking about the phone call she was going to make to Scott. For days, she worked on what to say, and by now she was pretty confident about how it would go. She was nervous, sure, but she was excited.

The moment was actually here, and suddenly a tidal wave of doubt surged through her.

She was terrified.

Closing her eyes tight, she forced herself to take long slow breaths.

I saw the way he looked at you, Megan had said.

Linda opened her eyes and pressed her lips together in a tight line. She had made a promise to her daughter and she was damn well going to keep it. Suddenly, for the first time, she realized there was more to it than that: this had become a promise to herself.

She turned off the music and tried to get comfortable on the couch. Then she picked up the phone and dialed, surprised to see that her hand was shaking.

God, she hoped Megan was right. Please, please be right, Megan!

After the fourth ring, Scott's answering machine picked up. She hadn't expected that. She was debating whether or not to leave a message when Scott's live voice suddenly cut in. He sounded agitated and out of breath.

"Hello! Hello! Don't hang up! I'm here. This is Scott."

Linda bit her lip, too flustered to say anything.

"Hello? Is anybody there?"

"Hi, Scott."

"Who's this?"

She thought she detected disappointment, as if he'd expected it to be someone else. "It's me. Linda."

There was a confused pause. Then, "Linda *Hillis*?"

"That's right."

"Wow... You're about the last person in the world I..." his voice trailed off.

"Expected to call?"

"Something like that..." He sounded guarded. "Why *are* you calling?"

The speech Linda had been working on for days promptly went out the window.

"Uh... I was wondering if... maybe..."

"Yes?"

She blurted, "I was wondering if I could meet you someplace where we could talk."

"What did you want to talk about?" His voice had become a whisper.

"Well, I... wanted to apologize. About when you came over the other week. For being so short with you. It was late, I was tired and I—"

"You have nothing to apologize for," he said. "It was pretty presumptuous of me to say the things I did that night. In fact, I'm the one who should be apologizing to you."

"I don't blame you if you're feeling bitter. And I certainly don't expect you to—"

"I don't feel bitter in the least toward you," he said. "You're right, I was hurt. But I'm a big boy. Things don't always turn out the way I want."

She felt a surge of panic in her chest. This was not at all going the way she expected. "But—I thought that... if we could just meet. Even for a few minutes. I—"

"Linda, I'm so sorry, but I have to leave in a few minutes. I am really so sorry."

With those words he hung up.

Linda stared at the phone in disbelief. She sat back, trying to comprehend what had just happened.

"'I reach out and he hangs up on me!" She realized she had said these words out loud.

A cauldron of emotions boiled up inside her. She felt stunned and hurt. Confused. Humiliated.

But mostly, she felt angry.

Chapter 19

THE STORM

Scott perched on the edge of his leather chair watching live TV coverage of the massive snowstorm that was beginning to engulf the Puget Sound Region. He was supposed to be flying in a couple of hours, but he couldn't seem to move. Since Linda's phone call, he hadn't stirred an inch from where he sat, thinking about the phone call and what a fool he had made of himself.

"—as Seattle braces for what could be its biggest weather event in over a decade," said the anchor, sounding both grim and gleeful to be delivering such ominous news.

Scott glanced at a swirling mass of snowflakes outside. Here on a ridge top, the snow was accumulating faster than it was down in Poulsbo, at sea level. There must have been at least four inches on the ground already, but it was hard to be sure in the dark.

Television news cut to a live report from the airport. As thick, wet flakes cascaded around her, a female reporter in a hooded jacket announced, "We've just been informed by the Director of Operations here at SeaTac that, for all intents and purposes, the airport is closed. The rest of today's outgoing flights have all been cancelled. All incoming flights have been rerouted to Portland. And right now, word is that it will remain that way through at least part of tomorrow."

Scott breathed out a sigh. Strangely, he felt something that he hadn't expected—*pure relief.* He turned and looked down at Jake, who was lying on his side dozing happily in front of the blazing fire.

"Looks like I'm not going anywhere." Jake opened one eye and looked up. "And you won't be getting boarded at the vet's."

The dog closed his eye and resumed snoozing. Scott wished he could do the same, but the words he'd spoken on the phone were echoing in his head. He couldn't understand why he'd said those things to Linda. All this time, he'd been longing for her, wishing she would change her mind, and now she'd called him – and what did he do? He'd told her to go away.

He had begun to understand his fears of getting involved, but he'd thought he was past them, that he was ready to take another person into his life, ready to love. Now he knew how frightened he was of being left, of feeling the terror that had been his when his parents died. Of allowing someone to come in close, and risk losing them. He had believed that acknowledging this, understanding this, would change him. But instead he'd said nothing when she'd called. He hadn't said how happy he was to hear her voice, nor that he would always love her, always miss her. No, he'd turned back into the robotic version of a man that he'd been for all these years. And this time, there would be no second chance.

There was a sudden pounding at the front door. Jake jumped up and began to bark. Scott hit the mute button for the TV and went to open the door.

Linda stomped into the house. Her hair and the jean jacket she wore over her sweatshirt were mottled with fresh snow, just from the short walk from her car to the door.

"You've got some nerve!"

Scott backed away as she marched toward him. He wanted to shout, *I love you, please don't ever leave me*, but he couldn't even speak.

Caramel eyes flashing with anger, she came to a halt in front of him. "You come over to my home and wait in the freezing cold to confess your undying love for me. And then a couple of weeks later, it's suddenly 'Sorry, gotta run!' Like you couldn't care less. Who in the hell do you think you are?!"

He knew he should be apologizing to her, begging her to stay, but what he heard himself say was, "What did you expect? I went to your house and poured my heart out, *bared my soul to you!* And what was your response? *Sorry, pal, but I need a break from men.*"

Jake sat off to the side to watch the two human beings quarrel.

"Don't try and change the subject. What you said to me was insulting and a cop-out."

"You drove all the way up here in the snow just to tell me that?"

"Oh, I'm just getting started!"

"How do you know where I live?"

"I finally get my nerve up to call you, and you can't get me off the phone fast enough!"

They both stopped shouting for a moment and stared at each other. Finally, in a quiet voice, he asked, "What do you mean, 'get your nerve up'?"

Linda's anger seemed to subside. He noticed the gleam of a tear in the corner of her eye.

"Megan told me she thought you and I would make an amazing couple."

"She said that?"

Linda nodded.

His voice grew softer. "What else did she say?"

Linda stared at him a moment before replying, as if trying to decide what more to divulge. She took a breath and said, "She thought I had another chance with you, and that I should take it. She said that we need to hold on to second chances with all our might. That's why I wanted to meet with you. I was going to ask you for that chance. I was going to beg you if I had to. But before any of that could happen, you blew me off like you were swatting a fly."

"Linda, I..." He loved her, he wanted to beg her forgiveness, but once again he couldn't find the courage.

"You don't have to say anything at all." Then a note of finality entered her voice. "And maybe we should just leave it at that."

Fighting back tears, she turned toward the door.

"Linda, wait. Don't go."

She stopped and looked back, now noticing the luggage stacked near the front door.

"Looks like you're going on a trip."

"Yeah, I was trying to get out of town before the storm hit. That's why I sounded so abrupt when you called. Turns out they just closed the airport." He gestured at the muted television where a live camera showed snow-covered runways.

Linda looked over at Jake. There was a candle flame of warmth in her voice as she said, "Is that your dog?"

"Jake, meet Linda."

She got down on her knees, and started scratching the side of his neck. "Hello, Jake. I've heard about you." He exposed more of his neck for her to scratch while watching her with serious brown eyes.

The phone rang. "I'm sure that's the airline calling to tell me my flight's cancelled. I'll just let the machine pick—"

The answering machine kicked on in the kitchen, just loud enough for them to hear the message being left. *"Hey, Scott! It's Betty down here in sunny Arizona!"*

"I think maybe I should get that," said Scott, dashing into the kitchen.

"Are you still coming down?" Betty's voice continued on the machine. *"Because I just saw on the news that Seattle is getting buried in—"*

He grabbed the phone. "Hi, Betty, it's me. Listen, I'm afraid I won't be coming down after all. ...Yeah, they just closed the airport. ...I'm sorry, too. Listen, can I call you back in a few minutes? Something urgent has come up that I need to take care of. ...Thanks."

He hung up and hurried into the living room.

But Linda was gone.

He ran out the front door in time to see the taillights of her ten-year-old Toyota Camry disappear down his snow-covered driveway.

The winding tree-lined road that led to Scott's house could be tricky enough to navigate in heavy rain during the daytime, let alone in snow at night. And there were no streetlights.

The wind had picked up considerably since Linda had arrived. Snow was blowing horizontally, making it that much harder for her to keep her bearings as she drove down Ridgetop Lane. To make matters worse, her anger had returned—not so much at Scott, but at herself, which didn't help her driving any.

"God, I should've known!" she shouted into the air. Wind-whipped snow caught by the headlights did a chaotic dance in front of the car. "*Why*, Linda? Why did you come up here?! You stupid, stupid woman. You never should have—*shit!*"

Heading down a slope on a hairpin turn, the Camry suddenly lost traction. In what seemed like slow motion to Linda, her car spun around 180 degrees and slid sideways off the road into a ditch. When it came to rest on its passenger side, she found herself hanging by her seatbelt at an awkward angle.

"It's okay," she said to herself in a shaky voice. "Don't panic. You can do this."

The engine was still running. Fearful of a fire, she turned off the ignition, and managed to unbuckle her seatbelt. Taking a moment to catch her breath, she was able to shove the door open just wide enough for her to crawl out of the vehicle.

As she got to her feet, she was grateful that she hadn't been hurt. And except for it being on its side, the car appeared to be relatively undamaged. But she was definitely going to need a tow truck. She reached into her pocket for her cellphone.

It wasn't there.

With a dull shock, she remembered leaving it on the nightstand in her bedroom as she'd unpacked. When Scott hung up on her, she'd been so mad that she'd grabbed her coat and stormed out the door.

She forced herself to remain calm as she thought about how to get out of this predicament. The most obvious thing was to walk to the nearest house and ask for help. But this was a sparsely populated road. She didn't see any houses. And she didn't have a flashlight. Moving around in the dark, she could easily wander off the road and get lost.

Fortunately, the headlights of her car were pointed back up the hill. And right at the very edge of the light, she could see something metallic that *might* be a gate that *might* have a house behind it.

It was a struggle to walk in the deepening snow. After a few minutes, she arrived at an electric gate, the entry to a large fenced property. The panic that had been building in her chest turned to relief.

Through the bars of the gate, she could just make out the shape of a massive house, completely dark in the swirling snow. She located the control buttons for the intercom.

"Hello!" she shouted into the box. "Is anybody home? Can you hear me? I need help! This is an emergency!"

No response.

She tried several more times, but no one answered. The wind had started to blow even harder and it was becoming increasingly colder. She had to make a decision. She was going to have to break into the house just to survive. If that meant setting off a burglar alarm, well, at least the police would come and find her.

She climbed to the top of the wrought iron fence and was lowering herself to the other side when a deep growl came out of the darkness below her.

Stifling a scream, she pulled herself back up and over the gate and dropped to the ground. A large black German Shepard that had been lying quietly in wait lunged at the fence, snarling and barking.

Linda scrambled away in terror. When she was able to catch her breath, she looked down the hill at her stranded car. The headlights were dimming.

The battery was going dead.

Shivering from cold and fear, she stood in the dark, snow-covered road, unsure what to do. The panic flooded back. She fought to keep it in check as she considered her options, none of them good.

She could try walking down to the main road to find some traffic. It was less than a mile away, and it was all downhill. But her clothes were wet from sweat and melted snow, so even if she managed to stay on the road, she might die of hypothermia before she made it off the ridge.

Another option was to try hiking up, back to Scott's house. Though it was over a mile away, her tire tracks could help guide her back, keeping her from straying off the road. The biggest drawback would be feeling for the ruts with every step. It would make for slow going. At the rate it was snowing, the tracks might be filled in long before she made it to Scott's.

The third choice was to climb back inside the shelter of the car until somebody came along—which probably wouldn't be until morning. She'd be in for a long, cold night. She could still freeze, but at least she'd be out of the wind and snow. It might just work. The only other danger, a remote one at that, was the possibility of a fuel leak in the engine that could—

Whumpf! The Camry flared into a yellow ball of fire.

Linda watched the flames consume her only realistic hope of living through the night. She was down to her last two options, but she knew that neither of them would do her any good. She was suddenly very afraid.

Her fury at herself came roaring back. She was probably going to die out here; God, what a dumb and pointless way to go. She gave a humorless laugh as she thought of what would be a perfect epitaph: "Here Lies Poor Linda Hillis, Victim of Death by Stupidity."

She watched as the flames gradually died down. Now she was shivering violently from the cold. Hoping for a last few minutes of warmth before she made her decision on which way to hike, she began walking down to the burning wreckage of her car.

At that moment, she heard something behind her. She turned and saw the glare of headlights rounding a curve; a four wheel drive vehicle moving laboriously. As it drew near, she frantically waved her arms, hoping she could be seen in the driving snow. It pulled even with her and stopped.

Scott rolled down the window. "Young lady, don't you know it's against the law to hitchhike in the state of Washington?"

She was so cold she could barely speak. "Very. Funny."

Only then did he notice the burning vehicle down the hill. "Jees, Linda! Are you all right?!"

"I'm just. Cold. Really really. Cold."

He leapt out, led her around to the passenger side and helped her in. Then he climbed in and turned the heater on full blast. He carefully backed the Range Rover up to the gated fence, where there was enough room to turn around.

"Where. Are we. Going."

"Back to my place."

"Can't. You just. Take me home."

"Linda. The storm. There's major road closures from here to Bremerton because of downed trees. We might not make it. Besides, you need to get warm—and fast! Don't worry, I promise you'll have total privacy. I've got a couple of spare bedrooms."

She nodded. A wave of exhaustion hit her and she closed her eyes. "What made. You drive. Down here."

"Toyota Camrys don't come with four-wheel drive. I was worried you wouldn't make it down to the main road."

She opened her eyes. "I didn't. Obviously."

"Driving in this stuff can be treacherous," he said. Afraid she might drift off into a hypothermia-induced sleep, he kept talking. "The first winter I lived here, my BMW got stuck every time it went below freezing. I'm a California boy originally. I've never felt real comfortable driving in the

snow. So, using my brilliant analytical abilities, I concluded that I needed a car with four-wheel drive. As an extra
precaution, I even have snow tires put on at the beginning
of every winter. It's worked out fine—until today. In all the
time I've lived here, I've never seen this much snow."

He looked over at her. She seemed—finally—to be warming up.

"I grew up here," she said. "And even I. Had no idea. It
was going to get. This bad."

"Neither did anyone else, apparently. The weather fore-
casters are all scratching their heads and making excuses."

The Range Rover lumbered steadily up the ridge. Scott
had to fight the wheel to keep the car on the road.

With his eyes focused ahead, he suddenly blurted out,
"Just so you know. I dated Betty up until over a year ago,
when she moved to Scottsdale. I hadn't even talked to her
until yesterday. I only called her because a certain person
had recently made it thoroughly, indelibly clear to me that
she wanted nothing to do with me."

"Maybe the airport will open. Tomorrow. You can go.
And see her then."

He was stung but tried not to show it.

"You really are. In a hurry to get down there. And see her.
Aren't you?"

"Only in about as much a hurry as you when you went to
Alaska to live with Captain Jack."

Linda turned and glared at him. "Now, wait just a minute," she said. "That's not fair and you know it. You were
the one who said 'some things just aren't meant to be', remember? You were the one who—"

"Linda. Linda. Easy. Tell you what. Let's call a truce,
okay? At least until it's safe enough for me to drive you
home. Let's promise to talk only about neutral things.
Pleasant things. Like religion. Or politics. Or terrorism."

His attempt to lighten things up worked. He saw the hint
of a smile out of the corner of his eye.

"Let's agree not to say anything that's going to push anyone's buttons, okay?" he said. "Let's just try and get through the night. What do you say?"

"I say truce."

"Good. Me, too."

An hour later, after a long hot shower and a bowl of steaming soup, Linda sat on the floor of the living room close to the fire, dressed in his sweatpants and sweatshirt, with a flannel robe over that. The fit was baggy but comfortable. Jake dozed close by and she was stroking his wiry fur.

Scott came in carrying two mugs of hot cocoa. He handed one to her and sat down.

"Thank you," she said.

"Your clothes are in the dryer."

She took a sip and enjoyed the heat moving from the mug into her hands. "Gee. I can't remember the last time I had cocoa."

"It's a perfect night for it."

A powerful gust of wind slammed into the big picture window, causing it to vibrate in its frame, and Linda shuddered. She took another sip and stared into the snapping flames. "There's something about a crackling fire on a cold, snowy night that I love. In Alaska, the winters are so long and dark that—" She caught herself. "Sorry. I think I just violated the terms of the truce."

"That's all right," said Scott. "It means you're warm and relaxed."

"I am. You seem pretty relaxed yourself."

"Do I?"

She turned and faced him. She peered into his eyes, as if seeing him for the first time. "Actually, yes. You do."

"Why are you looking at me like that?"

"There's something... different about you."

"I got a haircut the other day."

She laughed. "No, it's something else. I can't put my finger on it. You just seem more... at ease with things. With yourself. With me. I wonder why that is?"

"I haven't a clue."

She continued to stroke Jake's fur.

"I like hearing you laugh," said Scott.

She smiled. They settled into a comfortable silence, neither feeling the need to speak. Instead, they savored the cocoa and listened to the crackling fire mingle with the sounds of the storm beating against the house.

Jake flipped over onto his back, presenting his belly for Linda to scratch.

"Someone's in doggie heaven," mused Scott.

"I love dogs. I grew up with a passel of them."

"Why don't you have a dog now?"

"It wouldn't be right. To leave him home alone all day while I'm at work."

"I suppose so."

They were silent a moment. Then she said, "Thank you."

"For what?"

"For coming to get me."

"You're welcome. I'm sorry about your car."

"Yeah! Me, too. At least it was insured. And I've got some savings set aside so I can—oh!"

Linda gasped as the power went out, plunging the house into darkness. The only remaining light came from the fire, which illuminated the room with an orange, shadowy glow.

"I thought that might happen," he sighed. "Wait here while I round up some flashlights and candles." He glanced down at her and smiled. "If any wolves or bears try to get in while I'm gone, don't worry. Jake will protect you."

Twenty minutes later, Scott had placed candles all through the house. He stoked the fire into a blaze and sat back down beside Linda.

"With the power out, it's going to get cold tonight," he said. "There's an extra down quilt on the top shelf of the closet in your bedroom. I like to keep things ready in case my sister comes to visit."

"How often does she come and see you?"

"Uh, actually, she's never been here."

"That's too bad. Are you in some kind of feud with her? Because, believe me, I know sometimes families can be—"

"Oh, no, it's nothing like that. We get along fine. I go to Atlanta every couple of years to see them. But she and her husband have only so many vacation days a year. And her two boys like going to Disney World and the Florida beaches. Plus they're always tight on money, but they're so darn adamant about not letting me pay their way up here. So... I end up not seeing her very often."

They fell quiet again. The firelight and flickering candles made the room dark and mysterious, yet cozy and safe at the same time as the storm raged outside.

Finally Linda said, "Can I ask you something?"

"Sure. Just so long as it's neutral and pleasant."

"How come you never married?"

He shrugged. "I guess I just never found the right person." This wasn't even close to the truth, but he was too scared of breaking their peace to go into the real story.

"Have you ever lived with anyone?"

"Yes. Twice. Both very short-lived."

"Did you love them?"

Choosing his words with care, Scott said, "Yes, I suppose I did love them."

"You *suppose?*"

"Yes. But I was never actually *in love* with them."

"Hmm. You're saying there's a difference between loving someone and being *in love?*"

"Yes," he said, his eyes searching hers. "That's what I'm saying. You don't agree?"

"I never quite looked at it that way, but... yes, I suppose there is a difference."

"There's all the difference in the world."

They gazed at each for a moment. Scott was the one to break the quiet. He cleared his throat and said, "There's another reason why I never married."

"Tell me."

"I was a total workaholic. I didn't have time for much of anything else."

"Why were you a workaholic?"

"Huh?" The question caught him off guard.

"I said, why you were such a workaholic?"

"No one's ever asked me that before." He stared into the fire as he thought about it. "It was just the demands of the job, I guess... I liked to keep busy."

"And now, because you're retired, you can keep as busy—or as *not* busy—as you want."

"True. But, working or not, I still like having control over my life."

Linda's eyes darkened. "There's that word again."

"Look, I don't mean it the way you think."

"What way do you mean it?"

He thought about her question, trying to make sense of it himself. "When Danny died, it all came rushing back."

"Wait a minute. I'm confused here. Who's Danny? And *what* came rushing back?"

Tears came suddenly into Scott's eyes.

"Scott? What's the matter? Are you okay?"

His voice came out just above a whisper. "It's been a long time since I've talked to anyone about this."

Her voice was gentle. "About what?"

He took a slow shuddering breath. Then he said, "Have you ever heard the expression, 'Bad things come in threes'?"

"Of course. Why?"

He began to tell her about the year he turned fourteen. About his dog Sam. About his best friend Harry. About his parents.

She listened without speaking, occasionally uttering quiet sounds of sympathy and compassion.

"...I ran over to try and help them," said Scott, his voice strained. "To do something. Anything! But they were buried under the wreckage. The one thing I could see was...

was my mother's arm... sticking out from under the debris. It was covered with blood. I took her hand and... and..."

Linda took his hand as Scott struggled to compose himself.

"Mom and dad were the only people killed in the accident."

"My God..." said Linda, her voice very soft. "I can't even begin to imagine what you..."

"There was a big investigation into the cause of the accident. It ended up being a combination of a lot of different things: inferior steel from China; an under-experienced crane operator; defective anchor bolts; faulty support collars; city inspectors not properly doing their jobs. Any one of these... if they hadn't happened... or had happened in another, ever-so-slightly altered way... would have caused that crane to not come down *right where and when it did*."

He shook his head. "It really makes you think, you know?"

She didn't say anything, just let him talk.

"Anyway. That was the straw that broke the camel's back. Or, I guess you could say it was more like a sledgehammer. It was enough to make a fourteen year old kid have a breakdown. I just... shut down. Completely. I was institutionalized for a year."

"Oh, Scott..."

"After I got out, I went to live with Uncle Walter and Aunt Sally. Shelly was already there. They took good care of us. There was an insurance settlement, so we were able to go to college."

The fire crackled. The wind whistled.

"I've been told that when I was a kid, I was overly sensitive. That I took everything so seriously. So personally. But then after... what happened, I became just the opposite. I wasn't sensitive to anything. School—and then work—were my refuge. It was only after I stopped working and moved here that things began to change. Finding Jake. Getting to know Danny. Becoming friends with him..."

Linda shook her head, gently prodding, "I still don't know

who...”

“He owned Danny’s Tavern?”

“Of course. I’ve sold a ton of his ale at the Food King.”

“That’s the guy. He died over a year ago. Fell off a ladder while changing a light bulb.”

“What?”

“Yeah. That’s when it all came rushing back to me. I felt like I was going to... shut down again. But then, meeting Megan... And then you... I think it pretty much kept me from going off the deep end.”

Linda smiled. “That’s nice of you to say.”

He looked intently at her. “I mean it.”

“...Okay.”

A note of urgency entered his voice. “So *that’s* what I mean when I say I like to have some control over things in my life. Maybe I can at least minimize the chances that people—and dogs —” Scott nodded at Jake asleep on the floor— “who’ve come to mean something to me don’t suddenly get killed in some totally random, meaningless, *preventable* way. It may or may not be possible to do, but, still, I have to at least *try*.”

Embarrassed by the passion of his tirade, he shrugged. “Sorry. I didn’t mean to get so worked up.”

“Oh, Scott, that’s okay. Now I understand why you—”

An ear-splitting crash came from very close outside. The ground shuddered. Jake jumped up barking out of a dead sleep.

“God, what was that?” Linda sounded terrified.

“It must have been a tree coming down.”

He got up and grabbed a flashlight. With Linda at his side, they went to the front door and opened it. He shone the beam out into the surrounding forest. A hemlock tree at least fifty feet tall lay about a hundred yards from the house.

“Wow! The trees are top-heavy with snow,” he said. The two of them stood in the doorway watching the trees bending in the wind. “I wouldn’t be surprised if more come down. But don’t worry. When I built this house, I made sure that—”

There was another huge *craaack*. The entire house shook as a hundred-foot Douglas fir crashed to the ground less than thirty feet away. Crying out in fear, Linda clung tightly to Scott.

"It's okay," he said, suddenly aware of her body's warmth and softness pressing against him. She was trembling. He closed the door and put his arms around her in an effort to calm her. "We're safe," he whispered. "I was just saying that, when I built this house, I made sure that... no trees would be..."

She looked up into his face continuing to cleave to him. The whiteness of the snow coming in through the windows provided just enough light so they could see each other's eyes. Her breath was warm and sweet. "...would be in striking distance of... of... "

The power of his feelings for her could no longer be denied. He pulled her to him and their lips came together through no conscious decision. He had been fighting the inevitable for too long, and perhaps she had as well. Now it was impossible for either of them to keep up the charade any longer. Their kisses seemed as natural as rain falling from the sky or the sun rising in the morning.

Then they were in Scott's bed, neither of them having any idea how they got there. They removed each other's clothes with breathless urgency. With a desperate hunger, Linda pulled Scott to her. Oblivious to the wind that circled and lunged at the house like a wild animal, they made love with a passion and ferocity neither had ever experienced. Now and then another tree would come crashing down, but the terrifying sound would make them cling together ever more tightly. Finally, completely spent, they fell into a deep, exhausted sleep.

They awoke next morning in a tangle of arms, legs, pillows and blankets. The wind had stopped and there wasn't a cloud in the sky. Crisp, clear sunlight flooded into the room through the windows.

Linda snuggled up close and rested her head on Scott's chest. "Good morning," he said.

"Good morning, yourself," she said with a sleepy smile. Her eyes were closed against the light.

"Now that's what I call a truce," he said.

Her quiet laughter was both shy and lascivious.

"Maybe we should keep this truce thing going for a while," said Scott. "I mean, it's only right that we do our part to promote world peace. What do you think?"

"I'm all for world peace."

"Not as much as I am."

"Oh, I don't know about that..." She finally opened her eyes and started to stretch. She caught a glimpse of what lay outside the windows and sat upright. "Oh my God..."

Everything as far as the eye could see was covered in snow that sparkled like it was made of diamonds. In the distance, the Olympic Mountain Range soared glistening into the heavens, backed by a sky so intensely blue it was almost purple. Gazing out at the magical landscape, Linda felt as if she were in a fairy tale.

"I've never seen anything so beautiful," she whispered.

"Neither have I."

She glanced at him and saw that he was drinking in the sight of her naked body. With her tousled hair and soft, silky skin, she looked dangerously sexy. She crawled back under the covers and pulled close to him. Her scent was a sweet, dusky blend of sex and dried sweat, and he found himself becoming aroused.

"So. Where were we?" she said, as she ran her hand over his body.

He caught his breath and swallowed. He managed to say, "I think we were talking about world peace..."

When her hand found him, she whispered in delight. "Yes. Now I remember..."

Later, emerging from a post-coitus haze, Scott noticed Jake standing next to the bed.

"Well, good morning, Jake."

The dog flapped his ears, huffed at them, and trotted out of the room.

"That means he's got to go out."

Scott put on his robe, stepped into his slippers and followed Jake down the hall.

Linda lay in bed a few minutes longer staring at the view. As beautiful as it was outside, the power was still out and the house was very cold. She shivered as she pulled on her sweats and her robe, and then wrapped a down quilt around herself. When she walked into the living room, Scott had just come back in with Jake.

"Boy! You weren't kidding when you said it was going to get cold!" she said. As if to emphasize her words, she could see her breath when she spoke.

"Yeah. The fire's completely out."

"How long do you think it will be before the power comes back on?"

"Hard to say." He knelt down and toweled the snow from Jake's legs and paws. "I bet a lot of power lines got turned into spaghetti last night. It could be some time. Maybe days. In the meanwhile, it looks like we're going to have to rough it. Are you game?"

"Sure," was her cheerful answer.

"I'll get the fire started. You can boil some water in the fireplace for a sponge bath. I think I have a box of Cheerios. We can have that for breakfast. Or..."

He walked over to the wall next to the entrance to the kitchen. He opened a panel and flipped a switch. Somewhere outside, the motor of a generator coughed to life. The furnace came on within seconds.

"...how about a hot bath and eggs benedict instead?"

"What! You mean you had a generator all along?"

He shrugged and his eyes sparkled. "Guilty as charged. The power goes out all the time up here in the winter."

"But then—why didn't you turn it on last night?"

His smile was wicked. "Because there's something about a crackling fire on a cold, snowy night that I love."

She narrowed her eyes. "Scott Northwood."

"Yes?"

"Do you mean to tell me you were *planning* on something happening between us last night?" she said.

He was suddenly uncomfortable. He hoped he hadn't screwed up. "I can't say I was planning on anything. That something might happen, I mean. . ."

She didn't say anything. Just watched him with those eyes of warm and tremulous caramel.

"I hope you're not sorry about any of it," he said, aghast at the thought. "Because if you are, I don't know what I—"

"I'm not sorry." She walked toward him. Her face broke into a smile as she stood looking up at him. He touched the crooked corner of that smile, and her voice became a delicate whisper. "...As a matter of fact, what I am, is very, very happy." A single tear trailed down her cheek. Scott reached out and embraced her, holding on as if he would never let her go.

And so it happened that for the first and only time in his 53 years of existence on this earth, Scott Northwood fell genuinely in love.

He and Linda were snowed in for three perfect days. During that time, no one else in the world existed but them. He tried to recall any time in his life when he had been happier. Nothing even came close.

They spent most of each day outside playing in the snow like kids. They built snowmen and had snowball fights and snow-shoed through the woods with Jake.

Nights, they would build a fire and cook a leisurely meal together. They ate by candlelight and talked far into the evening. They enjoyed each hour they spent getting to know each other.

Then it would be time for bed. Their physical attraction

was a force of nature. From the first time they'd made love, it was as if they had been let in on a vast and amazing secret, as if a door to another dimension of life suddenly swung open. There was an intensity to their lovemaking that bordered on desperation, a craving so powerful it felt as if their bodies were trying to make up for all the years they had been apart. At times, the pleasure they experienced was so deep and exquisite that it crossed over into a kind of pain.

By the evening of the third day, the temperature warmed enough so that the next storm system came in the form of rain, turning much of the snow into slush. The next morning, they were able to drive down the ridge and rejoin the human race.

As the days went by, they were shocked at how quickly and intensely things progressed between them. They spent every possible moment together. Their compatibility was so eerily perfect that they decided it might be wise to pull back a little. They agreed to try and limit seeing each other to only a couple of times a week.

They failed miserably at this.

When it became obvious that they were never going to spend a night apart, Scott insisted—over Linda's vehement objections—that she quit her job, rent out her house, and move in with him. As the weeks went by, her protests weakened, and then stopped altogether. She finally gave in and it turned out to be the best decision she had made in many years. Living together drew them even closer. Megan had wanted her to be happy, Linda thought one night as she snuggled up next to Scott on the couch. If only she could see her now.

Scott continued taking Jake on his daily walks, and now Linda came too. It became a ritual of beauty and peace. Yet every now and then, something strange would happen on the trail. Jake would come to a stop and begin huffing and barking at something that only he seemed to see, something that made his tail go back and forth in broad happy strokes. Scott paid it no mind. He just racked it up as being another of his dog's many eccentricities.

He stopped watching reality TV shows; his own life had become so much more real with Linda in it. He did continue to watch local and national news, since she too was a bit of a news junkie. Most evenings, they would sit together with a glass of wine to see what events had transpired in the world that day. Because they each had their preferred stations, there were minor spats about which one to watch. More often than not, Scott just handed Linda the remote.

They were watching the local news on an unseasonably warm April night when it happened. Linda was flipping between several stations when Scott recognized a series entitled *Where Are They Now And How Are They Doing?* The series consisted of interviews with local people who had been in the news because something traumatic had happened to them. These shows updated how those folks were coping—or not coping—with their new, often drastically altered circumstances. Most of them were depressing to watch.

But not this one.

Scott caught a glimpse of someone interviewing a smiling Max Grabowsky just as Linda changed the channel.

"Could you turn that back?"

"Don't you want to see the weather?"

Something made him want to see the rest of it. "Just for a minute. Please."

She rolled her eyes and gave an exaggerated sigh, but returned to the segment.

The reporter was in the middle of a question. "—see how you're doing since that extremely close call you had last year."

"This may sound crazy," said Max, "but my brush with death was the best thing that ever happened to me."

"How so?"

"Well, the story got picked up by the national news. After it aired, the outpouring of donations from people around the country was incredible! I was able to buy a fleet of trucks and vans. Not only that, but dozens of restaurants throughout Puget Sound asked to be included on my food runs. I've been able to hire drivers to make sure all the food we pick up gets to needy families. It's fantastic! Plus, I've been working with folks in other cities who are interested in starting a similar charity. Some of them are already up and running. It's been so busy, I had to quit my day job so I could put all my energy into this full time!"

The reporter looked into the camera. "In case some of our viewers missed that remarkable footage taken from a bank's security camera, here it is."

The black and white footage appeared of Scott's flying tackle of Max Grabowsky a micro-second before his van was obliterated by the Cadillac.

"I still can't believe what happened," said Max, shaking his head. "I downloaded that video onto my iPhone. You know, whenever I start to feel stressed out or discouraged about something, I watch it. It really helps keep things in perspective. I'm just thankful I was given another chance to do the work I was put on this earth to do."

"Did you ever find out the name of the person who saved your life that day?"

Max took out his iPhone and fast-forwarded through the video until he found what he was looking for. He freeze-framed on the black and white image of Scott. The TV camera zoomed in on the grainy, out-of-focus shot.

"Nope. I never saw him again..."

"Scott..." said Linda. Her voice sounded strained.

The news camera continued to hold on the image.

"That's okay," Max went on, "I just chalk it up to being one of life's mysteries. But deep down in my heart, I am extremely grateful to him, whoever he is..."

The news camera panned back to the reporter. "Reporting from Pioneer Square, I'm—"

"Scott!"

Surprised at her outburst, he muted the TV and looked at her. "What's the matter?"

"...It's you."

"What are you talking about?"

"The man in the video. It's you!"

"That's impossible."

"Scott. Listen to me. I've gotten to know you so well. Every part of your face and body. Every crease. Every strand of your hair. Every little mole. Not to mention that old coat."

"Linda, that picture was so dark and blurry, it could be anyone."

"I'm telling you that it's you."

"And I'm telling you that it's not me."

"How can you be so certain?"

"How can I—Linda, listen to yourself! Look. If I *did* dive in front of a speeding car, I think I'd have a pretty clear memory of it. But I don't. Nothing like that has ever happened to me."

She continued to stare at him, unsure whether to believe him or not.

He rubbed the palms of his hands along his jeans. "I'm not lying to you, Linda. I would never lie to you."

"Then what *were* you doing that day?"

His face became damp with perspiration. He stood up and paced the room. "How the hell do I know what I was doing that day? I don't keep a diary. If you don't believe me, just say so."

She stood up and went over to him, placing her hands on his shoulders and looking into his eyes. "If you say that's not you in the footage, that's good enough for me."

"Okay. So can we drop this?"

"Yes. Please. Let's drop it. I'm sorry if I upset you."

He began to calm down. "Apology accepted." They embraced and held onto each other.

Finally she said, "What do you say we go make dinner?"

"I think that sounds great."

As the weeks and months went by, she sometimes thought back to that moment. She had never seen him so worked up. But she figured it was best to just let it go, and so she didn't bring it up again.

249

Chapter 20

JAKE

On a warm and sunny day in July, Scott, Linda, and Jake were out on their walk when they came across another couple with a dog. Other visitors to the park were so rare that people invariably stopped to chat—usually about dogs.

In their sixties, these people were tall and trim, with easy smiles. Their black Labrador retriever panted quietly as he shuffled along several steps behind them. His muzzle was gray with age. Jake hurried forward to greet him. Both tails wagged as the two dogs bumped their snouts together.

As the couples talked, Scott and Linda learned the lab's name was Konig. They also learned something else.

"Konig's a rescue dog," said the man. "We just got him last month."

"Rescued from where?" Linda asked.

"The Kitsap County pound."

Scott was confused. "Why would a dog need rescuing from the pound? It's a non-euthanasia facility."

The man and woman exchanged a sober glance.

"Not anymore," the woman said.

Scott was unable to hide his shock. "Are you sure?"

"I'm afraid it's true," said the man. "They started putting dogs down a couple months ago."

"Why?" said Linda.

"Budget cuts," the man answered. "That, combined with an increase in abandoned animals that they take in."

"Now they keep dogs for just a few weeks before... before putting them down," the woman chimed in.

"Oh, that's horrible!" said Linda.

Scott looked distressed. He watched Jake and Konig as they gently gnawed on each other.

Scott and Linda pulled out of the Autumn Lake parking lot, not saying a word all the way to the junction of State Route 3, the main north/south artery through Kitsap County. North would take them toward Poulsbo; south led to Bremerton.

He sat at the stop sign, thinking. Then, abruptly he turned south. He glanced at Linda, who looked back at him. She had a feeling about where he was headed and nodded her head in approval.

When the Range Rover pulled up at the Kitsap County Animal Control Services building, he got another shock. The last time he was here was almost seven years before—the day he'd come looking for a dog to adopt but instead had taken Jake in. It looked like the structure hadn't had any maintenance done in all that time. The paint was faded and peeling. Metal window frames were heavily rusted. An inch of moss had built up on the roof. Scott took something from the glove box and put it in his pocket, then strode toward the front door with Linda right behind him.

Inside, there was no one behind the counter. A steady cacophony of barks, whines, and yips came from dozens of unseen dogs somewhere in the back. A strong smell of feces and urine filled the air. They walked up to the Formica counter. Its surface was stained and cracked. A bell sat next to a crudely drawn sign that read, "RING FOR SERVICE." Scott hit the bell a lot harder than necessary.

A moment later, an overweight, exhausted-looking girl entered the room and stepped behind the counter. She wiped the sweat from her forehead with her dirty sleeve and said, "Yeah?"

"Who's in charge here?" he asked.

Linda realized that he was struggling to keep from losing his temper. She laid her hand on his arm.

"That would be my supervisor, Harlan Sweeney."

"And where would Mr. Sweeney be?"

"He's in back. Want me to get him?"

"Please."

She disappeared through the door.

Scott and Linda listened to the nonstop barking and howling. After several minutes, Mr. Sweeney came through the door. He was a lean, perpetually frowning man about Scott's age. His shirt was damp with sweat. As soon as he got behind the counter, he squeezed a blob of Purel into his hands from a giant plastic bottle. His demeanor was brusque to the point of rudeness.

"What do you want?" he said.

"Why are you killing the dogs?"

The man sighed in exasperation and his frown deepened into a scowl. He shook his head from side to side, then turned away from Scott and headed toward the back.

"Look, buddy, I've got work to do. If you wish to file a complaint with the county, you need to—"

"Hey!" shouted Scott, startling him, and causing him to stop and turn around. "Look, *buddy*! I asked you a question! I'll ask it again! Why are you killing the dogs?"

In a loud voice, Sweeney said, "'*Why?*' Do you think I enjoy it? Do you think I have a *choice?*"

It was Scott's turn to be startled as the man continued. "I'll tell you *why* we're killing the dogs. It's called cutbacks. Drastic cutbacks across the board. Which means no money. Which means letting staff go. Add to that an explosion in the number of unwanted animals and presto—I've got no one to help me take care of them, except Kelly back there. Christ, I'm barely able to feed the poor creatures."

Scott could tell from the anguish in Sweeney's voice that he was not so much angry as frustrated.

"I'm doing everything I can to find a home for these dogs.

But a lot of them are old or sick or have too many problems. I even adopted five of them myself. That's all me and my wife have room for. Our backyard's pretty small. In fact, in a lot of ways, these dogs are much better off when we... when we..."

Tears appeared in the man's eyes. Embarrassed, he tried to cover by shouting. "So don't lecture me, buddy! We're hanging on here by a thread. And I don't need—"

"How much?"

"How much what?"

Scott reached into his pocket and pulled out the object from the glove box—his checkbook.

"How much would it cost? To hire people who will take good care of the dogs and provide them with decent food for, say, the next two months?"

"A lot."

"Give me a figure."

Sweeney did some quick mental figuring. "You're talking around thirty thousand dollars."

Scott already had his pen out. "Do I make it out to Kitsap County Animal Control Services?"

Unprepared for the direction this had taken, it took a moment for Sweeney to respond. "Um, yes. That's correct."

Scott handed him the check. Sweeney stared at it, then looked at Scott, suddenly suspicious. "Is this any good? And please don't lie to me. You'd be surprised at the number of nut cases that come in here!"

"I suggest you take it to your bank," Scott said. "They'll let you know if I'm crazy or not." The barking and howling of the dogs grew louder, as if underlining his words.

A glimmer of hope appeared in Harlan Sweeney's eyes. Scott suspected hope was something that hadn't been around here for a long time.

～～～

As he and Linda left the building, she asked, "What happens after the two months are up?"

"The dogs come to live with us."

Her eyes opened wide in surprise. "Just like that?"

"Just like that." He gave her a searching look. "You did say you like dogs."

"No." Linda took his hand in hers and smiled. "I said I *love* dogs."

At twilight that evening, Scott and Linda walked the acreage surrounding the house and talked about their plans for the dogs. Jake ambled behind, inspecting shrubs, tree trunks, and rocks for olfactory evidence of squirrels and chipmunks.

The sun was setting behind the distant Olympic Mountains. Much of the snow had melted, revealing craggy granite peaks that were tingeing blue in the play of light and shadow. The air was warm and pleasantly humid, and felt soft to the skin.

"I've got ten acres sitting here doing nothing," said Scott, looking out at the view. "Meanwhile, down the road in Bremerton, there's a building filled with scared, hungry dogs, living in filth, waiting to be killed." He turned and looked at Linda. "But that's going to change." His voice was edged with quiet determination.

"Any idea what you're going to call it?"

"I haven't thought about it."

"I have a suggestion."

"What?"

"How about Jake's Joint?"

The dog looked up at the sound of his name. Scott smiled down at him. "I like it."

Wanting to move fast, Scott and Linda were up early the very next morning calling contractors and landscape designers. Within a week, two acres of land had been cleared. A week after that, the foundation for the structure that would house the dogs had been poured. By the time a month had gone by, construction of Jake's Joint was well underway. Work had also begun on a network of trails that meandered through the property. The final phase would include erecting a tall, sturdy fence to keep out deer, raccoons, and coyotes, not to mention the occasional bear. But that was still weeks away.

Jake's easygoing personality quickly won over the various work crews. He wandered from job to job where he would sit for long stretches of time, quietly watching forms get built, concrete poured, plumbing installed. His serious, watchful manner inspired the workers to start referring to him as "The Little Foreman." Lunchtime was especially rewarding for the dog as crew members handed out potato chips, slices of lunchmeat, or beef jerky to The Little Foreman.

At ten o'clock one morning, a truckload of lumber and another of gravel arrived simultaneously. Because Scott and Linda took a hands-on approach to the project, they scrambled to make sure that deliveries ended up in the right locations. Linda, as a guide, ran ahead of the dump truck full of gravel that was to be spread onto the trails, while Scott directed the lumber truck in another direction. As the gravel truck began backing up to the spot where it would dump its load, Linda's cellphone rang. Focused on the truck, she didn't answer but glanced at the screen to see who was calling.

It was Jonathan in England. She whistled for the truck to halt and answered the phone.

"Hello?" She felt herself automatically start to tense up. ". . . Yes, Jonathan. Is everything all right?" She had to cover one ear to hear over the deep idling of the dump truck. "... You're *where*—? ...*What* about Megan?"

Scott was fifty yards away overseeing the unloading of the lumber when he saw Linda running toward him. She was waving her arms and shouting. At first, this alarmed him, but as she came closer he could see that her face was lit up with joy.

"I just got off the phone with Jonathan!" she shouted, breathless. "Megan had her baby!"

"That's wonderful! It's about time she had her little girl!"

Linda practically knocked him over as she rushed into his arms. "Scott, we've got to go see them! Can we? Please?"

"Of course we can! There's nothing here that can't wait for a week. We'll leave tomorrow."

"Thank you!" she said, bursting with delight. They were both thinking the same thing as they held each other. It was nice, so nice, to have happy news about Megan for a change.

⌒⌒⌒

Later that night, after their excitement had settled down, Linda lay in bed trying to read as Scott slept beside her. She was groggy from the bottle of Dom Perignon they had drunk in celebration of the day's news. After reading the same paragraph for the third time, she gave up and turned off the light.

She was just drifting off to sleep when it hit her. Suddenly wide awake, she sat up and turned on the light. Jake groaned in annoyance, but Linda ignored him. She shook Scott's shoulder.

"Scott. Wake up."

His eyes opened in tiny slits. "What?" he said, his voice a little cranky.

"This morning. The phone call from Jonathan."

Scott shifted onto his back and closed his eyes. "What about it?" he grumbled.

"Megan and Jonathan didn't know if the baby was going to be a boy or a girl. They wanted it to be a surprise."

"You woke me up to tell me that?"

"When I told you Megan had her baby, you said, *It's about time she had her little girl.*"

"Yeah. So?"

"How did you know it was a girl?"

He opened his eyes and blinked at the ceiling. "Are you sure you didn't tell me that first?"

"I'm positive."

He was silent, staring at the ceiling. "Huh. Just a lucky guess, I suppose. Chances were fifty-fifty I'd be right. Those are pretty good odds."

"But you sounded so sure, like it was a foregone conclusion."

"Maybe I just assumed it would be a girl. It does seem to run in your family."

"Maybe."

He turned on to his side. "We need to sleep. We've got a long flight ahead of us tomorrow."

She reached up and turned off the light. "Good night."

"Good night."

But he didn't go to sleep right away. He lay awake thinking about what she had said.

∿∿∿

After arriving at Heathrow and clearing customs, they took a taxi to Megan and Jonathan's flat. Megan looked absolutely radiant.

Linda was anxious to meet little Rowena, which was the name the couple had chosen for their daughter. Jonathan went into the kitchen to make tea while Megan led her mom and Scott into the makeshift nursery. When they entered, crying was coming from the crib in the corner. Megan bent down and took Rowena into her arms.

"She's been fussing and crying like that from the start," Megan said. She enfolded the baby and gently patted her back. But the crying only got louder.

"Is she okay?" Scott asked.

"The doctor said she's perfectly healthy, that we just need to keep a close eye on her." Megan frowned with a young mother's worry. "But if she keeps on like this for more than a couple of days, we need to take her in for tests."

"Can I hold her?" Linda leaned in toward her daughter

and granddaughter.

"Of course you can."

Linda took the baby and spoke to her in soft coos. "What's the matter, Rowena? There's no reason to be upset."

The tiny face was red and moist from crying. "You're being silly, Rowena. Did you know that? You're being awfully silly." Linda cast a troubled glance at Megan while continuing to talk softly to Rowena, but nothing would pacify her.

Linda turned to Scott and said, "Would you like to hold her?"

He looked at her in surprise. "Me?"

"Yes. You."

Suddenly uncomfortable, he said, "I've never held a baby before."

"You're kidding," chuckled Linda. And then more seriously. "Aren't you?"

"No. I'm not."

"Jesus, Scott," said Megan, looking at him. "You look terrified!"

But Linda was already holding Rowena out to him. "Oh, come on. You're being a baby yourself."

Scott took her as gingerly as if he were being handed a live explosive. He looked at the two women in mild panic as Rowena continued to cry.

"Go on," said Linda. "Talk to her."

Scott looked down at the squalling infant in his arms. "Hey there, little baby," he said in a gentle voice. "Hey, Rowena. There's nothing to cry about. Everything's fine. Linda and I came all this way to see you, so that's no way to act."

At the sound of his voice, the baby stopped crying. She opened her eyes and looked at him. The directness of her gaze was startling. Scott found he couldn't look away. The two stared intensely into each other's eyes as if mesmerized.

"Wow," said Megan. "What in the world did you do?"

He didn't reply. Just continued staring at the little girl. Then, with a physical effort, he broke his gaze away and looked at Megan and Linda. Tears suddenly formed in his eyes.

"My God," he said in a whisper husky with emotion. "She's *amazing!*" He looked back down at the tiny infant, who was now smiling at him. *"She's absolutely amazing!"*

Linda and Megan both took it in with quiet wonder. Linda shrugged, shaking her head as if to say, *"I've never seen this side of Scott."*

Scott and Linda stayed for a week, enjoying every minute of their time. Then, all too soon, it was time to head home.

On the way back from the airport, they stopped and picked up Jake from the vet's boarding facility.

The contractors and crews showed up bright and early the next morning to recommence construction. Because either Scott or Linda always needed to be onsite to handle any unforeseen crises, they took turns sneaking Jake out to Autumn Lake for his daily walk.

Scott called Harlan Sweeney at the pound every day to keep him apprised of the progress. In return, he kept Scott informed of the condition of the dogs. Because they were now receiving proper care and nutrition, they were all doing fine. He told Scott that on the day Jake's Joint opened, he would personally drive the oldest and most frail of them to their new home. Scott said that he couldn't think of a better way to kick things off.

They had been back from England for less than a week when the construction of Jake's Joint once again came to an unexpected halt.

On a golden morning in late September, it was Scott's turn to take Jake for his walk. The stillness of the forest was a welcome respite from the noise and chaos of construction. Scott moved even more slowly than usual to prolong their time together in the quiet of the woods. Sunlight seeped like warm butter through the broccoli-green branches of the Douglas firs lining the trail. Overhead, the sky was a soft and perfect blue.

Jake was ambling about twenty paces ahead of Scott with his nose to the ground when suddenly he jerked upright and began to tremble violently. Moving stiffly, he turned to face Scott, a look of fear and confusion in his eyes. A strange, high-pitched whimper came from deep in his throat.

Alarmed, Scott quickly walked toward him. "Jake—?"

The dog took three faltering steps toward Scott and fell over on his side.

"Jake!" Scott sprinted to his dog and knelt beside him. Jake's breathing was very shallow. Scott stroked his neck.

"What is it, boy?" he said, his voice quavering. "What's the matter?" Jake turned his head and looked into Scott's eyes. He gave his hand two licks, laid his head on the ground and stopped breathing.

"Oh, Jake..." Scott whispered as he watched the life fade from the dog's eyes. "My poor Jake..."

Linda was consulting with the painting contractor when she noticed Scott's Range Rover pull in. She went back to studying the paint samples with the contractor. After a moment, she realized that the sounds of nail guns and power saws had stopped. She looked up and saw all the workers looking in the direction of Scott's car. She turned to look.

Scott stared at Linda with eyes that were like open wounds. He walked toward her with Jake cradled in his arms, his scruffy brown head hanging loosely to one side.

"Oh, no..." she said. The binder of paint samples slipped from her hands and she ran to him.

Scott was barely able to talk. "He just... collapsed and died..."

"Oh, Scott! I'm so sorry. Poor Jake..."

The two looked at each other in mutual shock and pain. Linda reached out and said, "Would you like me to take him?"

He nodded. She took the dog into her arms with infinite tenderness, then turned and carried him toward the house. Scott followed in a daze. Inside, she partly wrapped Jake in a towel and laid him on the couch with his head and neck uncovered. Scott sat beside him and rested his hand on Jake's shoulder.

"Scott, I'm so sorry."

Scott kept his hand on Jake. " .. I guess I was trying to ignore the fact that he was getting old. It looks like... like his heart just finally gave out."

They couldn't take their eyes from the still form.

Outside, the work crews quietly packed up their tools and drove away in their trucks. As they departed, more than one crusty construction worker was blinking back tears at the passing of The Little Foreman.

After the last truck was gone, in the softest voice she could summon, Linda asked, "What would you like to do with his remains?"

Scott looked up blankly as if she were speaking a foreign language. "Huh?"

"Have you ever given it any thought?"

He finally realized what she was saying. His voice carefully controlled, he said, "Yes. I have, actually. I'd like to have Jake cremated, and then scatter his ashes in the place where he was happiest. The thing is, I never thought... that this moment would..."

Linda's voice was a soothing whisper. "I think the sooner we do this, the better."

He nodded, and she went into another room to call the vet and arrange to drop off Jake's body. When she came back in, Scott spoke in an unsteady voice. "Do you mind if I stay here while you take him?"

"Are you sure?"

He nodded without looking at her.

"I don't mind. Will you be okay until I get back?"

"I'll be fine." But he knew he wouldn't be fine. He was losing control fast and he didn't want her to see him break down. As if sensing his thoughts, she quickly gathered up Jake. Holding him close, she went out and closed the door.

Scott listened to the sound of her steps fade as she walked to the car. When he could no longer hear them, he buried his face in his hands and let the sobs come.

Linda returned to find Scott sitting on an outcropping of granite, watching the sun set over the Olympics. A glass of wine was in his hand, the half-empty bottle resting on a flat spot beside him.

She got another bottle and a glass for herself, and went out to join him. They sat close without speaking, watching the sunlight slowly fade behind the mountains.

When it was almost too dark to see, she stood up. "I'm going inside," she said. "Don't be long."

Scott nodded, and she went back to the house.

She was in bed when he came in. When she saw him, she sat up in alarm. "You're bleeding!"

Scott looked down and saw the nasty scrape on his forearm. The blood had already dried.

"I tripped climbing down off the rocks," said Scott. "Must've banged my arm on something."

She started to get out of bed. "You want me to bandage it?"

He examined his arm more closely. "No. It's just a scrape. Already scabbing over. I'll go wash up."

She lay back down. When Scott came out of the bathroom, she was already asleep. He got into bed, turned off the light and curled up beside her. He reached out to pat Jake who was no longer there.

Chapter 21

THE EIGHT

Next morning, she was roused from sleep by Scott calling her name. "Linda…" His voice sounded different. Whispery and thin. Frightened. "Linda, wake up."

She turned over and looked at him. "What's the matter?"

"…Something's wrong! Look at my arm!"

It had turned a yellowish purple and swollen to twice its normal size. She felt his cheek. His skin was hot and dry. "My God, Scott, you're burning up!"

He had trouble speaking. "I… don't feel so good." His breathing was shallow. He suddenly jerked away from her, leaned over the side of the bed and vomited.

Linda grabbed the phone and dialed 9-1-1.

By the time the ambulance arrived, Scott was unconscious. The paramedics found his blood pressure dangerously low, his pulse rapid and weak, his heart rate erratic. His body temperature was 104 degrees. The chief paramedic called for an emergency helicopter evacuation. He was afraid that Scott wouldn't survive the drive and ferry ride to Seattle.

As soon as the copter touched down on the roof of Harborview Medical Center, he was rushed to the Emergency Room, where doctors quickly discovered a massive and deadly infection raging through his body. Unsure of the cause, they delivered a full spectrum of antibiotics into him intravenously, hoping one would be the magic bullet to counter the infection.

Scott's condition began to stabilize. His vital signs slowly reverted to levels that, though still far from normal, were no longer life-threatening.

For now, anyway.

As he drifted in and out of a delirious consciousness, he was transferred to Intensive Care, where he would be closely monitored. Even though the treatment seemed to be working, his situation could easily take a turn for the worse. The next twenty-four hours were going to be critical.

The day had passed in a nightmarish and exhausting blur for Linda. Except for when Scott was in the Emergency Room, she hadn't left his side. Now that he was in the ICU, she stayed close as he thrashed about in the hospital bed, mumbling and shouting incoherently in his fever. Every so often, she would wipe his brow with a cool damp cloth and whisper soothing words into his ear. After several hours, he finally settled into a fitful sleep.

The door to the ICU was propped open. A nurse padded in to do her hourly check on his vital signs. Linda curled in a chair watching the woman study the various monitors and make notations on a clipboard.

"How's he doing?" Linda asked.

"No change," said the nurse as she finished writing her notes. She turned and took in Linda's red, puffy eyes. "The question is, how are *you* doing?"

"I'm fine."

The expression on the nurse's face suggested she thought otherwise. "Why don't you go down to the cafeteria and get yourself something to eat?"

"I'm not hungry."

"Some coffee, then. Maybe wash your face and comb your hair. It'll make you feel better."

Linda stared blankly at the nurse as if emerging from a trance. She gave a tired sigh and ran her fingers through her hair. "Maybe you're right. I should at least stretch my legs."

The nurse smiled sympathetically. As they left the room together, she told Linda how to get to the cafeteria, then headed down the hall in the other direction to finish her rounds.

After they had gone, a gruff East Coast voice sliced through the fog of Scott's fevered sleep.

"Hey. Wake up."

Scott's body shuddered involuntarily at the sound. In his delirium, he couldn't tell if he was dreaming or awake.

"I said wake up, bright eyes."

When Scott opened his eyes, they focused on a man in a charcoal overcoat standing over him. There was something vaguely, disturbingly familiar about him.

As the man's dark glistening eyes bored deep into his own, Scott felt a wave of dread wash over him. The man leaned down and brought his face inches from Scott's. In a strangely intense voice, he said, *"You do know who I am, don't you?"*

A dam suddenly burst. Full knowledge of everything that had been previously erased from his mind came roaring back in a flood of memories and sensations. It was accompanied by such searing pain that he cried out.

The sudden restoration of memory was so disorienting that he wondered if he had gone insane. But as the pain subsided and he was able to sit up and look at Patrick, the realization that he wasn't crazy didn't comfort him much. In some ways, it might have been preferable to deal with insanity.

"I bet you thought you'd seen the last of my ugly mug," smirked Patrick.

Though the pain in Scott's head was dissipating, it still felt like the worst headache he'd ever had. That, in combination with his current fevered state, didn't make him very sociable. "What the hell are you doing here?!"

"We need to talk. It's about our deal."

"Some deal that turned out to be! Linda and I haven't even

had a year together."

"Hey, it was you who set the terms."

"And a key provision was that *I not know I'm going to die right after Jake!*"

"Yeah, sorry about your mutt. Could be he was a lot older than he looked."

"This isn't making it any easier, Patrick. Why couldn't you have just let things alone?!"

"Something's come up."

"Shit, my head hurts. I hurt everywhere."

Patrick raised an amused eyebrow. "I'm not surprised. Your time is just about up. You're right on the verge of croaking."

"*I know that now,*" said Scott through gritted teeth. "Why are you doing this!?"

"Something's happened that might interest you."

"What is it?" Scott enunciated each word with a precision born of pain.

"I'm here to tell you that, if you want, you've been given the option to stick around a little longer."

"What do you mean, 'stick around'?"

"As in continue to breathe." Patrick words were coated in sarcasm. "Stay alive. Not die."

"How *much* longer?"

Patrick held up a single finger. "One year."

Scott regarded him with suspicion. "What's the catch?"

"No catch. This is a one-time offer. Zero strings attached."

"Why would you do that?"

Patrick gave a laugh. "Believe me, Northwood, it wasn't my idea! I was fine with the deal we struck. But I didn't have a choice—I got overruled."

"Overruled? By who?"

"Your counterparts."

"My what?"

"Remember the eight other Implementers?"

"Of course. But how could they—"

"I told them how you so unselfishly gave up all but a tiny

portion of your time. They were so touched by your generosity, they each chipped in some of their time to give to you now, in case you changed your mind. It adds up to exactly one year. Matter of fact, because of you, there's been a freakin' palace revolt! Those people are dolin' out time like there's no tomorrow. Hey, get it? That's pretty funny. They even gave some more time to Max Grabowsky and Olivia What's-her-face?—Johansen. Said they're doin' such a good job, they also deserve to stick around a while longer. All of which translates to even more feathers in my cap, right?"

"Max and Olivia are still alive?"

"Both will still be kickin' for at least another year. Anyway, as for you, you can take the year they've offered, but that's only if you want to. You can always stay with the original—"

"So what you're saying is… I'm getting *another chance?*"

"Call it whatever you want."

Even with infection ravaging his body, Scott was able to smile.

"And while we're on the subject," Patrick added, "there's somethin' I wanna say to you. Somethin' personal."

"Then say it."

Patrick cleared his throat and then said, *"Thank you."*

This was so out of character that, even through his pain, Scott had to ask, "You're *thanking* me? For what?"

"Apparently the deal I made with you, plus what's happening with the other Implementers, scored me some major Brownie points. They went a long way toward paying off my karmic hit man debt, or whatever you wanna call it. It's gonna help me get out of this freakin' limbo I'm stuck in. My days of babysitting Implementers are coming to an end!"

"I can't believe you're actually thanking me for something."

Patrick suddenly looked uncomfortable. "Yeah, well, deal with it."

Scott was able to summon a brief grin. "You're welcome. So does that mean you'll be moving on soon?"

Patrick frowned. "Not soon enough. The way these things work, it could be a while. Months, or even years! But just knowing this gig has an expiration date? I can live with that. Pretty cool, huh?"

Scott grimaced through his pain, but the derision came through in his voice as he managed to utter, "It warms the cockles of my heart."

"So come on, Northwood," Patrick said, suddenly impatient. "The clock's ticking. You're scheduled to croak in a couple minutes. You got a decision to make. What's it gonna be?"

Scott tried to gather his thoughts. "Jake's dying hit me hard... harder than I thought it would. If I didn't have Linda, I would probably stay with the original deal. But having her in my life has changed everything. So, Patrick, here's my answer. It's the easiest decision I've ever made. If I can have one more year of life with her, you better believe I'll take it!"

Patrick nodded. "I figured as much. Okay, you know the drill. All you gotta do now is go to sleep. When you wake up tomorrow, you'll feel good as—"

"Wait a minute," said Scott. It was suddenly difficult for him to talk. He felt himself fading.

"You don't have a minute!" said Patrick. "You need to—"

"Patrick, listen to me!" Scott was struggling with every breath. "I want you to leave my memory intact! I want to remember... *everything!*"

"But—that means you'll know exactly when you're gonna die!"

"That's right. I *want* to know when I'm going to die."

"That's crazy! *Why?*"

A monitor began to beep.

"So I can treasure each and every day of the year I have left with her... Not take one minute for granted. Do we have a deal?"

Patrick didn't respond. *Another* monitor began to beep. Scott's voice was suddenly very weak. "*Answer.* Deal?... Or not?"

"Yeah, we have a deal." Patrick put his hand in Scott's and

shook it. Scott watched him. "So now will you close your goddamn eyes before—*oh, shit!*"

"Yeah, we have a deal." Patrick put his hand in Scott's and shook it. Scott watched him. "So now will you close your goddamn eyes before—*oh, shit!*"

Scott followed Patrick's startled gaze toward the door. The last thing he saw before falling into the deepest sleep was Linda standing frozen in the open doorway, staring at him.

He had no idea how long she'd been there.

Two nurses charged past her into the room just as he lost consciousness.

Scott woke the next morning in perfect health. His doctors were stunned and jubilant. Their course of treatment had worked beyond their wildest dreams.

Scott couldn't get home fast enough.

That night in bed, he and Linda lay in each other's arms. In the dark, she could feel the beating of his heart.

"Linda," he said.

"Yes?"

"Can I ask you something?"

"Of course."

"It's... a little awkward."

"You know you can ask me anything."

"Last night. At the hospital. When you were standing in the doorway. Did you happen to overhear me say anything? Because I was pretty out of it, and I think I was saying some pretty bizarre things. I mean, like, really crazy stuff. And the last thing in the world I would want is for you to think I'm crazy. Because I'm not."

She could tell from the seriousness in his voice that whatever she said in response was of the utmost importance to him. Her reply came from deep in her heart.

"First, let's get something straight right now. I definitely *do not* think you're crazy. In fact, you are the sanest, most wonderful person I've ever met. So, are we clear on that?"

She felt most, but not all, of the tension flow out of his body. "Yes. We are. Thank you. But..."

"But what?"

"You didn't answer my question."

"Yes, I did."

"No. You didn't. I asked you if you'd overheard anything I said."

She was quiet.

"Well?" said Scott.

"No," she lied. "I didn't hear a thing."

She felt the rest of the tension ease. She ran her hand gently down his shoulder, across his chest, over his stomach. She knew just the way to touch him.

"Now, I believe we were talking about getting something straight..."

⌃⌃⌃

Later, as he slept soundly beside her, she lay awake thinking about the lie she'd told him. She had never lied to him before, not about anything. But this time, she felt she had no choice in the matter.

As she'd stood in the doorway of his hospital room, she had overheard quite a lot. If she'd witnessed this earlier in their relationship, she absolutely would have doubted his mental stability. But she had seen enough unusual occurrences involving Scott to know that there were deeper things about him than met the eye. A lot deeper.

Remembering the first time she'd laid on eyes on him, she thought back to that day at Harborview Medical Center, when Megan lay near death. Linda had entered the hospital room to find a stranger standing over her comatose daughter saying the oddest things. She could remember some of what he'd said very clearly:

"...If I truly can shave some time, say, a few months, or even a year, from my own existence in this world and give them to you, I'll do it. I don't know you very well. But I know that you deserve this. I don't even know if it'll work.

But what the hell. It's worth a shot, right?... "
And then, shortly after that, there was the meteor storm in Poulsbo. Linda remembered a man and woman being interviewed on television. They insisted they'd met a man at the casino who had predicted the storm just before it happened.

The woman had described him as "*. . . a nice-looking man. In his late forties. Nice head of hair, starting to go gray. He wore one of those outdoorsy field coats, like you would see in a L.L. Bean catalogue. It was a faded green color.*"

"*And he said his name was Scott,*" the man had said.

"*That's right. Scott...*"

But more significant were Megan's dreams. On both occasions when her brain tumor disappeared overnight, Scott had appeared to her in a vivid dream. Each time, her recovery had baffled doctors who had found it nothing short of miraculous.

The recoveries occurred exactly one year apart.

Linda remembered the footage of Max Grabowsky being shoved out of the path of a speeding car by a mysterious stranger. To this day, she was convinced that Scott was that stranger, even though he'd sworn to her he had no memory of it.

And he had known that Megan's newborn baby was a girl.

Linda had had time to think long and hard about these incidents. Taken together, they couldn't be ignored. She believed that Scott was anything but crazy. If he was convinced he had only one year left to live, she would be the last person in the world to doubt that it was true.

But there was something else that solidified her undying devotion to Scott Northwood. In that doorway, listening to his one-sided conversation with unseen, unheard 'Patrick,' she overheard something that affected her profoundly. It was his desperate plea to know exactly when he was going to die, "*...so I can treasure each and every day of the year I have left with her... Not take one minute for granted.*"

She looked at his sleeping form beside her. She loved him

more than anything on this earth. Whatever his trials and tribulations in the past, she would do anything to make him as happy as possible, for as long as he lived. God knows he deserved it.

So yes, she had lied to him. But she wasn't sorry. She'd lied to protect him from the knowledge that she had overheard him at the hospital. She didn't want him to spend one second of their final time together worrying about whether she thought he was crazy or not.

Then she made a vow to herself.

She knew what was coming, and when it got here, they'd deal with it together. But until that happened, she too would treasure being with him for the time that remained.

She, too, would not take one single minute of it for granted.

Jake's Joint was in the final stages of construction. Scott threw himself into the work with abandon. The hard physical labor helped him deal with the grief of losing Jake. It kept his mind occupied during the day. And at night, his exhausted body would descend into a deep sleep.

When the project was nearly complete, he felt he was as emotionally ready as he ever would be to do something he'd been putting off. He asked Linda to come with him. "Of course," she said. "Would you like to do it now?"

He nodded, a somber look on his face. "I'll get his ashes."

"I'll meet you at the car."

Scott emerged from the house with the small green urn cradled in his arms. "Do you mind driving?" he said. "I just want to hold him one last time."

She nodded.

The Range Rover pulled into the dirt parking lot. It was a cool, overcast October day. They walked in silence along one of the trails until they arrived at the edge of Autumn Lake. Scott held the urn. He stared out at the still, silent lake. Linda stood close by.

Tears swam hot in his eyes as he glared up at the sky. "You

take good care of my dog!" His voice rang through the trees. "You hear me?! You take damn good care of him!"

As Scott's shout died away, a deep and pervading silence settled back over the forest like a thick, soft blanket. He opened the urn and poured the stream of coarse gray ashes into the lake.

When the last nail had been driven, the last brushstroke of paint applied, the last wheelbarrow of gravel spread on the paths, Jake's Joint was ready. Scott and Linda had already interviewed, screened, and hired several fulltime caretakers who would see to the animals' every need. Now all that was missing were the dogs.

There were more than a hundred of them. Scott, Linda and a grateful Supervisor Sweeney ferried carloads of dogs to their comfortable new home. It took most of the day.

As the first days went by, what surprised Scott the most was that the dogs' barking—so loud and continuous at the pound—nearly stopped altogether. Of course, there was no way he could prove it, but he believed that they could sense they were no longer in danger of being killed.

Any and all abandoned dogs were welcome to live at Jake's Joint. Every one of them was eligible for adoption at no charge. Thanks to a low-key but well-organized, ongoing publicity campaign, several dogs a month were placed in good homes.

Scott and Linda enjoyed their easygoing canine company, and walked over to visit several times a day with treats in hand. Every time, a wall of smiling dogs and wagging tails would greet them.

A few days after the grand opening, when things had settled down, Scott lay in bed early one morning watching Linda sleep beside him. It was time for him to decide what he was going to do with the rest of his shortened life. How in the world was he going to pack three decades of living and loving into a single year?

The answer came as soon as he asked the question.

Exuberantly!

He reached out and stroked her cheek. She opened her eyes and gave him a sleepy smile. He smiled back as she stretched like a cat and then embraced him with her warm, welcoming body.

～～～

For the next few months, their lives went into overdrive: they traveled everywhere and did everything, making trips to England to see Megan, Jonathan, and little Rowena. They traveled to many different countries, visited every major city. They trekked through exotic parks and nature preserves, rested and played at the most beautiful resorts, sought out the finest restaurants. Always moving, never holding back, they strove to enjoy life to the utmost.

During their travels, Scott was pleased and amazed at how well they got along—better than he could have imagined. They didn't argue about anything. Linda commented on it, too, expressing surprise at their perpetually cheerful compatibility. She told him that even the most companionable couples argued some time, and that it was probably even good for the relationship. He vigorously disagreed with her, thus prompting their one and only argument.

But after many weeks of living a fantasy existence, he experienced a shift in his thinking about what made a full life. Returning from a trip to the Galapagos Islands, he felt an overwhelming longing to be back in the Pacific Northwest. Linda agreed; she confessed she missed being home. So they booked a flight to Seattle.

Back in Poulsbo, they eased into a routine that let them live consciously and deliberately. Their days were spent taking walks in the woods, caring for the dogs, going on long drives in the country, and—on clear days—drinking in the sunsets. Nights, they cooked hearty meals together while they talked and joked and laughed. They took their time at dinner, savoring the food, washing it down with good wine. Every night, they slept wrapped in each other's arms.

On a rainy and gloomy Valentine's Day, Scott asked Linda to marry him. Happy tears streamed down her cheeks as she said yes.

They were married on a sun-flooded June day, holding their ceremony on the bluff in the backyard. The dramatic sweep of the Olympic Mountains made a perfect backdrop. Megan and Jonathan brought Rowena, and Scott's sister Shelly came with her husband Ben and their two sons. Scott was ecstatic that they had finally come out to see him.

To celebrate their honeymoon, Scott and Linda took the car ferry from Port Angeles across to Victoria, British Columbia. They drove along the wooded coast of Vancouver Island to an isolated cabin. For one beautiful week, they enjoyed the long days, the cool nights, and the amazing gift of each other.

Other than the wedding, no major events took place in their lives. And this was just how they wanted it. Indeed, their final months together turned out to be rich, full—perfect.

Chapter 22

DUSK

Slowly, steadily, inexorably, the months Scott had left shrank to weeks. Then days. And then, one dark, chilly morning in September, their final 24 hours together dawned. When he opened his eyes, he knew that the great, strange, wonderful dream that had been his life would end on this day.

He reached out for Linda, but the other side of the bed was empty. She was already up.

He lay gazing at the ceiling for a few minutes. Eventually, he got up, put on his robe, and went out to the kitchen where she was making scrambled eggs. She turned and smiled at him.

"Good morning."

He kissed her lightly on the lips. "Good morning."

He noticed that her eyes were red and swollen.

"Have you been crying?"

"No. It's just allergies."

"In September?"

"Ah! Sometimes they come out of nowhere. In fact, because of them, I didn't sleep very well last night at all."

"Neither did I," he whispered.

He poured himself some coffee and sat down at the kitchen table. Linda's back was to him as she continued cooking. He took a sip, then noticed that her shoulders were shaking.

"Linda?" he asked in alarm. "Are you okay?"

"No. I'm not okay."

He set his cup down. "What's the matter?"

Her back was still to him. "Don't die, Scott..."

"—What?"

She turned to face him. She was crying. "Please don't die!"

He stood and took her in his arms. They held each other for a long moment. Finally, he asked, "How long have you known?"

"I heard everything that day!" she said, sobbing into his chest. "I'm sorry I lied to you... I heard everything..."

"Ssh..." said Scott. "It's okay... It's okay..."

~ ~ ~

Later that day, they took a long, rambling walk at Autumn Lake where Scott explained to her how Patrick had come into his life. He told her about Enablers, Implementers and Prospects. He described the deal he had made.

"...which, in hindsight, turned out not to be a very good one." He gave her the wryest of smiles. "It may, in fact, be the worst ever."

Linda stopped and turned to look at him.

"But, Scott, *why* did you give away so much of your time?!"

"You have to realize that this was before we were together. I didn't think we would ever *be* together."

"But can't you get it back? At least some of it?"

"No. I'm afraid it can't be reversed."

"But—I still don't understand. *Who* in the world did you—"

Linda stopped herself and stared at him with those fawn-colored eyes.

He said nothing. Just watched her as she put it together.

It was several moments before she was finally able to speak.

"...*Oh, my God, Scott...*" she breathed, pressing her face hard against his chest, holding him close. *"Oh, my God..."*

Dusty shafts of sunlight streamed down through the trees as they stood clinging to each other. Small birds chirped and flitted among the branches.

Eventually, they resumed walking in silence, holding

hands very tightly. After a while, he said, "You know, it's a funny thing…"

"What is?"

"I was thinking about when Jake and I would come out here. Even though Patrick was supposed to be invisible to everyone but me, I swear that dog could sense when he was around. Jake would start to huff and bark, then he'd plant that butt on the ground and his tail would just go crazy!" He smiled at the memory.

In bed that night, they held on to each other. Light from the full September moon burst in through all the windows of the house, flooding every room with a luminescence so bright it was otherworldly. In the distance, the Olympics glowed a blueish silver.

"Linda," said Scott in a whisper. "I want you to know something. Whatever happens, my time with you has been the happiest of my life. By far. Before I met you, I'd been living my life in black and white, and I didn't even know it. But being with you every day has put my life in color… In gorgeous, wonderful color…"

She held him all the closer.

Then, lying there with him, she had an idea. It didn't make any sense, but right now nothing made any sense.

She decided not to fall asleep. If she slept, she'd wake up and it would be morning, and he might be gone. But if she could somehow stay awake all night with her arms wrapped around him, nothing could happen.

After a while, Scott began his quiet snore. Yes, she'd stay awake all night. Nothing would happen as long as she was watching over him.

The minutes stretched into an hour. Then two hours. He continued to snore.

Not long to go now, she prayed. Almost there. Dawn's just around the corner… And then everything will be okay…

Linda opened her eyes and sat up with a start. It was raining steadily outside. Dull gray morning light filled the room. She turned to Scott, who lay on his side facing away.

"Scott—?"

She hesitantly reached out to take his shoulder and shake him gently awake. But as soon as she touched him, she jerked her hand away.

His skin was cold.

"Oh, no. Oh, Scott. Oh no. No, no..." She could see that his flesh was tinged a soft pale blue.

She curled her body around his still form, and began to cry, softly at first. But soon, she clung to him, sobbing as if the world had ended.

The county coroner determined that he had died of a massive brain aneurysm that had come out of nowhere. Linda posted an obituary in the *Kitsap County Herald* that described the relatively modest accomplishments of his life. It was accompanied by one of her favorite pictures of Scott—a photo she'd taken of him and Jake out at Autumn Lake.

The obituary mentioned that Scott was most proud of having built Jake's Joint, a refuge where unwanted dogs could live out the rest of their lives in peace and comfort.

A small memorial service to celebrate his life was planned for the following week. The only people coming for certain would be Megan, Jonathan, and Rowena from her side of the family, and Shelly, Ben, and their two sons from Scott's side. Linda decided it was only right to allow for a few possible stray acquaintances and grateful dog owners who might wish to stop by and pay their respects, so she rented a room in the Sons of Norway Hall, a public meeting place on the edge of pretty Liberty Bay in Poulsbo.

She was realistic; she wouldn't be terribly surprised if no one else showed up. Scott's death seemed to have passed unnoticed.

Then things took an unexpected turn.

Derek Styles, a Seattle TV news producer, lived on nearby Bainbridge Island. He had ridden the ferry to work for many years. On the crowded commuter runs, Derek boarded the boat early to snag a decent seat and work on his laptop during the crossing.

One night, a late September storm knocked out power to several grids on the island. Because of that, Derek's alarm clock failed to go off in the morning. But he had an important meeting scheduled first thing. He rushed out the door forgetting his laptop and was the last passenger to board, lucky to find the last unoccupied seat. As he was about to sit down, he noticed an abandoned newspaper. Having nothing else to do, he opened up the *Kitsap County Herald* and began to read.

As the ferry docked in Seattle, Derek sat lingering over Scott's obituary, his producer's wheels turning. He'd heard about Jake's Joint from other dog owners on the island. Everybody had wonderful things to say about it.

Always on the lookout for a good human interest story, Derek Styles had just found his next one.

⌒ ⌒ ⌒

Max Grabowsky sat at the bar of a restaurant discussing the next day's pickup with the manager. Behind the bar, a flat-screen television was tuned to the local news. Max's conversation was interrupted by the sound of barking dogs coming from the TV. They both glanced up to see a woman passing out treats to dozens of excited dogs at some animal shelter.

"Carlos, could you turn that down?" said the annoyed manager.

The bartender grabbed the remote and hit the mute button. "Sorry, Boss."

Max was about to resume his conversation when something on the TV caught his eye. The woman, her eyes slightly red, showed a photograph of a grinning Scott holding a hammer.

Max's jaw dropped. The blood drained from his face. "It's *him*... That's the guy! Carlos! Turn that up! Quick!"

Carlos complied, and the woman showed more photos of Scott in various phases of the construction of Jake's Joint.

"...was a labor of love for Scott. Every bit of Jake's Joint was paid for out of his own pocket..."

Max stared at the television. "I don't believe it," he breathed. "It's really him."

Confused, the manager said, "I don't understand. Who's 'him'?"

Max continued to stare at the TV. "I wouldn't be sitting here right now if... *That's the guy who saved my life.*"

≈ ≈ ≈

Carrying a stack of mail in one hand and her checkbook in the other, Olivia Johansen slid onto a stool at the kitchen counter and, with a weary sigh, flipped on the television. In her hectic life that was filled with caring for all her kids, the half hour she set aside each week to pay bills was the only time she got to watch the news. She changed the channel from a cartoon network to a local news program. A sad-eyed woman talked to a reporter on a wooded bluff.

". . . decided to name it Jake's Joint, after the dog Scott owned for many years."

Olivia opened the first envelope: a whopping electricity bill. Thank God they had plenty of money in the checking account. She gave a silent thank you for their good fortune, something she did a dozen times a day. She wrote the check and signed it while listening to the TV.

The reporter was talking. ". . . so, all in all, not a bad legacy for a man some people might call reclusive, perhaps even a little eccentric."

"... No, I suppose not..." said the woman.

When Olivia glanced back at the TV, the camera had zoomed in to Scott's obituary photo. She gasped and dropped her pen.

She was staring at the man and dog from her dream. The

one she'd experienced as she was coming out of her coma.

"A small memorial service for Scott Northwood is planned at Sons of Norway Hall in Poulsbo this Saturday, the reporter said. "For more information, please go to our website. Reporting from Jake's Joint in Kitsap County, I'm Rick Reynolds."

Olivia opened her laptop and powered it up.

In a bar at the Eagle Harbor Casino, a television was tuned to the same channel.

"...Reporting from Jake's Joint in Kitsap County, I'm Rick Reynolds."

Back for their yearly visit with their son, the couple from Kentucky sat at the bar watching the TV, their mouths agape. They turned and looked at each other.

"That was him," said Bill.

"Yep," said Marilyn. They raised their drinks to their lips and took a sip.

The next morning, there was steady rain in Puget Sound. On Mercer Island, Jason Epstein stepped out into the gloom to get the morning paper from the front steps. He liked to read the comics with his cereal.

Now 17, the musical prodigy had grown into a tall, skinny, good-looking young man. Long, curly black hair framed his face, but what people noticed were his sensitive brown eyes.

The front steps were built of rough Pennsylvania bluestone, so rough that the third step collected a small puddle whenever it rained. Unfortunately, the delivery person had tossed the newspaper so that it landed partly in the puddle. Water seeped in under its plastic bag.

"Oh, great!" said Jason as he stooped down to retrieve *The Seattle Times.*

In the kitchen, he separated the pages and spread them on the floor to dry. He never read anything except the comics, but those pages were the wettest.

With a frown, he poured milk on his Cheerios, grabbed the driest section—the local news—and took a seat at the table. As he scanned the headlines and started eating, something caught his eye. The spoonful of Cheerios froze halfway to his mouth.

He stared at the picture of Scott and Jake. The article combined the obituary with an account of Jake's Joint.

Jason carefully put the spoon back in the bowl and leaned forward to study the photograph and read the article. As he did so, a melody from a dream he'd once had began to play in his head.

Saturday dawned gray and gloomy. The service was scheduled for two o'clock. Linda had booked the smallest of the three meeting rooms at the Sons of Norway Hall. At 1:30 she, Megan, and Jonathan arrived and began arranging a couple of dozen folding chairs in front of a podium. Rowena, a toddler now, was a bundle of energy as she scurried about the room. Her squeals and laughter added a welcome bit of cheerfulness to the somber preparations.

Shelly, Ben, and their two sons also came early to help. At the side of the podium, Linda set up an easel with a large blowup of Scott's photo on it. Beside that, she set up a small folding table with a vase of white roses and a burning white candle. And that was it. She knew Scott would have wanted this to be as low-key as possible.

It was now 1:45. Linda and the others stood around talking quietly as they waited for people to show up—assuming, of course, that anyone would show up.

"Are you doing okay?" Shelly asked.

Linda smiled. "I'm doing okay..." After crying herself out over the last week, her grief had subsided enough so that today, for the first time, she felt that maybe, just maybe, she had weathered the worst of the maelstrom.

"Have you thought about, you know, what you're going to

do when we all head back home?” Shelly asked.

“Yes, actually. I have…”

“Hmm. Do you want to tell me?”

“Sure. It has to do with dog shelters. The TV story about Jake’s Joint went viral. I’ve been getting calls from people around the country interested in doing something similar. They want to meet with me to talk about how to go about it. I imagine that’ll keep me busy for a while.”

“That’s wonderful!”

“Yes. I think so, too.”

It was now two o’clock, and still no one had shown up. The thought had crossed Linda’s mind more than once that morning that they might end up being the only people present for Scott’s service. It seemed the others were thinking the same thing. Linda suggested they wait another ten minutes before starting the service, just in case. They all struggled to maintain an upbeat chatter.

“You know, it’s kind of odd, really,” said Shelly with a nervous laugh.

“What’s odd?” said Linda.

“I was just thinking about a message Scott left on my answering machine once. This is a few years back. He’d gone to the funeral of a friend that day and had downed a couple glasses of wine afterward.”

“What was the message?”

Shelly hesitated, as if suddenly realizing that this might be the wrong thing to bring up.

Her curiosity piqued, Linda repeated the question. “What was the message?”

“Well,” said Shelly, smiling nervously. “He said that when he died, he didn’t think anyone would bother to come to his funeral. It was such an absurd thing for him to say that I’ve never forgotten it. I mean, *of course*, someone will show up, right?” Tears welled in her eyes.

No one said anything. They stared at the ground or looked at the walls. All except for Linda, whose smile was gentle. “Of course, someone will show.”

There was a squeak of hinges as the door opened. Mike, the produce guy from Central Market, poked his head in the door. He looked at the giant photo of Scott.

"This must be the place," he said. He nodded at the photo. "Mind if I come in?"

"Please do," Linda said.

Soon more people trickled in: Harlan Sweeney and his wife, followed by a couple of his assistants from Kitsap County Animal Control Services. Pam, Barbara and the other barmaids from Danny's Tavern arrived. Jeff from the video store showed up with his girlfriend. Brenda and Gus from the Cedar Rock Bar and Grill arrived together. There was happy chatter as Megan hugged them and introduced Jonathan and her adorable granddaughter. Greg, the pleasant older man from Linda's notorious Thanksgiving dinner, turned up alone and gave her a long hug. Bill and Marilyn from Paducah, Kentucky, looking fraught with apprehension, appeared at the door. Even though Linda didn't know them, she welcomed them inside.

The noise level shot up dramatically as many of the contractors and construction crews from the building of Jake's Joint arrived en masse. And Derek Styles, the TV producer from Bainbridge Island, made his way into the suddenly crowded room. Touched by the creation of Jake's Joint, he felt it was only right to come. He also had a message for Linda as he made his way toward her.

He practically had to shout to be heard above the growing din. "Does this building have a bigger room?"

"Yes," said Linda. "Why?"

"I think you're going to need it."

"What do you mean?"

"When I pulled into the parking lot, a couple of buses filled with people were coming in behind me."

"What?! Here?"

It turned out that Max Grabowsky had offered anyone who had benefited from his charity over the years the chance to attend the service with him, to honor the man who'd saved his life. He'd ended up having to charter two buses to accommodate those who wanted to come. Olivia Johansen arrived behind them with her beautiful family of special-needs kids.

Fortunately, the largest meeting room in the hall was not in use that day, so they were able to relocate the service. The sound system would be needed in this vast space. Jeff and Mike spontaneously teamed up to set the sound levels so everyone would be able to hear.

Linda's son-in-law Jonathan assumed the role of master of ceremonies. His pleasant, British-accented voice carried to all corners of the room as he invited anyone and everyone to come up to the podium and share memories of Scott. For the next two hours, one by one, dozens of people told their stories.

It was a warm and heartfelt service. As the event was finally coming to an end, Jonathan asked if anyone else wished to add anything. No one spoke or moved. But then a young man made his way up from the back of the hall. Jonathan waited for him to reach the podium, but he was surprised when the curly-haired fellow walked past it over to an old, funky piano tucked in a corner of the room.

Jason Epstein sat down, closed his eyes, and, for a moment, stayed very still. Just as people were starting to shift and cough, he took a deep breath and began to play.

In the years to come, many in attendance that gloomy October afternoon would never forget hearing the fiercely haunting, beautiful melody. Listeners were transported by it. Even Jason's parents, who'd been pestered by their son, and had finally—in exasperation— agreed to drive him to a stranger's memorial service, had never heard him play like that.

Jason seemed to be in a trance as his fingers pirouetted across the keyboard. It was as if the piano had become a portal to another dimension. When he played the final chord, it shimmered in the air before fading away. There wasn't a dry eye in the room.

Without a word, the boy got up from the piano and walked back to his parents. As he did so, he noticed eight familiar-looking faces in the back row. He wasn't at all surprised to realize that they were the other people from his dream.

He nodded to them as he took his seat. They nodded back, their faces glowing with approval.

Chapter 23

BRANDON

It was an unusually warm day in late September when Brandon Spencer shuffled into the gymnasium of North Kitsap High School along with a line of other people. He sighed in exasperation and asked himself for the umpteenth time why in the world he'd decided to come to this stupid thing. He had been to only one other funeral in his twenty-one years and had hated it. He much preferred weddings. Some of his friends had gotten married. Weddings were fun, the beer was free and there were always pretty girls. But this just plain sucked. Plus, he hadn't even seen Ron McGregor since graduating from high school three years before. Brandon was sorely tempted to get up and leave.

But when the service for the beloved biology teacher finally began, he had to admit he was shocked by the number of people who—like himself—had decided to sacrifice a perfect spring day for this. He suddenly felt less cranky. Mr. McGregor had been a good guy. He deserved this last measure of respect. It was the least Brandon could do, he realized.

Ron McGregor had been killed in a head on collision with a drunk driver, Brandon had read in the newspaper. What a stupid, meaningless way to go. Poor Mr. McGregor. He didn't deserve to check out like that. And now that Brandon thought about it, McGregor was the one who had encouraged him to enroll in Olympic Community College, where his interest in electrical engineering had taken hold. He was getting good grades and would be transferring to the University of Washington in the fall.

Again he looked around at all the people. There were *hundreds* of current and former students, and many of their parents—some of whom McGregor had also taught. The entire high school staff was there including the janitors. Plus dozens of friends and family.

Until this moment, Brandon had no idea how many lives McGregor had touched. And now this good man was gone, his life cut tragically short. Seeing all these people brought the craziest idea booming into Brandon's brain: If there were a way, some way, he could change it so that Mr. McGregor didn't die, he'd do it.

As the service continued, he began to feel as if someone was looking at him. He turned around and craned his neck. There. In the doorway. Some jerk in a green coat was staring at him. Why in the world was he wearing a coat on a day like this? And there was a dog sitting next to him. Dogs weren't allowed on school property. Yeah, he thought, this guy's got one wheel in the sand.

When he turned around to face the front, he did a slow burn. Why was that guy staring at him? It gave him the creeps! He had a good mind to go over there and—

He turned back around to glare at the man, but he and the dog were gone.

. . . Weird, he thought. Where the hell did he go? Well, no big deal...

Brandon surprised himself by staying in that hot, crowded gymnasium for the rest of the service, listening to the stories told by those who'd known Ron McGregor. He forgot all about the man in the green coat.

For the moment, anyway.

Chapter 24

THE TRAILS OF AUTUMN LAKE

On a bright, crisp day in early October, Linda, Megan and Rowena walked down the trail toward Autumn Lake. Because of his busy work schedule, Jonathan had returned to London earlier in the week. His wife and daughter were staying on a few more days to see Linda through the aftermath of Scott's memorial service. Their flight to England was scheduled for early the next morning.

Rowena was having trouble negotiating the uneven terrain and held tightly to her mother's hand.

"Where are we going, Granmum?" asked Rowena in her distinct British accent. It was startling to hear coming from a toddler. Linda still hadn't quite gotten used to it. She smiled every time her granddaughter spoke.

"To a special place."

"Do you think Lucy will fancy it?"

The scruffy black puppy trotting at Rowena's heels looked up at the mention of her name.

"Yes," said Linda, stifling a smile. "I think she will fancy it."

Stately Douglas firs towered all around them. Interspersed among the evergreens were a number of big leaf maples. Now in their full autumnal glory, they blazed yellow, red, and gold.

"I've never been out here before," said Megan. "It's beautiful!"

"I've always thought so." Linda adjusted the strap of the canvas satchel hanging from her shoulder. "Scott and I came out here every day.”

“I seem to remember a story about these woods when I was little,” said Megan. “That they were haunted.”

“Haunted?” repeated Rowena, a single worry line creasing her brow. “Oh, dear.” Even though she probably didn’t know what the word meant, the tone of her mother’s voice was cause enough for concern.

“No, Rowena,” smiled Linda. “This forest isn’t haunted. Far from it.”

They soon arrived at Autumn Lake. A newly installed bench was perched near the edge of the water. On one side of the bench, a shiny brass plaque read:

In Loving Memory of Scott Northwood
And May Jake Be Forever At Your Side

“Are you okay, Mom?” asked Megan.

“Yes,” said Linda as she stared out at the lake. “Yes... I’m fine.”

Megan and Rowena sat on the bench as Linda took the satchel from her shoulder and removed from it the ceramic vessel that held Scott’s ashes. She took the lid off the container and stepped onto a thick, moss-covered log that jutted partway over the lake. Taking her time, she gently poured the ashes into the silver water.

When she had finished, she stepped off the log and sat down on the bench between Megan and Rowena. She put an arm around each of them and held them close. Tears streamed down her face.

“Please don’t cry, Granmum,” said Rowena.

“Rowena,” said Megan, her voice quiet. “It’s okay if your grandmother cries.”

The three of them sat very still, watching the play of light and shadow reflecting from the sky and forest onto the lake. After several minutes, Lucy started to bark at something behind them. They turned to see what it was.

But there was nothing there except for a stand of big leaf

maples.

Lucy continued barking like mad.

"Lucy! What in the world are you barking at?" Megan shook her head. "What's got into that dog?"

Lucy stopped barking as abruptly as she had started.

Megan and Rowena turned their eyes back to the shimmering lake in front of the bench.

But Linda kept watching Lucy, who continued to stare at the bright grove of trees. Then the little dog sat down, ears and eyes alert.

Her tail suddenly started to wag like crazy.

Linda looked at the spot Lucy was watching.

A lone breeze began to blow softly through the stand of maples, causing the trees to turn into continents of quivering, golden butterflies.

With tears trembling in the corners of her eyes, Linda smiled in the direction of the maples. It was a slightly crooked smile, with one corner of her mouth rising a little higher than the other.

About the Author

Dave lives with his wife Marigene on an island in Western Washington, surrounded by water, mountains, and forests. Although weather in the Northwest tends to be a little on the wet side, Dave never tires of it. Indeed, he finds the ever-changing nuances of gray to be a source of daily inspiration.
***'If I Could Give You A Day'** is his first novel.*

www.daverichardsbooks.com

9 781942 661535